CU00797521

ISOLATION

Jared Grace

ℐCKNOWLEDGMENTS

To my daughter, Jordan. You are the reason I have fought so hard for success. From the first moment that I held you, I knew I needed to be the best father and man that I could be. Your passion and charm are infectious. Here's to you. May all your dreams come true.

To my son, Wyatt. Watching you grow up is one of the biggest highlights of my life. You are one of the funniest people I know. Hearing you laugh fills my heart with joy. You're a really special person, and I can't wait to see what the future holds for you. Love you, Goose.

To Rob Morgan for always being a great friend and a great ear. Your sage advice has pulled me back from the brink many times. Thank you for that. To the moment of this writing, you are the only person to fully complete this book cover to cover, and your words of advice and encouragement helped me through all the times that I believed this book would never come true. You are truly a friend for life. Thank you for everything.

To Jo Kratman for keeping me focused on writing and always making me see things from a different point of view. You're a vital part of my growth as a writer and a person. We need more writing nights in the future. Let's get you published as well!

To Jamie McDonald for being the best girlfriend in the world (that is what you told me to write, right? Haha). Your encouragement and support of my goals mean the world to me. Thank you.

To my student, LJ Flateau, for bringing a little made-up town in northwestern New Hampshire to life with your beautifully drawn map. When you created this, you were only a freshman. Keep art at the front of your heart. You have so much beauty to show the world.

To Stevie Warf, who took the photo of me that graces this book. You did a wonderful job with a less-than-perfect model. Thank you so much for everything.

My brother, Joel Grace. My sister-in-law, Brenda Sieng. My sister, Jenee Aguilar. My brother-in-law, Jhony Aguilar. My mother, Jill Petit.

My step-father Steve Petit. My step-brother Adam Petit. My step-sister, Stacey Proctor. My step-brother-in-law, Pat Proctor. My nephews: Owen Proctor, Pierce Grace, Casen Aguilar, Jack Proctor. My nieces: Samantha Proctor, Corah Aguilar, Eliyana Sieng.

Adam Weafer, Kamal Rowe, Elizabeth Lis, Chrissy McCabe, Aubrey Kelley, Laurie Lindsey, Theresa Beste, Stephanie Marston, Amanda LaFond, Jessica Quinn, Mike George, Merrill Marshall, Uncle Gordy, and Aunt Patty. Thank you all for everything you've contributed to my life. You've helped me find my place in this crazy existence.

And finally, to my father, John Grace, who passed away on July 20, 2015. You are forever missed. I know you're up there somewhere, traveling through eternity like Picard or Kirk. Your memory lives on with your children and grandchildren. We love you and miss you dearly.

TABLE OF CONTENTS

ISOLATION

Wimpah Hill

Legend:

1 Appleton Elementary
2 Sandlot
3 Myrtle's
4 The Dusty Bookshelf
5 The Back in Time Cafe
6 Bryce's
7 Miles'
8 Sarah's
9 Wally's General Store
10 The Dinsmore's
11 Forest Walker's
12 Adam Hunt's
13 Jimmy Delaney's
14 Mrs. Felders's
15 McNeil's Auto Body
16 McNeil's House
17 Stanley's Kitchen
18 Moonbeam Sleepaway Camp
19 Storage Units
20 EAS Station
21 Church
22 Russell's
23 Tom Richmond's
24 Mitchell Freemore's
25 Herman Roberson's
26 The Crowley's

PROLOGUE

The red '78 Ford pickup truck sped down Main Street going just a bit faster than the posted thirty MPH speed limit sign demanded.

It had a dented bumper, and the paint was chipping off in some spots, but, dammit, it was a hell of a truck. The driver's side window was cracked open, and a cigarette could be seen dangling between two fingers, ashes being flicked onto the road. In the cab, Jamison Crowley (James to those that called him a friend) turned the radio's volume higher as he drove past *Wally's General Store*, *The Back In Time Cafe* (home to the best damn coffee in town), and Mike Walker's quaint bookstore, *The Dusty Bookshelf*.

The distinctive voice of Steven Tyler blasted from the speakers, and Jamison leaned back without a care in the world; he was in an exceptionally good mood this morning. He had come home from work last night to a three-course meal prepared for him by his beautiful wife, Eve. After helping himself to seconds of her famous barbeque chicken, she took him upstairs, undressed him, and stripped off her own clothes. Eve pushed her husband down on the bed, climbed on top of him, and massaged every knot out of his forty-three-year-old, ever-aging back. Just as he began to wonder what he had done to deserve such a night, she asked him to roll over where she, again, climbed on top of him and relieved any excess stress she may have missed with the massage.

It was early November, and the rifle hunting season had just opened. He was ready for a day in the woods where he hoped to bag the fourteen-point buck that he had seen last weekend while out on "The Hill," glassing the terrain.

Jamison had always loved the outdoors; it comes with the territory when you live in northern New Hampshire. You either embrace the wonders of nature, or you move down to the city where the most natural thing you're likely to see is a drunk college student pissing on the one tree that graces his walk back to his overpriced and very undersized studio apartment.

Jamison had thought he needed a change of scenery in his late teens and moved to Boston, albeit temporarily, to pursue a college degree. For those that live in rural communities throughout the country, it seems as if this is a rite of passage. Discovering yourself as you discover adulthood. Jamison lasted one semester before he realized the noise of the city was too much and that he'd rather listen to the sounds of millions of insects copulating than hear one more middle-aged woman asking to see the store clerk's manager because he wouldn't accept her two-month expired coupon. Or one more homeless person asking for change. Or one more half in the bag, aggressive forty-something day trader laying on his horn because the mom trying to rush her three kids—two of which she has on leashes—across the street into *Neiman Marcus,* where she'll buy three more sweaters she'll wear once and never look at again, took too long to cross the road.

"No, sir," Jamison confessed one day to his roommate. "This isn't for me. I'm heading back home. The quiet life for me."

Jamison left just after Christmas break and returned to Isolation, New Hampshire, population 577. He moved back in with his dad, God rest his soul, and got a job fixing cars at *McNeil's Auto Body,* where he works to this day.

"McNeil is a real ball-buster," Jamison told his dad one day. "But that man knows everything there is to know about cars." Ball buster or not, McNeil was a man that was known for his kindness and fair prices. Local businesses needed to make sure they kept the local clients. Couldn't have people going to get their cars fixed down in Berlin. No, McNeil was a fair and honest businessman.

Mr. McNeil died a few years back, leaving his shop to his only son, Joshua. Unlike his dad, Joshua knew jack shit about cars, so when he asked Jamison to run the day-to-day operations for him, he accepted as a personal favor to the late Mr. McNeil.

Early last week, Herman Roberson, Jamison's long-time friend and longer-time drinking buddy, came into the shop just before lunch. Herman was a tall man with a long, red and white beard that hung to his chest. With skin pale enough to almost be described as transparent, Herman's gaunt figure gave him a ghoulish look.

Herman grew up just down the road from Jamison; the two had known each other casually throughout their childhoods. Though never close as kids, they were pleasant and would exchange hellos and even, at times, ride their bikes together down by the sandlot where the older kids would play baseball most summer afternoons. The innocence of children means you don't need to be the best of friends to play together. Companionship is learned at such an early age.

During one of their trips to the 'lot, a few of the older kids asked them if they wanted to take a swig of their booze (really, it was one of their father's booze that was snuck out of the house). They glanced over at each other, smiled, and took a sip. They were both thirteen. From that day forth, they became closer by the day.

When Jamison left for college, Herman became depressed but found relief in a bottle. When Jamison came back, they celebrated with the same stuff they had drank that day all those years ago—Jack Daniels. Since Jamison's return, the pair had made it a Sunday ritual to watch the Patriots and share some fine Tennessee whiskey.

"H'yah, James. Listen, I'm gunna head on up ta the hill this weekend. Do a little glassin', check out the game before the season opens, ya know. Feel like taking a ride Sat'day mornin?" Herman's accent, a combination of urban New Hampshire (if indeed you call anywhere in New Hampshire urban) and backwoods Maine seemed thicker this morning than most.

"What time you thinking about going?"

"Probably be on the road 'bout five AM."

"Shit, Herm, on a Saturday?" Jamison said, running his hand through his hair.

"Early bird gits the worm and all that shit."

Jamison considered for only a moment longer before the quiet of the woods appealed too strongly. He hadn't been out in what seemed like ages, at least since he took over the shop. He deserved a nice, quiet morning.

"Yeah, alright, Herm, five AM. Swing by the house?"

"Will do," Herm said as he turned back toward the old coupe with the front bumper hanging slightly askew—remnants of the accident he had gotten in a few weeks before when a doe ran out of the woods just in front of him, smashing headlong into the car. Herman gave a wave and a toot of the horn before turning back onto Second Street and heading (most likely if he knew Herman, and he knew Herman) to the cafe for his late morning breakfast, not brunch. Brunch was for women on Sundays.

Saturday morning came, and Herman showed up just before 5:00 AM. Early bird and all that shit. They spent the better part of the day hiking up "The Hill," stopping several times to warm themselves with the coffee that Eve had supplied in two separate thermoses. They talked, they glassed, and Jamison caught sight of his buck.

"That there is mine, Herm."

"That's a mighty fine buck there, James. Whatcha gunna call him?"

Jamison turned and looked strangely at Herman as his friend took a sip from this thermos.

"Why, that's easy, Herm. I'm going to call him dinner."

The hunting bug had bit, and its bite was ferocious.

The leaves, already well into their beautiful death cycle, covered the sidewalks as the pickup continued down Main Street and headed out of town toward Wimpak Hill.

Leaves danced in the wind as Jamison drove past a sole runner out in the early morning hours. *The early bird gets the worm,* Jamison thought. As the truck got closer, he saw that it was Russell Tolliver, out for his typical pre-dawn run. He gave Russ a wave as he passed and got a quick one in return.

Jamison flicked his cigarette out the window and rolled it up—a chill beginning to creep into his bones. Putting the heat on in the cab, Jamison let his mind wander to the buck that he had already started to cook for dinner in his mind. He could smell the deer meat, and his mouth began to salivate.

So focused was Jamison that he hardly noticed the clouds ominously rolling in over "The Hill." He hardly noticed the trees waving in the wind, waving him back from whence he came. And he certainly didn't notice the dark figure that seemed to dart between the trees in the blink of an eye. No, in fact, as he pulled over to the side of the road at the base of Wimpak Hill, only one thought played in his mind—a nice, hot venison dinner.

Yup, he thought, *today is going to be one fine day.*

CHAPTER 1

Wispy pink clouds floated silently above Isolation, signaling the official start of a new day. The sun slowly rose, awaking from its slumber, and the people within the houses along Allen Street did so in kind. Bathroom windows began to steam up from blistering hot showers, the smell of coffee wafted down hallways leading to still darkened bedrooms, and somewhere lovers held each other close, fighting off the cold air that threatened to overtake them once they left the warmth of their bed.

The sounds of waking birds (the ones that were brave enough to not have begun their long flight south for the upcoming winter) could be heard in yards, chirping a warning to the animals that took up residence in the wilderness that surrounded each house, that there was an intruder among them. Leaves fell in cascading rainbows as the creatures took flight, ready to warm their blood against the frigid breeze.

A doe, grazing with her fawn in the backyard of Mitchell Freemore's place, raised its head, heeded the warning of the birds, and darted off into the woods. The cascade continued, covering the quiet, welcoming street in a kaleidoscope of color as Russell was urged forward by the thought of a warm cup of coffee and a day of writing.

Russell loved getting up before the sun to begin his morning run. The crisp air filled his lungs and, with every exhale, sent a fog across his eyes that lent a sense of surrealism against the backdrop of his picturesque neighborhood. Russell's footsteps were thunder claps against the silence of the dawn as he rounded the corner onto Allen Street. The birds, now barely audible over the sound of his heartbeat, sat amongst the skeletons of the Red Maples and Birch trees lining the road.

The wind picked up, blowing an oil slick of leaves across his path, causing his sweat-drenched shirt to cling to his body. A chill, numbing to the bone, crept through him. He closed his eyes, bracing himself against the raw, late autumn New England air, not noticing the leaves swirling around him. As his foot landed upon a frosty collection that had congregated in his path, Russell's leg slipped out from beneath him, buckling his right knee and sending a shock of pain and fear throughout him. His panic subsided only slightly as he bent over at the waist, hands on his thighs, gasping for breath.

"Shit!" he exclaimed.

He began to bend his knee, testing the durability of it. When the knee did not bite back too hard, Russell straightened up and placed his weight on the throbbing leg. A slight pain (more discomfort, really) arose, signaling caution. "Maybe I'll walk from here," he mused.

Slowly and not without a limp, Russell began walking toward his home. Thankfully, the damned leaves had decided to play their evil prank only a few houses down from his own. Even as the ache from his knee continued to send slight tremors to his brain, Russell couldn't help but recognize again that this street was as picturesque as any Thomas Kinkade painting he had ever seen. Russell's beautiful and kind-hearted wife's favorite artist was never his cup of tea; he was a bit too commercial for Russell's taste. (What ever happened to the starving artist?) Even still, Russell couldn't help but draw a comparison.

Russell moved his family to Isolation only six months ago, but it had felt like home the first time they had laid eyes on the serene beauty of the area.

Russell and Marie had been married for the last six years, but they had been together since college. They moved into a small two-bedroom apartment just outside Boston while in their senior year. Nestled within the affluence of Chestnut Hill, Boston College offered a more quiet option to most of the other colleges in the area; though rent prices were much higher than two struggling college students could afford, they had to move a bit further away from the school than they would have liked. The apartment was perfect for the two of them. Even if the location wasn't ideal, they had each other.

After graduation, Russell worked at a marketing firm in the heart of the city, but at night he pursued his real passion: writing. He honed his craft night after night, and finally, after just over a year of diligence, he produced his first novel: *Beyond the Autumn Leaves*.

It took a few weeks to get going, but when word got out about the new novelist whose debut was part John Muir and part Stephen King, he began to climb the literary charts. Critics praised him, readers bought multiple copies for friends and family, and his own friends bragged about knowing the new hot author.

Russell asked Marie to marry him a week after the novel was released. They were married six months later at the church Marie's family had gone to her whole life. They flew to Peru for a much cherished and much-needed honeymoon. The two of them relaxed on the beaches, took in all the tourist attractions, and even saw the wondrous Machu Picchu-a lifelong dream for Russell. For two solid weeks, they ate, made love under the stars, and embraced the sounds and culture of the area. Who knew heaven came next to an alpaca?

When they returned home, Russell's publishing company began pushing him hard to produce another book. They were a small publishing house, and because of the success of Russell's first book, he was able to push off the expectation of a second novel until after the wedding and honeymoon. Now that he had returned home from his time in paradise, their patience was wearing a bit thin.

"You need to strike while the iron is hot, Russ. And make no mistake, it's already cooling off. If you don't, you'll be forgotten by next year," his agent pleaded. Russell knew this was true. *Beyond the Autumn Leaves* had fallen out of the top ten books by debut authors months ago, and while it was still critically acclaimed, the buzz surrounding it had certainly died down. Russ knew that he needed to produce something to appease the publishing house, so weeks after returning from the honeymoon, he began taking an hour each night to write.

The bones of a story began to develop, but they seemed to be coming as slowly as a frappe being sucked through a straw, the effort immense, but the satisfaction when it hit your tongue, or in this case, your eyes, made it all worthwhile. But when Marie became pregnant, priorities changed.

In an effort to please the publishing house while supporting Marie during her first pregnancy, Russell was able to strike a deal that allowed for two novellas rather than one full-length novel. Russell was able to write during the day, go to Marie's appointments with her during the afternoon, and edit at night.

By the time Marie was six months on, Russ had produced his next work—*Under the Stars*. He wrote this book as a tribute to his wife, to the love they made in Peru. To the beauty and femininity that he saw each time he looked at the swell of her belly. Russell realized that there was nothing as attractive as his pregnant wife. The way she shuffled off to the bedroom at night, her hips widening each day. The way her belly stuck out as she lay next to him. Her breasts full and heaving after even the slightest exercise. *Under the Stars* was a tribute to the beauty of women and the feminine virtues within.

Unfortunately, readers didn't quite embrace the novella in the way that he had hoped. It was released to tepid reviews. Certainly not the worst reviews he had ever seen, but nothing close to the critical acclaim of *Beyond the Autumn Leaves*. Russell didn't care. He wrote this book for his wife, his love. He didn't need critical acclaim to feel pride in his work.

Marie gave birth to a boy, Sam, three months later. Sam came in the middle of the night and was far quicker than anyone had expected. Marie had woken up around midnight to a wet bed. Confusion struck first, followed by panic, and then a sense of duty and calmness sank in as she woke Russell. They got to the hospital and were taken right into a room where pictures of happy mothers holding their newborn babies hung, between sporadically placed, stenciled balloons on the wall. The doctor checked Marie's dilation and prepared her for her stay.

By noon, Sam was screaming at the top of his lungs. A shrill scream that only a baby can produce, one that only a parent can love on this joyous day but brings nightmarish frustration to everyone not long after. Sam was carried over to Marie, all cleaned up by the doctors and smelling that baby smell, placed on her chest and held tightly. Russell looked at his family and smiled.

Less than a year later, Russell produced the second of his novellas. Unfortunately, this one was reviewed even worse than the first. In fact, several critics posited whether Russell Tolliver was simply a "one-hit wonder."

Though Russell knew he shouldn't read the social media posts or take the critics too seriously, they stung. Russell took a break from writing after this. Well, not so much a break, as he just *couldn't* write.

A year passed.

Then two.

"Writer's block is a real ass kicker," he said during one of his bi-weekly therapy sessions. "I have all these…these pieces rattling around in my head, but I can't put them together. It's like my brain is all clouded. I can see what is right in front of me, but when I take a step, it disappears."

"You know Russ, maybe the answer is as simple as a fresh start. You've been talking about getting out of the city for as long as you've been coming here. Hell, even your novels are nature based. Sam's getting bigger. You're going to need to get a bigger place sooner or later. And, at the risk of being unprofessional for only a moment, you need to get back to what you know. Back to the writing that made you successful."

"Maybe you're right," Russell said after a few moments of contemplation.

"I am, Russ. Remember, my advice is what you pay me so handsomely for."

"We need a bigger place, Russ," Marie said after Sam's fourth birthday party. "We've talked about it for almost a year now, and I don't want to raise Sam in the city. Hell, neither of us wants to be in the city anymore. We haven't for a while. This place was fine when it was just us, but it's time we start a life somewhere new. Somewhere Sam can grow," a car horn blasted just outside the window, and a stream of curse words flew from a man's mouth who had apparently been cut off by some "out of state piece of shit."

Russell glanced out of the window and shook his head. "Maybe a place a little quieter."

Russell had left his shrink's office that night last week, knowing he was right but struggling with the change.

The only great writing I ever did was here. What if I move us to a new home, and it gets worse?

Gets worse, the voice in his head said, *you've barely written a word in years. Stop being a stubborn asshole and make a change. You know the definition of insanity is…*

Russell nodded and walked over to Marie, putting his arm around her waist and kissing her head. "Why don't you spend some time looking for places and let me know what you find?"

"Oh, sure, I'll do that right after I do everything else around here," she said with a wry smile on her face.

There was a bang in the living room, followed by Sam crying. "I'll go check on him," Russ said as he returned her smile.

"Thank you, honey. Love you lots." She slapped his butt as she walked down to the bedroom.

Marie was always so positive. Russell often thought the universe must have been watching out for him when it brought Marie into his life.

Russell and Marie had only a general sense of what they wanted in their new home: a quiet neighborhood, a large yard for Sam to play in, and a fireplace. They were determined to head north, where they could disappear into the green areas that enveloped the state on every map they looked at. However, they looked at half a dozen houses from Nashua to Concord, and none satisfied the visualization that Marie had created in her head. Until one day, while making an impromptu search online, she found it.

"Russ! Oh my God, come here!"

Russell ran into the living room, panic-stricken. "What happened?"

"I found it," Marie said, not taking her eyes off the screen.

It was perfect and within their price range. A three-bedroom (but one can be used for an office, the listing stated) home in a quiet neighborhood surrounded by nature. **"A large yard,"** the listing stated, **"for children to play in or for you to watch the crystal clear night sky."**

"Marie, it's beautiful, but it's pretty far north. I mean, I've never even heard of this town."

"What does it matter? I've been home with Sam, and you just need an office to write. What's keeping us here? This is it. This is the one."

The next morning Marie called and set up a meeting with the agent in charge of the house; they took the long drive north that same week.

As they toured the home, Marie walked with Sam around the yard. Sam rolled around in the grass as Marie laughed and talked with the real estate agent. Russ walked into what he had already marked in his mind as his office and gazed out the window that displayed what he would come to discover was Wimpak Hill.

They put an offer in that same day.

The serenity Russell felt in this town was real. More real than anything he had experienced in Boston. More real than the first autograph he was asked to sign. This house, this street, this town gave Russell the solace he and Marie had been searching for. Solace that, he was sure, would help him write his next novel.

The town's name held in stark contrast to Russell and Marie's previous life. The name held them close, wrapping the family up in its warm embrace.

Isolation.

CHAPTER 2

Marie had always been a city girl. Yet, growing up just south of Boston, in Dorchester, Massachusetts, she never felt quite at home amongst the cramped streets where she lived.

Marie was an only child and reaped all the benefits that came with that title. Doted on and praised, Marie never seemed to let the affection go to her head. She was always appreciative, never expectant.

While her family was hardly wealthy, on Marie's eighth birthday, when all she hoped for was horseback riding lessons, Marie's parents made sure she had the best instructor they could find. Her love for horses stayed with her into adulthood, and she could often be found cruising the internet for funny horse videos (forget those cat videos, they were played out) or volunteering at the local horse farm when the opportunities arose.

Marie's riding developed quickly. She competed in several horse shows in which she placed in the top three. She did allow her pride to swell in these circumstances. She had worked very hard at such an early age for success, and success she had. When she dismounted, she would always pet her horse's nose and kiss it before feeding the mare carrots, her favorite treat.

Unfortunately, caring for a horse was too expensive for Marie's parents to maintain for long. When they told Marie that she would have to give up the lessons and shows (at least for a while), she held the tears in and accepted the decision as a child beyond her years.

For her Sweet Sixteen, Marie was given a slightly used Toyota Corolla (the salesman promised that it was in tip-top shape and could they really argue with the price?) even while the family car was seemingly falling apart piece by piece. She drove that car everywhere. She loved going out to the beach at night and sitting with the windows down, listening to the waves crash on the shore. Oftentimes she'd bring her friends as well, and they would walk along the sandy dunes. The grainy pieces of sand slipping their way in between Marie's toes was one of her simple pleasures in life.

At seventeen, Marie's parents reluctantly told her that if she wanted to go to college, she would have to find a way herself; they simply couldn't afford it. As she had always done, Marie took the news in stride. She wasn't afraid of a little hard work, and so she reached out to the horse farm where she had once ridden and later volunteered years before.

The woman was kind enough to bring Marie on as a paid employee, knowing her love for the animals and her familiarity with the farm. Marie would get up early so she could go to the farm before dawn and get work done. She would get home with enough time to shower and grab a coffee before heading to school. On the weekends, she allowed herself to sleep a little later, but she would spend most of the day there mucking the stalls, cleaning the corrals, and feeding the horses. It was incredibly hard work, but Marie loved it.

When it was finally time to apply for college, Marie had her grades (which she always kept up, despite the hard work on the farm) and a great letter of recommendation from the farm, and she applied to

Boston College with the hopes of admission; a scholarship or two wouldn't hurt either. When the acceptance letter came, and the Whites were gathered around their daughter in the living room of their modest home, Marie's father, Ron, could not hold back the tears; his baby girl had done it. Pride swelled within him as he hugged her close.

Joan, Marie's mother, stood on the other side of her daughter, clutching her tightly and whispering that she was so proud of her and "Let's go get some ice cream," a staple in the White family household since Marie was a child. Ice cream was the celebratory treat of good news. Marie had declared long ago that she was never too old to go out for ice cream.

Marie's first day on campus was hectic but full of anticipation and excitement. She discovered she was dorming with a beautiful and bubbly blonde named Amanda Tyler (call me Mandy though, please and thank you), who was the complete antithesis of Marie, yet, they simply worked. Mandy had the type of beauty that made men drop to their knees and kiss the ground she had just walked. It was a timeless beauty-Marilyn Monroe meets Audrey Hepburn.

Mandy and Marie would go out every Friday night to celebrate another week completed at school. Usually, M&M (the nickname for the pair given to them by their sorority sisters during pledge week) would head down to Quincy Market to shop, sample the delicious food, and watch as the boys on their skateboards would try to do tricks to impress the two-often crashing both figuratively and literally. Marie paid the skaters little mind; she had far too much going on with the sorority and classes to be bothered with boys that spent their Friday nights cracking their heads open on sidewalks. Besides, any boy that wore a chain connected to his wallet was just not her style.

The two would often find a nice cozy cafe, grab an appetizer, and chat about everything they should be doing back on campus. But it was Friday night, and the girls needed to blow off steam somehow. Occasionally, M&M would forgo their trip to the Quincy Market shops and restaurants and really cut loose at one of the many nightclubs scattered around the city. These nights were reserved for the weeks that were more stressful than others.

Marie was always a bit more modest than Mandy. Mandy often sported a low-cut T-shirt and skin-tight jeans that she would fight to pull up over her considerably amazing ass. Marie was jealous of Mandy's body, but Mandy would always say, "Marie, be proud of what you have. Besides, you have the tits. I have the ass. Together no man can resist our," Mandy paused and thought for a moment, "charm." Marie would blush at this but decided early on that giving a little smack on Mandy's backside served as a better conclusion than hiding her face in embarrassment.

Russell had met Marie on campus in the Fall of their junior year. Russell had been on campus for three years now, and yet, he had never seen a woman until that moment. When he first laid eyes on her, sitting in the grass under one of the large trees that speckled the campus, his heart caught in his chest. She was with several other girls (likely her roommates, he suspected at the time), but at that moment, they could have been the only two people in the world. When Russell began walking over to her, reciting what he planned on saying, his voice caught in his throat. Marie looked over and saw him staring in her direction, a stunned look covering his face.

She smiled at him, and Russell's heart melted. He gave a gentle, albeit awkward, wave and took the final steps toward the woman that he had already decided was the prettiest girl in the world. He gathered his courage and asked her out that day. Later, Mandy would ask her, "Why him when she had been so dismissive of all the guys on campus to that point?"

"I just knew," Marie replied. "I just knew."

Their love was passionate, and it was real, and Russell believed himself to be the luckiest man in the world. They spent nights alone among the crowds of people in downtown Boston. They spent weekends at the beach rolling amongst the dunes and letting the waves crash over them.

These were the days Russell and Marie would reflect back on that were the most carefree of their lives. When love, laughter, and peace came easily. But at some point, life tries to disrupt the ease of things. It is during these times Russ and Marie would remark to each other that it is best to have a rock to fall back on.

A partner to confide in.

A strong wind to blow away all the debris that threatens to get in your way.

CHAPTER 3

As Russell approached his house, he heard a familiar voice calling, "Heyah Russ, how ya doin'?"

Snapping out of his thoughts, Russ looked to his left and saw his neighbor and an overall hell of a guy, Tom Richmond. Russ walked over, still favoring his knee, arm extended. "Morning, Tom. You're up early."

For an older man, Tom cut himself a pretty solid figure. Over six feet tall, broad-shouldered, and the best damn beard Russ could remember laying his eyes on, Tom always had a smile on his face and sage advice to offer. The day the small family had moved in, Tom came bounding out of his house to introduce himself and grab a box.

Tom's eyes hid horrors of an unspeakable nature, though. Tom had served as an Army infantry soldier during the Vietnam War. While he didn't often speak about his deployment, at times, usually after a few stiff drinks of whiskey, Tom might let slip some small tidbit of information. Some long forgotten or long ignored memory of his time in the jungle. Then he would get a glazed look in his eyes and say, "Ahyup. Best be gittin' home now. Alcohol is gittin ta mah head."

"Ahyup. Headin' out towahds Wimpak Hill this mahning." It always amazed Russ how some people in New England had far thicker accents than others. "Hopin' to get me a deeyah. Wintah's comin' and ain't nothin' like a nice venison stew to warm the ol' bones."

For the six months that Russ had known Tom, he made it a point, at least once a week, to head out into the woods-sometimes to hunt, sometimes to wander.

It seemed surprising that a man who had so many seemingly awful memories of war would want to be out with a rifle. Then again, it's what Tom knew. Tom knew guns, and the woods offered Tom the same thing it offered Russ: solace. Besides, who was Russ to assume he knew another man's heart more than the man knew his own.

"The deer seem to be coming into town more and more lately. Just saw a couple over in Mitchell Freemore's yard this morning. I'm sure an old deerstalker like you won't have any trouble."

"Don't you doubt that. I may be getting old, but I've got the patience of a snake waitin' fowah the perfect chance to strike." Tom mimed his rifle in hand, scanning the woods for a target. "When I get to makin' the stew, I'll be sure to send some ovah to you and Marie too. Maybe give some to yah boy as well. Put some meat on him so we can take him out inta tha woods too."

"Ha, thanks, Tom. Sam is still a little young to go hunting, though. Marie would have me strung up and gutted like a deer if Sam went anywhere near a gun."

"Well, hell Russ, we don't gotta take the boy huntin'. Just a nice walk will do the boy some good. This is beautiful country up heah, Russ."

Russ nodded and considered what Tom had said, "Listen, I have to head in and get in the shower. It's chilly out here, and the sweat is freezing me to the bone."

"Could use summa that stew now, I reckon, haha. My best to Marie and Sam."

Russ turned and gave a wave over his shoulder. "Good luck out there today, Tom."

"Sayah Russ," Tom called as Russ approached his front steps, "when ya gunna finally come along? I may know those woods bettah than I know my own ass, but a little comp'ny would be nice too."

All summer, Tom had been on Russ about hunting. Russ continually dismissed the thought, unsure if he even had the will to shoot a deer.

"The old know-it-alls in town say to stay away from there, you know. Aren't those woods supposed to be haunted anyways?" Russ chuckled. He looked back to Tom, a dark look of seriousness crossed over the old man's face. Russell's smile fell from his face as he watched the old man. "Maybe one of these days, Tom," Russ called back, trying to ease the tension that had crossed his friend's face.

"That's what you've been tellin' me," Tom closed the bed of his truck, realized he had forgotten his chewing tobacco, and mosied back inside.

Just as Russell opened the front door, a shiver shook him from head to toe. The warmth of the house was a welcome gift but not nearly as welcoming as the aroma of coffee and bacon coming from the kitchen. The smell carried him down the hall where Marie was standing, over the sink, looking out the window into the backyard and off toward Wimpak Hill some miles in the distance.

He always loved how her hair, still tussled from a deep sleep, looked and the way her pajama bottoms stuck to her ("I don't know why you like my ass, it's nothing special." "I like your everything, Marie."). Russ came up behind her and wrapped his arms around her waist, kissing her neck.

"Oh Russ, you're soaked, and you smell like a wet dog."

"Well, good morning to you too," he said, crossing his arms over his chest and doing his best impersonation of a man deeply wounded.

"Good morning, honey." She leaned over and kissed him, and Russ wasn't unaware of the gentle movement of her breasts under her T-shirt. "Breakfast is on, and coffee is brewing."

"Sam's not up yet?" he asked as he glanced at the time on the stove.

"Not yet. He has a few more minutes before he needs to get up for school."

Russ took a few steps closer to Marie and placed his hands on her hips. "A few more minutes, huh?"

Marie leaned in and kissed him as Russ let his hands wander over the back of her pajama pants. "Honey. Honey. You really do stink. Go take a shower."

Giving him a quick peck on the nose, Marie returned to the bacon and eggs. "You're a cruel person Mrs. Tolliver. Evil to the core."

"I know, honey. Hey, wake up Sam on your way past his room," she called back to him as he made his way down the hall.

Russell didn't know what was more uncomfortable at that moment, the shirt sticking to his body or the ache that he now felt in his crotch. He was sure, with his time in the shower, he could take care of both.

"Hey bud, time to get up," Russ called as he knocked on Sam's door, pushing it open slowly. Sam was already awake, dressed in his favorite red flannel button-up, and playing with his Legos. Russ was amused to see that Sam was growing up to be a morning person like himself.

"Hi, Dad, good morning. Looky what I'm doing."

Russ walked over to where his son was sitting in the middle of his bedroom floor, criss-cross applesauce, and sat down next to him. "Wow, bud, that's great."

"Yeah, it's a house in the woods, with trees, and animals, and water so the animals can drink. It was in my dream last night, and I wanted to make it to show my friends."

The excitement of a five-year-old can be infectious, and Russ couldn't help but smile as he looked at his son's masterpiece. "Sure, bud. I'm sure they'll love it."

Realizing that he really did smell like the back alleys of Boston's Chinatown district, he said to Sam, "I've gotta get in the shower. Do you need to use the bathroom?"

"Nope, I'm fine. Hey, do I smell bacon?" As Sam darted from the room, faster than Barry Allen's alter-ego "The Flash" (a poster hanging above Sam's bed, as well as bed sheets and pajama pants flung in the corner of the room showed anyone that dared question who should have a larger role in the DC Universe, what Sam Tolliver, five-year-old, thought), he shoved the bedroom door hard against the wall, almost knocking down the lava lamp placed on the bedside table.

"Hey pal, don't run."

As Russ started to get up, movement past a small window of the Lego house caught his eye.

At that very moment, the wind outside seemed to die down, though Russ hardly noticed. The squeals of joy coming from Sam as he shoved the first slice of bacon in his mouth seemed to fade away into a silence so heavy the weight of it threatened to crush him. Russell lay on his stomach and inched closer to the small window on the side of the Lego house.

As he peered inside, he saw a small, all-black figure standing in the corner of the toy living room. Russell's focus became hyper-sensitive, and his head began to swim. The strangest thing about this figure was that it seemed to…vibrate. As though there was something within that was trying to stay hidden or, maybe, trying to come out.

The wind began again, blowing the leaves around and slapping them against the window. Suddenly Russ was very aware of the chill that had crept back into his bones, but he couldn't take his eyes away from the little figure in the cabin. His hand reached for the roof of the toy home. He had to see it closer. He had to hold it in his hands. He had to know that it was real.

"Russ," a slightly aggravated voice called from behind him.

Russ jumped so much that he nearly knocked over Sam's masterpiece. "Honey, sorry I didn't hear you. What's up?"

"Will you get in the shower? I need to get in there before work, too. What are you doing down there anyways?"

Russ turned back to the Lego cabin and saw that the figure he had become so transfixed with was no longer there. "Nothing…nothing. Sorry. Shower, yes." Russ jumped up. "Love you." He ran by his wife, kissed her on the lips, and began peeling his shirt off before the bathroom door was even closed.

CHAPTER 4

As Russ walked by his office, he peered in, mentally preparing himself for a long day of writing. He ran through, in his mind, the last chapter he had written and thought about what was next as he went into his bedroom and closed the door.

The sound (slightly muffled) of his wife finishing her morning routine while Sam laughed playfully, watching his morning cartoons, was only a distant background noise registering somewhere in the deepest recesses of his mind. As he sat at the end of the bed, he found himself lost in thoughts of the figure that he had seen hidden in the shadows of the little Lego house.

He must have been seeing things. Too much energy expended on his morning run, too little food in his stomach, and too much sexual frustration built up within can cause a man to go crazy. He shook his head and rubbed his hands across his cheeks, attempting to refocus himself. He stood up and put on his boxers, jeans, a tank top, and a nice button-up shirt. Russell had decided long ago that if he was going to work from home, he would keep to a routine of getting up and putting actual clothes on. He wasn't going to be one of those people that stayed in pajamas all day. He did, however, decide that wearing his slippers while he wrote was perfectly acceptable.

A man is allowed some comforts, after all.

He left the bedroom and started toward his office. SpongeBob SquarePants was on some ridiculous adventure with Patrick, and it sounded like Plankton was doing what he always does, failing in comedic fashion.

He closed the door and walked to the window just above his desk. He adjusted the shades, sat down in his chair, cracked his knuckles, and looked at the typewriter. It beckoned him as he contemplated the next chapter. Ultimately, Russ did take his therapist's advice, well, at least some of it, and went back to his wheelhouse. He steered away from the truly romantic tales and drifted toward more dramatic tales with a supernatural twist. Russ knew he could write another masterpiece if he just stayed focused.

Okay, masterpiece is a little much, don't you think, the voice in his head reacted.

"It's all relative," Russ responded to the empty room.

It was not lost on Russ that the small town setting in his story slightly mirrored the town around him. Russ thought it remarkable that a change in scenery had done so much. Pulling imagery from Isolation really helped to get the creative juices flowing, even if the setting was slightly different.

Russ enjoyed the simplicity of using a typewriter, even while most authors enjoyed the modern technology that would correct spelling mistakes and give word suggestions in real-time. Russ found that the steady *tap, tap, tap* of the typewriter keys often lulled him into a hypnotic state where the words would simply flow. Besides, there was something rhythmic, almost erotic, watching the teeth slap the wet ink across the paper.

Marie opened the door to kiss her husband goodbye. She looked beautiful, and he thought that the country life really suited her. She just seemed so…happy. And even though they had been together all these years, he would still catch himself staring into her eyes on occasion and see an almost childlike joy brimming within.

"So what's going to happen with the Riley boys now?"

"Huh?"

She looked down at the typewriter while she put in her earrings. "Oh, well, I can't just give that away. You'll have to wait and see, just like everyone else."

"Tease," she said with a smirk crossing her lips. "I'll see you later tonight. Don't forget to pick Sam up from school."

"You got it. Hey Sam!" The sound of thumping shoes running down the hall is something that can bring joy or annoyance to any parent; today, it brought joy.

"Yeah, Dad?" he asked, a piece of bacon still in his hands.

"Love you, bud. Have a great day at school."

Sam smiled and shoved the rest of the bacon into his mouth before running over and grabbing onto Russell's neck. "Have a great day with your spooky story, Dad." Sam ran out of the room, thudded down the hall into his own room to get the Lego cabin, and ran to the front door. "Come on, Mom, we're gonna be late."

Marie kissed Russ on the cheek one last time before she left the room, calling back over her shoulder, "You know you're going to let me read it before you finish. You always do."

"Well, maybe this time I'll have enough self-control to not be affected by your womanly charms."

"Ha, not likely. Love you."

Russ listened as her heels clicked down the hall, the jingling of keys as she passed the counter, and the click of the latch as she closed the door. He heard Sam call out a good morning to Tom (Mr. Bridges to Sam), who was finally pulling out of his driveway, packed and loaded, ready to find his buck. Marie's car started shortly thereafter, and he followed it with his ears down the road. The smell of Marie's perfume hung in the air while Russ looked back to his typewriter.

"Alright, boys, what are you up to today?"

Jamison had arrived at "The Hill" almost an hour ago and had made his way in the direction where he had glassed his buck the previous week.

The woods that made up Wimpak Hill, even in the daylight, had an aura of eeriness to them. The trees seemed to have their own personality. When they swayed, they spoke in long groans and whispered conversations only intelligible to those that chose to listen.

Yet, oftentimes, these secret conversations were the only noises that could be heard in the woods. There was wildlife to be seen, but even the scattered rustlings of the squirrels and chipmunks seemed muted most days. A person could yell into the silence, and the trees seemed to grab the noise before it could go too far, holding it tight so as to not allow a disturbance in the serenity. This is what made hunting up on "The Hill" so difficult. Animal calls were few and far between. To hunt on "The Hill," one had to rely heavily on their intuition.

Jamison had great intuition.

Jamison's camouflage hid his form almost perfectly against the backdrop of the late autumn trees. As he edged closer to where he had spotted his target previously, the wind picked up the leaves that had collected all over the forest floor. They swirled around him, and Jamison couldn't help but be mesmerized by the beauty of the red and orange leaves circling him in their dance.

Jamison was brought out of his hypnotic state by the movement of something between the trees. The wind stopped. The leaves fell back to the ground. Jamison's eyes focused on where he had seen the shadow. As he crouched down, he reached for his rifle slowly. He edged closer to a downed tree a few feet in front of him, hoping to not be left out in the open when his prize emerged.

His breath slowed to a practiced repetition: *breathe slowly, in through your nose, out through your mouth*. His eyes were that of an eagle locked onto its prey.

Tom pulled up to the trailhead just north of town. Tom had known these woods most of his life-hiking, then hunting them whenever the mood struck. These woods were second nature to him, but when he pulled up to the trail and saw an old Ford pickup already there, his hair stood on end.

There was no reason, no reason at all, for Tom to be concerned. No reason at all to think anything was out of place. Nothing was wrong. Just another hunter or maybe a hiker enjoying the beautiful morning. But when Tom parked next to the pickup, something felt wrong.

The woods, always quiet and serene, took on a sense that Tom had never felt in all his years coming up here. The trees were ominous. So quiet they seemed to almost hum. Clouds slowly rolled in above Tom. Dark, dangerous clouds. When Tom turned to look toward town, the sky was blue, and the sun shone, but directly above, the clouds added to the feeling that lay on him like a madman staring into the abyss.

Jamison took his eyes off his target's location for only a moment to glance up at the clouds that had appeared out of nowhere.

No rain in the forecast today, he thought.

A sound from behind him caused him to turn cautiously. A giant black figure stood behind him, towering over him like a grizzly facing a puppy. A wet stream of urine ran down Jamison's leg. Tears filled his eyes. His head rang out with fear as his mind tried to comprehend what his eyes were seeing. The last thing to escape Jamison's lips was a scream loud enough to pierce even the silence of the woods on Wimpak Hill.

And then there was nothing.

Tom was just grabbing his gun from the bed of his truck when he heard the scream off to his left.

Goosebumps started at his legs and ran all the way up to the back of his neck. Tom instinctually ran to the driver's side door and got in. He sat there for what felt like an eternity, trying to decide what to do. If someone was in trouble, he couldn't just leave.

Jesus H. Christ, Tom, quit being such a sorry sack of shit. Get out there and help. If this was 'Nam, you'd be out there.

"This ain't 'Nam," he said to no one. "I ain't never felt in 'Nam what I feel out theyah now."

You know these woods, Tom. You've been coming here your whole goddamn life. Quit being such a pussy.

"Ah, fuck you. Stupid fucking mind," he said. Tom took a deep breath, gave himself a couple slaps to the cheeks to clear his mind, and he stepped out of his truck.

The tapping of the keys stopped, and Russ listened intently.

Something in his mind, some primal part, sent waves of anxiety through him. Russ got up and walked toward the kitchen, though he wasn't sure why. It was almost as if he was drawn there. He went over to the sink and looked out his picturesque window and off toward Wimpak Hill.

The trees that led to a small patch of woods out back swayed in the gentle breeze. Off in the distance, dark clouds hung over "The Hill," though clear skies reigned above Isolation. The silence of the house was magical. There was almost a hum in the air.

The silence was broken by a murder of crows cawing in one of the trees in the yard. Several swooped down and pecked at the ground, likely looking for insects or worms that were just under the surface. He heard some kids, probably teenagers, from the language being used, walking by out front. A car passing by slowly. Russell imagined the driver staring out at the teenagers with a glare of disapproval. Russell heard all this, but he did not hear the scream coming from Wimpak Hill.

Russell leaned down and splashed water on his face, clearing his mind and shifting his focus back to the Riley boys. He gave one more quick, conciliatory glance out toward the beauty of Wimpak Hill and walked back to his office.

CHAPTER 5

Sam stared out the back window as they drove down the side streets of Isolation toward Appleton Elementary (named after the town founder Isaac Appleton, famed trapper, trader, and, though Sam didn't understand what it meant when he heard a couple teachers talking about it in hushed tones by the teacher's lounge, racist, rapist, and murderer).

The school kids in Isolation all learn that Appleton was one of the best trappers of his day. A regular American success story. Though at Sam's age, the lessons tend to focus on the legend of the man who created the town and gave his name to their school.

The furs that he collected from fox, coyote, beavers, and other critters that may be found in the woods of northwestern New Hampshire would be sold down in New York or Boston so that the fancy men and women in the city could show off their wealth to those that were far less fortunate.

As history has noted, Appleton took his earnings from he and his family's work in Boston and, seeing a vast wealth of animals to be had and very few people (there were the Native Americans, but they didn't understand how much money they had crawling all around them; hell, they didn't even wear clothes most of the time. How could they ever appreciate the furs he was capturing), Appleton decided he'd create his own little slice of the world. He named it Isolation.

Historians debate the true reason that Appleton decided on the small town's name, but the accepted reason is simply that Appleton wanted peace and quiet. After leaving the hustle and bustle of Boston in the mid-1800s and having so few people around, the name just fit. However, some of the older folks in town-the folks that you can find each Sunday morning gathered at the local rendezvous, *The Back In Time Cafe*-tell a far different tale of insanity and murder that once plagued the area.

Some of the older folks, such as Sarah Thornberg and Miles Gray, claim to have primary source documents that they keep at Bryce Callahan's place that detail, graphically, the truth of the legends. Most of the townsfolk simply dismiss them out of hand as the old town kooks who waste away their time telling these hand-me-down stories from their fathers and grandfathers.

Sam peeled his eyes away from the window and looked at his Lego cabin. If this was not the best building that any kid in any part of the world had ever made, well, he'd just have to meet that kid because *that* kid clearly had to be amazing. Sam lifted it up, inspecting every brick, making sure that nothing was out of place. His friends were going to be amazed. He could see the looks on their faces when they set eyes on this masterpiece.

"Wow, Sam," they'll say. "Where did you come up with such a great idea?"

Sam would walk proudly to each student, holding out his creation, making sure they all got a good look. The class would...wait...Sam noticed something out of place. He thought he saw something inside the cabin that hadn't been there before. He thought there was a character inside, staring out the window. The character was black as pitch, and he seemed to be shaking. Sam held the cabin close to his face, but his eyes couldn't seem to focus on what he was seeing.

The back roads of Isolation were very narrow, and the canopy of the trees, crossing over the road some twenty or thirty feet up, made the roads very dark. Sam placed the cabin down on his lap and rubbed his eyes. He picked it back up carefully and brought it close to his face. He was sure there was something in there now. He carefully lifted the roof off of the cabin; nothing could be out of place. He couldn't have something there that didn't belong. The roof slowly detached, and Sam looked in. Nothing.

"Sam," his mom called from the front seat, "didn't you hear me?" She was looking at him in the rearview mirror. "I asked if you were feeling Okay. You look like you're getting a little pale."

Sam sighed a little and looked out the window, confused by what he had seen, or at least what he thought he had seen. "Yeah, Mom, I'm fine."

Marie turned to look at Sam, reached back, and grabbed his knee— a comforting squeeze. When Marie turned back to the road, standing directly on the centerline stood a massive man. No, a creature. A shadow of pure darkness, broad-shouldered and awful. There was no face, just a terrible gaping smile. It screamed at the car, cracking the windshield.

"Oh shit!" Marie screamed as she swerved the car, somehow managing to miss the creature and the trees that lined the road. She slammed on the brakes and put the car in park. Sam was wide-eyed in the back seat, blissfully unaware of what she saw.

"Sam. Oh my God, are you alright?" Marie unbuckled her seat belt and turned to face him. She looked out the back window, terrified at what she might see. Her heart sounded like a drum beating in her head. Nothing but trees and the empty road was there.

"Mom, are you okay? What happened?" Sam asked, fighting off the fear that threatened to overwhelm him. Tears began to brim over and spill down his face.

Marie continued to stare out the back window, expecting to see something, anything, walk out of the woods and toward the car, but there was nothing.

"Nothing, baby. An animal just ran in front of the car, that's all. I'm sorry I scared you."

Marie, still shaking with fear, composed herself and took a deep, calming breath. Wiping the tears that were threatening, Marie took one more glance at the rearview mirror and slid the gear shift into drive. She eased out into the road and continued on toward Sam's school. Though she desperately tried to convince herself that she had imagined the creature in the road, her eyes continued to flick from the cracked windshield and toward the rearview mirror, searching the road for she didn't know what.

In the back seat, Sam's heart gradually slowed to a normal pace. His eyes drifted back to the trees. His mind wandered to childish things and how much fun he was going to have showing his friends his cabin. He stared out the window, looking deep into the woods, and within the small Lego house, a dark shape looked out at him.

CHAPTER 6

Built in the year 2000, Appleton Elementary is a small, one-story brick building that screams "small-town New England." Because of Isolation's low population, it houses grades K-8. Sam started there only a few months earlier and loved every moment of his days.

The grass, or what could be seen peeking out from the leaves that covered the ground, was always mowed. The flag pole towered over the students as they congregated out in front of the school. Trees lined the sidewalk, and, at this hour, the rising sun cast dancing shadows on the bricks at the front of the school.

Marie's Camry pulled up in front of Appleton Elementary just as the students were beginning to head inside. Several of the middle school kids remained sitting under a tree at the far end of the building. One of the boys punched his friend in the arm and then wrapped his arms around the girl sitting next to him. *Young love*, she thought, smiling.

Just as the last of the students were filing into the school (the ones that had actually gotten moving when the bell sounded, that is), Mrs. Granger, Sam's kindergarten teacher, came outside with a wave and a smile.

Annie Granger was a woman in her early thirties, not homely, but plain. She dressed in conservative clothes, and her glasses always sat just a little too low on her nose. She often wore her hair in a bun, but today it was down, blowing in the wind as the leaves crossed the field in front of the school. Sam struggled to open the back door of the Camry, pushing against the gusting wind as it tried to close the door, imploring Sam to stay in the car.

"Don't forget your backpack, honey," Marie called to him as he started to get out of the car.

Sam placed his masterpiece on the backseat while he picked up his backpack and hefted it over his shoulders. He cautiously picked up his work of art and pushed down a loose tile that was threatening to fall from the roof. Sam ran around to the front of the car and gave his mom a giant peck on the cheek.

"Have a great day at school, sweetheart."

"Bye, Mom. Love you," Sam joyously exclaimed as he ran toward his teacher.

Marie saw Mrs. Granger wrap her arm around Sam's shoulder as she guided him into the school.

As the door shut behind them, a dark figure seemed to be hiding in the shadows that lived in the doorway. Marie desperately tried to adjust her eyes to what she thought she saw, but the flickering rays of light played tricks.

When a knock came on her driver's side window, Marie's scream could have rivaled any of the "Scream Queens" she had watched during the slumber parties she had, growing up.

"Jesus Christ," Marie chuckled when she saw that it was only Eve.

Eve was the mother of one of Sam's friends at school. Eve was an altogether pleasant woman with bewitching eyes and lips that begged to be kissed by any man Eve deemed worthy enough to be in her orbit.

For the past several years, she had given only one man that honor, Jamison Crowley.

Eve worked down at the cafe during the week and as a waitress at a dive bar one town over on the weekends. Russ and Marie had met her and Jamison several times at *The Back in Time cafe*, where the women would talk about the town gossip, and the men would make plans to get together for a drink the way men do. And then forget about it by the time they left each other's presence.

Though she was pleasing to the eye and her laugh was often infectious, rumors in town swirled about Eve. *She's banging every guy at that bar for extra tips. She convinced her ex-boyfriend to throw himself off the bridge that separated Isolation from Errol.* Hell, Marie had even once heard, from a couple of high school kids as she walked down the aisle at the grocery store, that Eve was a witch. Marie really didn't know where kids got their imagination from. In Marie's estimation, Eve was a nice woman, even if Marie could slap her at this moment.

"Geez, Marie. A little jumpy this morning?"

Marie gave a pleasant smile. "I've only had one cup of coffee so far. I guess I'm a little bit out of it."

"Well, you know where to go. Go *Back In Time,* and I'll buy you a cup," Eve smiled radiantly at her.

Sometimes you just need to be in a special kind of mood to deal with some people.

"Ha, yeah, well, I'm a little late for work this morning, so the sludge in the office is going to have to do."

"Well, maybe tomorrow. Hey, Marie, I came over because I wanted to invite you and Russ over for dinner tomorrow night. James is going to grill up some steaks. We can have a couple glasses of wine…what do you think? Daniel would love to see Sam too."

Marie glanced down at the clock. "Sure, Eve, definitely. Listen, though, I really am running a bit late. I'll call you later?"

"Sure, babe. See ya," Eve called over her shoulder as she glided back to her SUV.

Marie adjusted her mirror, took a deep breath-still rattled from what she had thought she'd seen, and began to pull out from the parent drop-off portion of the school parking lot. She turned on the radio, and the melodic voice of Don Henley drizzled sweet nectar into her ears as he sang:

She held me spellbound in the night
Dancing shadows and firelight,

As an unnaturally foreboding feeling crept back over Marie, she held her focus intently on the road, choosing to ignore the hairs standing up on her neck. She turned the radio louder and held a duet with Don as they sang:

Crazy laughter in another room
And she drove herself to madness with a silver spoon.
Woohoo, witchy woman
See how high she flies
Woohoo, witchy woman
She got the moon in her eye

By the time Marie had pulled into a parking spot in front of the small real estate office, she had forgotten about the dark feeling that crept over her in front of the school; she had convinced herself that what she saw on the road was a figment of her imagination; and Eve Crowley was behind the wheel of her crushed SUV, her leg jammed by the engine that had been pushed into the cab by the impact against a tree.

By the time Marie sat at her desk and turned on her computer, a dark creature was approaching a screaming woman in a white SUV.

Chapter 7

Not so far from the devastation that was playing out Rainbow Road, Jimmy Delaney and his friends, Adam Hunt and Forest Walker, were skipping school and walking amongst the cabins of the abandoned camp on the outskirts of Isolation. This was a regular occurrence for Jimmy and his crew. Breaking windows in the cabins, pissing in the counselor's old offices, and lighting fires in the filing cabinets.

Jimmy loved fire. Sometimes, if the mood hit him just so, he would try to hit a squirrel or a bird with a stone, not hard enough to kill it, just to stun it. He'd run to his prey and pick it up, walk it over to the open file cabinet drawer, already ablaze, and toss it in. His favorite part was, after he closed the drawer, hearing the scratching of the little creature as it tried to get out. Adam and Forest would laugh and high-five while Jimmy sat in front of the cabinet, eyes fixated, just wishing he could see the fire consuming his sacrifice.

Jimmy Delaney was a very disturbed boy. What was perhaps the most confounding part of Jimmy's torturous habits was that they seemed to develop from nowhere. Jimmy had a mother and father that were happily married, a sister that was six years his younger and looked up to him, and a brain that most of his teachers would say was bordering on genius (if only he'd apply himself).

Jimmy grew up being loved and doted on and had a very close relationship with his mother and sister. His father worked a lot, and Jimmy's resentment toward him grew with each passing day. Especially if his father and mother would argue at night, as most do from time to time.

He loved playing baseball down at the sandlot with the other boys his age, and he sure had a pop in his bat, even by the time he was eight years old. His father would show up and watch him whenever he could, but it wasn't enough for Jimmy. And his resentment grew.

When he was ten, Jimmy was walking toward the sandlot, Adam and Forest in tow, when he came across a frog hopping across the street. Jimmy stopped and watched the frog do his *hop, hop, hop* to the shoulder of the road as he headed toward the marshy area below. Adam and Forest, stopping just behind Jimmy, were utterly confused by his fascination until Jimmy walked over, kicked the frog onto its back, and brought the baseball bat down on the poor creature as it tried to flip itself back over.

Adam and Forest jumped back, shocked at what they had seen Jimmy do. But Jimmy just pushed the bat down harder, fascinated as the frog's innards oozed out of the gaping holes that were now torn into its side.

As Jimmy rotated the bat back and forth, grinding the goo that was once the frog into the pavement, Forest finally built up the courage to step in, placing his hand on Jimmy's shoulder. Jimmy turned around with venom in his eyes, his lips curled back into a snarl. He raised the baseball bat above his head as if to strike Forest. Forest let out a scream and covered his face with his hands. Jimmy's eyes seemed to come back into focus, and he realized what he was about to do. He looked at the bat, covered in gore, smiled, and simply said, "Let's go play some ball." Too afraid to say no, Adam and Forest fell into step behind Jimmy and went off to the sandlot.

By twelve, the carcasses of animals had begun to show up around Jimmy's neighborhood. Many of the Delaney's neighbors spoke of the coyotes, or maybe even wolves, that must be coming into town to feed. What else would tear the animals up so? Squirrels, chipmunks, and even Mrs. Fielder's orange cat Milo all suffered under Jimmy's bat. Yet Jimmy, smart as he is, hid all his malicious tendencies from his family. No, Jimmy's mother and father had no idea what he was doing. His father might comment about how good he must be getting, playing baseball as often as he was, but no suspicion of his son's wicked tendencies ever came to mind. Jimmy would just smile and say something about making it to the majors one day.

Only once was there ever any suspicion of Jimmy's actions.

On Jimmy's sixteenth birthday, his sister Sarah had followed him as he headed down to the sandlot-not too close. Girls weren't allowed. When Jimmy went off the road and down into the embankment, Sarah cautiously and curiously followed.

The ground was marshy, almost a full-blown swamp-out of place considering the terrain just up the embankment. The sunny day seemed to darken as the canopy of trees hid the sunlight from view. There was a smell of mildew and rot that attacked her nose and flies that attacked the rest of her. Though there was no trail to speak of, Jimmy walked in front of her like a man who knew exactly where he was going.

A sharp bark, more of a *yip* really, pierced the silence of the marsh. She watched Jimmy as he walked over to a tree, where a fox hung upside down by his foot. The fox swung helplessly as Jimmy brought his face close, sniffing it.

Sarah watched, awestruck.

"You stupid fucking fox. You think you can come into my woods and not pay a toll?"

Jimmy stepped back and cocked his head to the side, almost as if he was listening to a response. The fox simply twirled around and around from its leg, its eyes wide with fear.

"Ha ha ha, no fox," Jimmy said as he got into his stance. "I'm afraid this just won't do."

Jimmy swung that bat as hard as he ever had before, treating the fox like a live piñata and splitting it in half with one swing.

Sarah screamed and began to run away. Jimmy turned and saw his sister before she had gone too far and, being much bigger and faster, caught up with her before she could reach the road. Jimmy explained that he had been doing the neighborhood a favor. This was the fox that had been attacking all those animals. He couldn't stand what had been happening, and wouldn't Mrs. Fielder be so relieved to know that Milo's killer had been taken care of.

Sarah looked into Jimmy's eyes, the eyes of her older brother, and understanding flooded her brain. Jimmy was protecting everyone. Jimmy was a hero.

"But Sarah, let's keep the details to ourselves. All anyone needs to know is that the murdering fox wouldn't be bothering their pets anymore."

"Sure, Jimmy. Stupid fox got what it deserved."

It was only recently that Jimmy had discovered the joys of fire.

The flame purified, it consumed, and it ate whatever was in its path. It was magnificent. Horribly magnificent, and Jimmy wanted to feed its fury. By this time, Adam and Forest had not only gotten used to Jimmy's actions but they were fascinated by them. The shock had worn off long ago, and now fascination ruled the day; they wanted to see what he could come up with next. It was as though the world was Jimmy's lab, and they were the assistants.

As they walked the camp today, an idea struck Jimmy. A wonderful, terrible idea. Jimmy had set up traps throughout the camp—just simple snare traps, but effective. When he saw that he had caught not one but two raccoons that had been looking for dinner around the trash barrels, his plan began to fall into place.

"Come with me, boys," he snarled, walking over to the terrified animals. As he approached, he pulled gloves over his hands with the fluidity of a practiced surgeon.

"Forest, go open the door to that shed over there. Adam, get the gasoline."

The two lackeys ran and did as they were bid while Jimmy lifted up both of the raccoons and carried them by their legs to where Adam stood.

The raccoons twisted and scratched but couldn't reach Jimmy's flesh. Their chattering was enough to drive Adam and Forest mad, but Jimmy hardly noticed.

"Douse 'em," Jimmy commanded, and Adam poured the gas all over the animals. They made awful, crying noises and tried desperately to get away. Jimmy only laughed as he walked over to the shed, threw them against the wall, and closed the door.

"Forest, you got your lighter?"

"Yeah, Jimmy…what are we doing here?"

"Adam, pour the rest of that gas on the door, then Forest, light it up."

Adam hesitated for only a moment before doing as he was told. Jimmy walked over to the window of the shed, seeing the animals stumbling around, disoriented and confused within. When Forest lit the shed ablaze, Jimmy watched as the smoke and flames began to engulf the panic-stricken creatures. Finally, a spark from the walls came free, landed on the smaller of the raccoons, and lit it afire. Jimmy stood at the window, gloves cast aside and hands to his mouth as he watched in pure elation. His pants began to bulge as his penis swelled with arousal. The flames danced for Jimmy, and Jimmy watched in ecstasy.

Jimmy Delaney was a very disturbed boy.

CHAPTER 8

By the time the flames were starting to catch at the old *Moonbeam Sleepaway Camp*, Mitchell Freemore was saddling up to a stool at *The Back In Time Cafe* and ordering his morning coffee. Mitchell stopped here every morning for the past five years, though typically much earlier in the morning; Christ, it was pushing nine o'clock. The cafe was always busy no matter the time of day. The room was small and packed with people. Muddled conversation and boisterous laughter filled the cafe as the sweet aroma of coffee and bacon flooded the patron's noses.

"Here you go, hon," Myrtle, the *Back in Time*'s dependable owner, said as she placed Mitchell's fuel in front of him. "You're later than usual. Busy morning?"

"Actually…no. I had the strangest dreams last night. Tossed and turned the whole night," Mitchell said, running his fingers through his hair as if trying to wake his brain up.

"Jesus, hon, what happened to your hand?" Myrtle asked as her eyes went from Mitchell's hand to his eyes.

Mitchell looked down at his bandaged right hand, the blood reddening the gauze ever so slightly.

"Oh, just a stupid mistake out near the hill yesterday afternoon. Mike and me were out and got us a nice big buck, biggest I seen in three years, at least. Anyways, Mike takes the shot and nails it right in the heart. Old boy falls down dead immediately. Best damn shot I ever saw." Mitchell sipped his coffee, putting both hands around the mug to warm up his fingers.

Myrtle stared at Mitchell, waiting for him to continue. After a few moments, she said, "So how does that explain your hand, Mitch?"

"Oh, right," Mitchell put down his mug on the counter in front of him. "Anyways, we go down to start cleaning out this buck. We're both on our knees, and I'm holding back a flap of skin while Mike is cutting. Stupid bastard slips with the knife and cuts me. Deep cut too. Bled like a son-of-a-bitch, but doc said it'll heal just fine."

Mitchell flexed his fingers as if to show Myrtle that it was nothing to be concerned about. As he did, his eyes started to glaze over. His mind drifted as he recalled his dreams; the chatter of the cafe seemed to drift away. The cut on his hand began to throb under the bandages, and Mitchell's gaze drifted down to his wound. The door opened just as one of Isolation's two fire trucks went screaming by, snapping Mitchell back into reality.

"Ha, sorry, Myrtle. I'm off in my own world today."

"Well, I'm glad you're alright, hon. Use it to your advantage. You know girls love scars."

She winked and walked down the counter to help the new customers as they pulled up a stool by the window. Mitchell laughed at the implication that any woman would find such a ridiculous story arousing. Then again, he did always seem to have a way with women.

Mitchell stood a commanding six foot four inches (okay, it was six foot three and a half, but who's really checking?) and had the build of an NFL linebacker. That's not to say Mitchell was a bodybuilder, but he certainly had muscles in all the right places. He was thirty years old, but his hair, which was long and hung just below his shoulders, was just starting to have signs of gray. His skin was a few shades darker than most of the inhabitants of Isolation. His eyes were a dark brown that seemed to glisten in the light of day and shine, cat-like, in the darkest nights. His grandfather always said you can tell the soul of a man from his eyes. Mitchell's eyes were powerful, yes, but they also held the ghosts of the past. His grandfather had once told him that all Wimpak have these eyes.

Trauma can span lifetimes.

Mitchell had grown up in Isolation. In fact, he lived in his family home on Allen Street. The Freemores were a staple in Isolation. In fact, they were the only Wimpak family left in an area that once flourished with native ancestry. That was before Mitchell's parents passed on several years ago; now, he was the only full-blooded Wimpak remaining, though he did keep in touch with some members of the tribe that had moved away to greener pastures. Though he grew up here, he still suffered the stares of some of the older generation in Isolation. The trouble, he assumed, wasn't so much that he was Wimpak but more that he had left Isolation only to come back.

While he did have a way with women, it didn't mean Mitchell was immune to heartbreak. And that is exactly what happened that prompted the sudden move. Mitchell had moved out to Southern California for college, where he had met a woman, fallen in love, and planned to remain. A few weeks before he was set to buy an engagement ring, Mitchell walked into his apartment to see his love atop the man who trimmed the bushes at their apartment complex. Mitchell decided, some would say rashly, that it was time to go back to what he knew. So he left his tech job and moved to the place of his ancestry to find himself again. He hoped that by reconnecting with his past, he could find himself presently and have a clearer vision of the future.

Mitchell turned around on his stool, facing away from the counter, and scanned the room full of familiar faces. Bryce Callahan was sitting in the corner with Sarah Thornberg and Miles Gray, talking about, what sounded like, the New England Patriots and their season.

"Brady's bringing another ring to New England this year. I feel it," Bryce said to the others.

"Probably," Miles responded. "But watch out for Green Bay. Rodgers is having a season as well."

Sarah sipped at her coffee and had a look of total disinterest.

Bryce was in his early seventies, Sarah and Miles only slightly younger. They liked to consider themselves the town historians. Bryce had lived here his entire life. Sarah moved to Isolation in 1952 and Miles in 1960. If you ever wanted to know what the weather would be like on a particular day or who had been sneaking around with who back in the seventies (when the girls were loose, the boys were high, and life was free), you just had to ask the historians. Mitchell swore they kept notes on everyone in town.

Mitchell's eyes continued to wander the room, taking in the usual sights and sounds of the cafe. Old newspaper articles, most of which were discussing, in one way or another, the happenings of Isolation through the years, were hung up on the walls. **Halloween festival is a big hit**, **McNeil's auto body under new management**, and **Best selling author takes up residence in Isolation** were all headlines that could be seen adding to the ambiance of the room.

The furniture, while dated, held a certain charm that only a local hot spot in a small town can manage. Even as a kid, Mitchell could remember sitting at the tables, wondering about the stories that these walls could tell. Mitchell's personification of things was a quirk he had held to his whole life. *If only these walls could...*

The last of Isolation's fire trucks went blasting by on the way out of town, startling the diners and coffee drinkers. At the historian's table, a coffee mug crashed on the ground and shattered.

"Christ alive," yelled Bryce Callahan. "What the hell is going on?"

Must be one hell of a fire to be going that fast through town, Mitchell thought as he turned back to the television that was playing some terrible morning talk show.

The Historians collectively got up from their table and gathered just outside the door, peering down the road until the fire truck was out of sight.

"Smoke. Out by the old camp. You see it, Sarah?" asked Bryce as he pointed down the road, finger following the path that the fire truck just went.

"Yes…yes, I do. I wonder what's going on out there?" Sarah responded, concern tinging her voice.

"I don't see any damn smoke," Miles complained as he craned his neck to get a better look.

"You dopey bastard, right there, over the trees," Bryce pointed with more intensity. "Shit, can't you smell the fire?"

"You know Bryce, you really are a bastard. You always have to be so damn…" The voices faded away as the door shut behind them. The historians and the argument continued out in front of the cafe. Mitchell shook his head and let his mind wander back to what he could recall from the dreams of the previous night. No matter how much he concentrated, he couldn't quite piece the dreams together. A flash of a knife in the sun; a woman crying; words being spoken in a language that was familiar, yet foreign, almost within reach but impossible to catch.

He continued to nurse his coffee when the phone rang. Myrtle Cuthbert, the giver of the sweet fuel of life, walked over and answered it.

"Hello…oh no…what happened…yes…oh no…well is she okay…okay, Chief, thank you…yes, I'll be down when my shift is done. Thank you for calling."

"What was all that about Myrt?" asked Mitchell, seeing the look of shock that came across her face.

"Eve was just in an accident on her way to work. She's in bad shape, Mitch."

"Christ. The chief say what happened?"

"No, of course not. They are still trying to figure all that out. Just said her car slammed into a tree off Main Street. She's conscious but in a good deal of pain. They are taking her to Coos County right now."

"That's awful, Myrt. Are you okay?" Seeing the look that remained on her face, he could clearly see she wasn't. "Myrtle, is there more?"

Sighing deeply and shaking her head as if to shake off cobwebs that had been spun in a matter of only a few moments, she looked at Mitchell. "Chief said she was screaming when they got to her."

"Well, she was just in an accident. Probably in terrible pain."

"No…she was screaming 'stay away,'" Myrtle turned and faced the mirror that was behind the bar, head down. "Please, stay away."

CHAPTER 9

Sam's heart was pounding, his palms were sweating, and his breath was rapid. He watched from his front-row seat as Emily Higgenbottom stood in front of the class, showing off her collection of dolls. Dolls with blonde hair, dolls with brown hair, dolls with red hair, dolls with polka dots, and dolls with stripes. Sam thought Emily Higgenbottom must have every doll that was ever made, and she brought them all in to show and tell today. Looking around the class, Sam saw most of the girls looking rapturously at the collection in front of them, while most of the boys either had their heads down or were looking out the windows as the clouds rolled in front of the sun. Sam was up next, and he knew that he would have everyone's attention when they saw what he brought.

"…and that's why Piper is my favorite of all my dolls. Thank you."

The girls in the class gave a round of applause, followed hesitantly by the boys.

Emily took a small bow and began moving her dolls, one by one, to the corner of the room where they could watch the remainder of the class before being brought back to their corner of Emily's room, where they would sit and be forgotten about for months at a time.

"Thank you so much for sharing your dolls with us, Emily," Mrs. Granger said, having a difficult time hiding the relief that threatened to reveal itself. "Next up, we have Samuel Tolliver, who has brought us his beautifully designed house…Sam, come on up."

Sam bounded from his seat and stood in front of the class, Lego home held out in front of him.

"Hi, everybody. I just wanted to show you the house that I built with my Legos. As you can see, it has a bright red door and big windows in the front."

"How come the top doesn't have any windows?" asked Emily Higgenbottom with pretension in her voice. A murmur of laughter spread through the classroom.

"Well, Emily," Sam said, not without a bit of pretension himself, "it was in my dream, and there were no windows on top."

"In your dream?" Emily Higgenbottom said, rolling her eyes.

"Yup. My mom says some of the most smart people ever sometimes see things in their dreams too. And then they make them. And then everyone thinks it's so cool."

Sam looked over to Mrs. Granger for approval, his eyes wide with excitement.

"Sam, that is wonderful," Mrs. Granger said with a smile spreading across her face. "Can you tell us a bit more about your dream?"

"Umm," Sam hesitated as he thought back to the night before.

"Well, I was in the woods with my dad and a couple other people, but I can't remember who they were."

"Oh, does your dad take you out hiking in the woods?"

Sam thought for a moment. "He has a couple times. I like going out in the woods. It's so quiet, and we like to see what animals we can spot."

"That sounds wonderful, Sam."

"Yeah, and we were all walking in my dream, and I saw the house. This house," Sam held it up for the class to see again.

"Maybe you saw that house one time when you were out with your dad?"

Sam didn't remember ever seeing a house in the woods. Especially one with a bright red door, but he nodded nonetheless.

"See class. Sometimes our mind remembers things when we sleep that we don't even remember when we wake up. Our mind is funny like that, isn't it?"

The class nodded and seemed to be very engaged in how their minds could do that. Sam looked around at all his friends (and Emily Higgenbottom) and saw them all thinking hard and not paying attention to his house.

"Then…"

"Sam, are you alright?" Mrs. Granger asked slowly, standing up behind her desk.

"Then something kept running between the trees. My dad saw it. He told me to run." Sam began to sweat, and his eyes welled up.

"Okay, Sam, I think that's enough about your dream. Class, let's give Sam a round of applause for his great house," Mrs. Granger said as she walked over to Sam and placed a warm hand on his lower back. Sam was completely rigid.

As the class began to applaud, Sam seemed to come out of his almost trance-like state. The color returned to his face, and the look of utter satisfaction came over him as he smiled and took a deep bow.

Emily Higgenbottom rolled her eyes deeply and turned to her friends as she mouthed *what a weirdo*.

In the back of the class, Alex Dinsmore allowed his dislike for Sam Tolliver to grow. He let it well up inside of him.

As Sam walked back to his desk, Alex knew what he had to do.

The fire had caught faster than Jimmy had expected. The dry leaves on the ground acted like tinder and spread the flames through a wide area around the camp. Jimmy and his crew watched from behind a boulder that had been placed there millions of years ago by the receding glaciers as the firetrucks worked to knock down the flames. A smile spread across Jimmy's face as he smelled the burning wood, saw the dark smoke rising above the trees, and the flames (admittedly smaller now) dance in the husk that was once the counselor's cabin.

Forest Walker sat with his back against the massive block of granite, head in hands, his stomach turning. Killing a couple stupid animals was one thing, hell the hunters go out and do that same thing all the time, but this fire was something else. People weren't likely to look too hard at a few dead rabbits or squirrels (easy enough to blame that on nature-only the strongest survive), but people were going to look into this.

Forest looked to Adam, standing behind Jimmy, his eyes focused on the destruction almost as intently as Jimmy. When Forest let his eyes find Jimmy, he found Jimmy staring directly at him.

"What the fuck is wrong with you?" Jimmy asked incredulously. "It's beautiful."

"Jimmy, man, this is bad," Forest said, standing up so as to not be beneath Jimmy's hateful glare. "The fire department is going to figure out that someone set this. There's going to be an investigation, and there are only so many people they are going to look at."

Jimmy stepped closer to Forest. "No one is going to find out anything."

"Jimmy, there is a fucking empty canister of gasoline sitting out there. They are going to know someone set this." Forest closed the distance even further between him and Jimmy. "And they are going to look at the high school kids that live here and see we were out today."

"Listen," Jimmy hissed in Forest's ear, "no one is going to suspect us if we keep our mouth shut, our head's down, and our story straight. If, and it's a big if, someone does come to talk with us, we'll tell them we needed some extra time to work on the research paper Mr. Turner assigned last week." Jimmy turned to Adam, " Adam, your parents are at work today, right?"

Adam nodded in confirmation.

"Perfect. We go to Adam's now. We sneak in the back, through the woods, so no one sees us showing up."

Forest's eyes showed Jimmy that he didn't entirely believe in this plan, but there didn't seem to be a better answer. Forest could think of dozens of ways this plan could fail, but if no one had seen them here yet, maybe it would work.

"Let's go," Jimmy said as he slapped Adam on the back and took the long way around the camp, heading toward Adam's home. Forest was reluctant to move but did so. The look he had seen in Jimmy's eyes today scared him. If this plan didn't work, there was no telling what Jimmy would do.

CHAPTER 10

Marie found her calling the day she found their home in Isolation. In the few short months between finding the home online and moving in, Marie studied harder than she had for any exam she had in college, took the real estate exam, and became an agent at a small office south of Isolation in the northern city (well, city may be a bit of an overstatement) of Berlin.

Berlin is an old mill town north of the White Mountains. It sits amongst the trees that welcome you to the North Country of New Hampshire, nestled right on the Androscoggin River. This geography helped to create a mighty mill and lumber town that thrived during the nineteenth century. Though the scenery was still beautiful, Marie often thought, looking out of her office window, that the heart of a once economically strong town was losing its will to continue beating.

Old mills lay empty, scattered along the river like discarded memories from one's past. Homes, once grand and beautiful, lay in dilapidated disrepair. Graffiti contaminated the outside of many of the stores. But there was beauty here. Beauty that didn't just come from the trees and rivers. If you allowed yourself a moment to look past the sometimes ugly facade, you could see the city that once was, perhaps the city that it will be again.

When Marie met Barney (owner of Barney's Real Estate—*Let us find your dream home*), he seemed like a sweet, albeit odd, man. Barney was a short, gaunt man whose past was worn on his face. The last decade had eaten away at him, causing him to have a slight hunch in his stance and a moderate limp in his walk. What Barney lacked in physique, however, he more than made up for in charm.

Barney was from the deep south, somewhere just outside of Savannah, where southern charm and manners were taught right alongside reading, writing, and Jesus. Marie thought that perhaps she was reading Barney wrong initially, that the odd vibe was nothing more than a product of cultural differences. However, the way he looked at her, the way he always felt the need to touch her on the shoulder or lower back when he passed, the pet names, it just never felt right. Nonetheless, he had taken a chance on Marie when she had no previous experience to speak of, and she felt she owed him a debt of gratitude for that.

Barney had decided some years ago to move out of the south, hoping to escape the seemingly constant oppressive humidity for a cooler climate with a larger variety of seasons. Hell, maybe even see what snow was all about. After his first winter in northern New England, he knew all about snow.

Barney's life-altering decision to move from the south came shortly after coming home from work one afternoon, unexpectedly, to find his wife bent over the kitchen table, his brother standing behind her, in the midst of a passionate affair that Barney later found out had been going on for quite some time. Barney exploded and threw his brother right out the second-story window of his home.

At this time, he had not yet had the wear of stress, hatred, and sadness eat away at his body. When he turned on his wife, rage had spread across his face, but he could not bring himself to say a word. He could not bring himself to raise a hand to this woman. But what he did bring himself to do, just as she was walking over to him, spouting something about being sorry and her love for him, was to spit in her face. She collapsed on the kitchen floor as he grabbed his jacket and walked out of the house. He only stopped a moment to cast a glance down at his brother, laying naked and bloodied in the yard, before getting in his car and driving to the local motel.

Barney sat in that motel for days, contemplating his next move. He could have simply moved locally and not uprooted his life in such an abrupt manner. He could have, but after that day, the south, filled with all its southern belles, seemed to sour in Barney's mind. The thoughts caused his mouth to fill with saliva. The kind of saliva that, if swallowed, will make you vomit your soul food all over the front of your shirt. The south was toxic to Barney now.

The next day he got in his car and drove north, never going back for a single article of clothing.

Let the bitch keep it all, he thought as he drove. *I hope she thinks of me every day. I hope she realizes what she lost.* Barney found that more and more, he would get lost in his own thoughts-dark thoughts.

For days he drank and dreamt of throwing his brother out the window. He thought of the sound the glass made as it shattered, the thump of his brother's body landing in the front yard, and the scream his bitch of a wife made when he turned on her. The last made him smile the most. His heart was broken, yes, but his rage was more powerful. He had loved her. She had loved him, or at least he believed that to be true at one point. He slammed his fist on the steering wheel and screamed, "Now I can't even stand the thought of that fucking town!"

He kept driving north until the snow-covered mountains of New Hampshire welcomed him. Maybe it was the crisp autumn air, maybe it was just exhaustion from driving, but Barney knew he was done running from his problems. Barney knew he could create a new life for himself. A life where he would never have to feel that hatred inside of himself again.

Barney kept that southern charm for a time, but his distaste and distrust for women hid just under the surface. Barney hated that side of himself and tried to push it down into the deepest recesses of his soul whenever it would begin to boil up inside.

Initially, he believed that the change of scenery had changed his thoughts on the fairer sex.

It hadn't. Behind his smile hid a darkness that was always threatening to boil over.

After a few months in the north, he decided to try to get back out into the dating world. However, after a few bad dates, one that ultimately culminated in the woman telling him she wasn't surprised that his wife had cheated, Barney's rage became impossible to quell.

She got out of his car and slammed the door. Barney pulled out of the parking lot of her apartment complex and drove away. He drove exactly the speed limit (not one mile an hour over) and sat in silence. His breathing came in slow, measured breaths. He drove with the smallest touch of a grin showing faintly on his face. When he arrived home, Barney shut his car off, walked over to his front door, fumbled for only a moment with his keys, and let himself in. He turned the lights on in the kitchen, walked to the freezer, and took out a bottle of vodka he had been keeping cold. He took a long drink from the neck of the bottle. Then another. In only a few seconds, half of the bottle of vodka was gone. And so was Barney's composure.

He threw the bottle against the kitchen wall, shattering it to pieces. He ripped his shirt in half and screamed terrible, heinous things at the walls. He punched his fist through the closet door and then punched himself in the jaw. Barney saw red, and red was a beautiful color.

When Barney finally began to calm down, tears streaming from his eyes, the shine of the shattered vodka bottle caught his eye. He walked over and picked up a large shard of glass that read "dka" in bold white letters and "Product of" in smaller black letters. He turned the shard over in his hands. Despair had never been so palpable. Fury, so unbounded. Barney carried the shard of glass into the bathroom and stood in front of the mirror. He stared at himself, shirt torn to pieces, a bloody cut still red on his lip, and he screamed.

"Fuuuuuuuuuck You."

He took the shard of glass and ran it from his collar bone to his left nipple. Barney may not have been able to feel the pain, but he was at least aware enough to not dig the glass in too deep. Blood streamed from the wound as it opened wider with every inch the glass tore further. He stared at himself without blinking the entire time. A twisted grin on his face.

Barney looked at the blood. Saw it begin to pool in the sink, and his mind flashed to his date that night.

I wonder if her blood looks any different, he pondered.

When he looked up again, realization crept into his mind. Realization of what he had just done and what he was just thinking. Barney's anger may have been justified, but some of the thoughts that accompanied that anger, even he couldn't reconcile.

He decided that perhaps he wasn't quite ready to start dating yet.

When he hired Marie, he thought that she could be the answer to all of his women issues. Marie was sweet, caring, and motivated, and when she came into the office for her interview, Barney couldn't help but think she may be the perfect type of person to get to know and reprogram his thoughts. Marie's energy seemed to reinvigorate Barney, and a youthful exuberance seemed to overcome him.

In the first few weeks that Marie had started to work with Barney, he began to change his diet, he began exercising each morning (well, it was more stretching, but as far as he was concerned, he was doing great), and he even thought that he may have been growing some of his hair back. Barney felt like a new man.

That is until Barney's heart began to betray him again. Barney knew deep inside that he was beginning to fall for Marie. He hated that he felt this way. Hated that she was married and couldn't be his. And hated more that he knew she would never reciprocate the thoughts that played in his head whenever she came into the office. Nonetheless, Barney's charm would be on full display for her each day.

Marie had noticed a change, however. His smile was there, but his eyes seemed to betray something else. Their once-easy banter seemed forced, and Barney seemed to be getting a bit too familiar. His advances, at least she thought they were advances, seemed to bolden as time went on. Thankfully, Marie's job didn't allow her much time in the office, so she tolerated the awkwardness as nothing more than a mild inconvenience. By the time she turned her computer on today, Barney was already coming over, cup of coffee in hand.

"Good morning, darling."

"Good morning, Barney. I'm only here for a little bit. I have a couple showings this morning."

"Well, that's okay," Barney said as he handed over the cup of coffee. "I'm just glad I got to see you."

Marie gave an uncomfortable smile that Barney took as genuine as she took the coffee and turned to her computer. Barney placed his hand on her shoulder gently. "I feel like I haven't seen you in weeks."

Marie shrugged, removing Barney's hand. "I was in here Friday, Barney. It's only Monday."

"Well, jeez, I guess you're right. I guess I just forgot," Barney said as he turned to walk back to his desk just across the room.

Marie quickly began going through her emails, deciding to respond later to those that weren't in need of an immediate answer. She glanced up and saw Barney staring at her from across the room.

Forcing a smile, and with as much politeness as she could muster, Marie said, "Well, jeez, Barney, is there something you want to say?"

At this directness, Barney hesitated, steeled himself, and simply said, "N-No, nothing. You just look mighty pretty this morning."

Marie closed out her emails, stood up, and said, "Thank you, Barney. I really have to go now."

She rushed out the door, feeling Barney's gaze on her the whole way.

Tom had walked for the better part of an hour in the direction of the scream. At least he thought he was heading in the right direction. Sounds carry funny in the woods, especially these woods. Tom had tried to convince himself that what he heard was just a trick of the mind. Maybe even an animal getting caught in a trap. He had almost convinced himself of that when he stumbled upon a matted-down area of grass under a giant pine tree.

The flattened area was roughly the size of a man, though Tom guessed it could have been a deer or small bear that had laid there. Tom searched the area, rifle extended just in case.

"Hullo," Tom yelled. "Anyone out theyah?"

Silence was all that replied.

"Jesus Tom, yah really ah losin' it now, ya know," he said.

Just as he was turning to head in the direction of his own hunting grounds, something shone in the sunlight just at his feet. He reached down and brushed the leaves away from the golden circle that had caught the sun's gaze.

He dropped to a knee to get a closer look, and horror overcame him. The golden circle was a ring, a wedding ring by the looks of it, and it was still secured around a man's ring finger. The finger had been torn off, or so it seemed, by the jagged skin that flapped around when Tom picked it up to examine it.

"Christ alive, what coulda done this," Tom whispered breathlessly.

A shadow passed in front of him through the trees. He stifled a scream, and the finger slipped out of his hand and landed among the leaves. Though he was too focused on the movement in front of him to even notice.

A scream, more ear-splitting than Tom had ever heard before, cut through the silence of the forest. At this, the shadow ran to another tree only a few yards in front of him. It moved faster than anything he had ever seen. He had known these woods his whole life, but he had no idea what he was looking at now.

A hand, blacker than charcoal, reached around the tree. Tom, shaking convulsively, lifted his rifle in the direction of the monster.

"Jesus help me," Tom whispered.

His finger rested on the trigger, though he seemed to not be able to call on it to pull. He had no idea if his rifle would even affect this, this thing, but it had stopped every other creature in these woods, so Tom thought it was a better chance than doing nothing at all.

His finger twitched slightly. Sweat began to run down his forehead. The wind picked up just slightly, and Tom's jacket flapped lightly with it.

With all the bravery of a vet who had seen his fair share of horrors, Tom took a deep breath and, with as much bravado as he could muster, yelled to the monster.

"Come on, ya sonofabitch. If ya think ya can take me down, ya bettah be ready fowah fight. This old bastahd don't go down easy."

The creature's head appeared from behind the tree. A leg proceeded as the creature stepped out from behind the pine. A nightmare from the depths of hell looked at him.

Oh, fuck me sideways. What the fuck is that?

Tom steadied himself and aimed.

"Come on ya muthah fuckah!!"

The monster screamed and darted back behind the trees. And suddenly, Tom was alone in the woods once more.

CHAPTER 11

Alex Dinsmore crept down the hall, peering over his shoulder to make sure no teacher was watching. All his classmates were outside at recess enjoying the crisp, cool air on the beautiful late autumn morning. Alex had been walking around behind the kids that were playing tag, behind the teachers watching with eagle's eyes. Quietly. On cat's feet.

As he got to Mrs. Granger's class, he gave one last glance before pushing the door open and slinking in. Alex walked with determination to the back, where the Lego house sat on the back counter, isolated amongst the shadows. Alex didn't really have anything against the Lego house. In fact, he thought it was pretty cool. He just couldn't stand the smug satisfaction that goody-two-shoes Sam Tolliver had spread across his face when he showed it off to the class.

Sam knew nothing of Alex's dislike. In fact, Sam had never even interacted with Alex, but Alex had been plotting a way to knock Sam off his high horse since the first day of school. He finally figured out how. *I'm going to smash that house into a million pieces,* he thought as he marched toward the back of the room.

As he approached the Lego house, an ominous feeling crept over him-as if someone might be watching him from the shadows. Alex chanced a look over his shoulder, expecting to see Mrs. Granger sitting at her desk, a disapproving scowl covering her face. Yet, when he looked, nothing was there.

Gooseflesh covered Alex's body as he stepped ever closer to the back of the room. The toy house seemed to have an evil feel to it, the way it crept back into the darkness. The closer he came, the more the house seemed to try to pull back, not wanting to be seen. Alex was sure his mind was just playing tricks on him, the way it does after he watches a spooky Halloween movie or when his older brother tries to scare him. He leaned forward and glimpsed what he thought was a little figure in the corner of the living room.

Alex reached out and picked the Lego house up carefully. As he did so, a buzzing sound began to resonate within his ears. It was as though a mosquito had gotten stuck deep within his ear canal. He brought the house close to his eye, straining against the dark room to get a closer look at what was lurking in the corner.

The buzzing got louder.

A low rumble vibrated softly over Alex's skin.

He glanced over his shoulder, sure there was someone there now. Sure he had been caught before he could teach Sam Tolliver a lesson. But again, no one waited behind him.

The incessant buzzing got louder. Alex stuck a finger in his ear, moving it around in an effort to make it go away.

The low rumble grew in strength. Alex's shirt fluttered with the growing pressure of it against his back.

A whispered breath. A raspy, gravely sound that seemed to come from within his own head startled him. The Lego house slipped through his fingers, but he was able to save it from smashing on the ground.

He lowered his head as his nose was filled with the stench of dirt and…something else. He smelled it once before when he went to the hospital to visit his grandmother. It made his head spin. His heart was beating between his ears, thunderous claps in the silent classroom.

He turned slowly, cautiously. Rays of light streamed into the class but seemed to die out in the darkness of the corners of the room. Alex knew shadows held secrets, some of them scary. The heaviness of the classroom weighed on him, and he knew the secrets that these shadows held were the scary kind. The shadows shifted and seemed to creep toward him.

The buzzing continued.

He looked at the desks in the front of the class, now covered in darkness.

The shadows crept closer.

Suddenly, a ball (one of the kickballs his friends were playing with outside, most likely) struck the window. Alex stifled a scream and looked toward the outside, thinking it may be a better idea to get back on the playground with his friends. If Mrs. Granger saw him, he would just tell her that he had to pee. Yes, that was why he was inside. And he had to go real bad, which is why he didn't have time to tell her.

Alex looked back toward the front of the class. The desks were bathed in sunshine. The buzzing in his ears had stopped, and the smell had disappeared. The light from the window seemed to be cast upon Sam Tolliver's desk especially, illuminating it in a glow that caused Alex to hold a hand up to his eyes. His resolve began to return, and his determination followed.

He took a deep breath to calm his nerves; he had a job to do, and he would see it through. Still clutching the little home, Alex thought, *you need to get it together, dummy. Show him that he's not better than anyone.*

Alex set the Lego house down on the counter and lifted off the roof, careful not to destroy it…not yet. He needed to see if something was there, tucked away in the corner, out of sight. The hairs on the back of Alex Dinsmore's neck began to stand on end again as he placed the roof down on the counter and looked in from above. Nothing appeared to be detached, nothing out of place. There was no figure hiding in the corner and no shadows creeping over the house.

The smell. The earthy, terrible smell returned as quickly as it had disappeared.

Deep breathing, almost a growl really, began to emanate from behind him. The boy's breath caught in his throat as he slowly turned around, sure to see a wolf, a bear, or some other forest creature behind him. He must have left the school door open, and it followed him in.

Stupid kid, he thought.

His eyes darted back and forth, trying to locate the source of the noise, and then his eyes fell on where it was.

At the far end of the room, standing amongst the darkness in the corner behind Mrs. Granger's desk and next to the file cabinet where she kept all of the past and future assignments, stood a dark figure. At first, Alex thought that it must be Mrs. Granger until he realized the sheer mass of it.

"Wh-what are you," he managed to stammer out as he backed up against the counter where the Lego home rested. When his body hit the counter, the roof fell off the shelf and smashed onto the ground. The figure in the corner let out a shriek, awful and terrifying.

Time slowed down. All the colors that decorated Mrs.Granger's classroom seemed to become muted. Alex's mouth became dry, and the high-pitched buzz returned, ringing in his ears. Tears streamed down his face as the figure from the corner stepped toward him slowly. Alex darted for the door, but the creature moved in an instant to block his way. Another shriek left its gaping maw. Teeth, razor-sharp, seemed to snap at the air as Alex backed up, body pressed again against the counter at the back of the class. Though the ringing in his ears made it difficult to tell for certain, Alex was sure the sound of his classmates outside was gone.

They must have heard that awful thing, he thought.

He scanned the room, looking for some way of escape.

His eyes fell upon the windows. Alex knew that if he could make it there, he could get away from this terror. He would be free of this scary thing he saw in front of him. He would leave Sam Tolliver alone from now on. Hell, he'd help Sam build his next Lego house. He just needed to run away. Fear threatened to take full control of his body. Alex may have been young, but he knew he needed to try. This was stranger-danger on a much higher scale. His mom always told him to run if he was in danger. He needed his mommy.

Alex sprinted with all of his might toward the window, never seeing the Lego pieces that had once been the roof to Sam Tolliver's perfect creation. Alex's foot landed on the mess and came out from under him. The last thing he saw before his head smacked against the corner of a desk was his feet appearing to touch the ceiling.

When he opened his eyes, he was convinced that what he had seen was nothing more than a trick of the shadows. He rotated his head as cautiously as he could, trying to fight off the nausea that threatened to overwhelm him. He felt sick. He was scared, but he was alone. No monster. No, Mrs. Granger. He could even hear the students starting to come back into the school from recess.

Alex's hand moved back to test the pain at the back of his head, and came back red and sticky. The low rumble returned. It made Alex's stomach sink. He rotated his head back so that he could see what stood behind him. Sharp, ripping teeth greeted him as saliva from the nightmare dripped down onto his forehead. Alex had time for one interrupted scream before the monster bit down on his head.

Alex screamed no more.

Mrs. Granger heard the scream and came running down the hall, bursting into her room. Some of the more curious students followed closely behind as she searched the front of the class.

The next scream came from Emily Higgenbottom just before she fainted in the back of the room. When Mrs.Granger rushed to the back, she saw a puddle of blood with one small brown boot in the middle. The foot still snug within.

Mrs. Granger retched next to the student's desks. She begged the children to stay back, but many had already gathered around her. Tears poured from the students that were frozen in fear. Many saw the sight and ran for the door screaming; other students simply ran when they saw the fear on their friend's faces as they headed for the door.

Mrs. Granger hoisted Emily Higgenbottom up as best as she could and rushed toward the front of the class and out the door.

Sam remained only a few moments longer. The earthy smell of something decaying and awful battered his nose. Sam saw the blood, but the sight didn't seem to register in his mind. What he was focused on was the destroyed roof of his masterpiece as it lay in a pool of Alex Dinsmore's blood.

CHAPTER 12

The students of Appleton Elementary all had their parents called, and shortly after, the police arrived and set up a perimeter. The sole remaining ambulance in town was diverted away from the fire out at the camp, having been there and realizing there were no injuries (at least of the human variety), and pulled in just before the first cars began pulling into the parking lot. Frantic parents sprinted toward the police tape that blocked the way to the front doors of the school.

One by one, students began to emerge from behind closed doors, escorted by their teachers to the loving arms of their mothers and fathers. Most students still had no idea what was happening. Many students had heard a scream, other students knew that a boy was hurt, but very few saw what Mrs. Granger's class had seen…what Sam had seen.

When Russell made his way to the front of the line of parents, the assistant principal, Mrs. Roth, walked Sam out.

"Sam, are you alright?" Russell asked as he knelt before his son, looking him up and down.

"Someone broke my Lego house, Dad," Sam's head was lowered, and you could tell he had been crying. "I think it was Alex. I saw his boot near it. There was blood…"

Russell grabbed Sam and pulled him close, squeezing him into his chest. He looked up at Mrs. Roth. "What happened, Judy?"

"Honestly, Russ, we have no idea. Annie took attendance when the kids got outside for recess. Everyone was accounted for, but then…"

Cries of pain and agony sprung up from behind the line of anxious parents. Ruth and John Dinsmore were rushing toward the school, crazed looks in their eyes. The police, recognizing the parents as those of the lost boy, rushed forward to meet them before they could reach the front of the line.

John Dinsmore was the first to reach the police. His eyes wild with panic, all he could muster was, "H-Happened? Where's he?"

"Mr. Dinsmore, Mrs. Dinsmore, please…come this way," said one of the deputies. Russell had seen him around town, but he couldn't place where. The deputy's stoic face threatened to break as he looked into the eyes of the parents whose child was almost certainly dead.

"What the fuck happened to my son!" screamed Ruth Dinsmore as she reached for the deputy's collar. Mr. Dinsmore, having enough sense to recognize that even a grieving mother shouldn't go around grabbing police officers by the neck, especially in front of a crowd of people, grabbed hold of his wife and pulled her close.

As he held her, listening to her sobs against his chest, he saw all the parents lined up in front of the school, each one barely keeping their emotions under control.

"What are you all looking at, huh? Go on! Take your children home! Go on, take them!" he yelled, his voice wavering.

"Mr. Dinsmore, Mrs. Dinsmore, please…" as the deputy held out his arm in the direction of his cruiser. The Dinsmores, held in each other's embrace, somberly walked over to the police car. Privacy a priority for the details that the deputy was soon to relay.

"Dad, what happened?"

Russell's eyes went from the Dinsmores' to Mrs. Roth, whose eyes could no longer hold back the flow of tears. She shook her head, turned slowly, and walked back to the front doors of the school.

"I have no idea, son."

Russell had called Marie shortly after he received the call from the school. She had been just arriving at her second appointment of the day when her phone rang. Marie immediately apologized to her clients, told them she would call to reschedule, got in her car, and arrived home shortly after Russell and Sam arrived.

Russ had relayed the basics of what happened but hadn't known enough to give Marie the details she needed. Her mind had gone crazy as she was racing home. Not knowing is always worse than having all the details; your mind piecing things together from minor, vague details can be torturous.

Marie ran over and hugged Sam so tight that Sam thought he might pop right then. She looked at Russ and asked what happened.

"The school doesn't seem to have any idea. They don't even have a body. Apparently, there was just some blood and a boot."

"His foot," Sam mumbled into his mother's chest.

Marie loosened her grip. "What did you say?"

"His foot, Mom. Alex's foot was still in the boot. That's why there was blood."

"Oh my God. Sam, I'm so sorry you saw that," Marie said as she pulled him close once again. She brushed his hair back and kissed his forehead. Russell kneeled next to both of them and held them.

Pressed between his parents, Sam finally began to cry.

Just before the sun set, Russ saw Tom's truck pull into his driveway. Russ sat at the kitchen table, staring out the living room window, as Sam watched cartoons and Marie cooked dinner. The scent of roasted asparagus and pork chops seemed far away as Tom stepped out of his truck and shut the door. Tom rested a hand on the bed of his truck. Even from this distance, Russ could see that he was disturbed by something. He glanced up at the Tolliver's home, shook his head, and walked toward his front door.

"Sam, come sit down at the table. Dinner's ready," Marie called.

The Tollivers did not eat well that night. Each with their own thoughts drifting through a fog that threatened to take over their reality. Sam could only think of the bloody boot, the bone sticking up like a push pop. Russell's mind focused on Tom. Tom, who had gotten out of his truck with such a strange look after a day out hunting. A look that told him he'd have to make a trip over in the morning. And Marie, who could only think of the creature she saw earlier that day on the road, suddenly appearing back in her mind. The dark figure she thought she saw again at the school. The darkness that seemed to lurk just out of sight in the shadows that were closing in around her.

CHAPTER 13

It took Sam a long time to fall asleep that night. Trauma makes people react in different ways. For Sam, it was hearing the students screaming every time he closed his eyes. It was the blood that seemed to surround the shoe in a way that resembled a modern art piece that he had seen his mother stare at when she took him to visit Aunt Mandy in Boston. But mostly, it was the smell that haunted Sam. The iron, the tinny smell of the blood, and something else underneath that. If fear had a smell, that would be it. A sort of earthy, humid smell that could be detected only if you chose to acknowledge it. That smell is what kept making Sam snap open his eyes. But, as he lay in bed, his eyes began to snap open with less fervor until, eventually, he slept.

Marie got into the shower, and Russ decided he'd get a bit of fresh air to clear his mind of the day's events. Or at least try to. As he stepped outside, the air swirled around him-chilly, but not entirely unpleasant. He stood there for a short time, looking up at the sky. It was one of those crystal clear nights where you can see to infinity. One of those nights that the stars seem to shine extra bright. The silence is deafening, and if you listen close enough, you feel as though you can hear the hum of eternity buzzing around you. One of those autumn New England nights.

Russell's breath swirled into the night sky, and a shiver crossed over his body. He looked over at Tom's house, quiet except for one lone light in the back corner of his home. Russ had been over there enough to know that Tom must have got his mind stuck on something to be in his office (really, it was a small living room, but Tom liked to call it his office—he thought it made him sound more fancy) at this hour. *At this hour* is a relative term in this case. Tom was in good shape and health, but he was still an older man. And older men tend to go to bed shortly after the sun goes down and rise shortly before it comes up again.

Russell started toward the end of his walkway, heading toward the mailbox. He was sure it would be filled with nothing more than junk advertisements for things he likely would never need. However, once in a while, the grocery store offered some good discounts on their meats (last week was $2.99 a pound for ground beef, and Russ thought that was just fine). As he reached in, he was surprised to find the box full. As he pulled at the clogged box, it seemed as though it was only one large envelope. Russ turned it over in his hands but couldn't make the writing out on the front.

Suddenly a loud crash broke the silence of the night, and Russ turned around to Tom's house. The light, now turned off, caused Russ a bit of panic. However, as he took a step toward the road to head over and check on his friend, the kitchen light flicked on, and he could see Tom standing at the sink. Russ thought he looked tired but not really any worse for wear. Russ turned back and headed toward the front door. As he turned the knob and stepped through the threshold, Tom Richmond collapsed onto his kitchen floor.

Jimmy Delaney sat on his bed that night, holding a daddy long legs spider down with the tip of a pencil and pulling its legs off one by one. As the spider squirmed, Jimmy smiled. He was so focused on his task that he didn't hear his father's knock as he entered the room.

"Hey bud, I'm going to be heading to bed soon," Jimmy's dad said as he saw the startled look on his son's face.

Jimmy quickly swept away the tortured body of the spider to the floor.

"Oh hey…yeah, sure, Dad. Goodnight."

His father paused at the door, looking his son over and struggling to find the words he needed.

"Jimmy," his father wet his lips with his tongue and took a step further into his room.

Jimmy looked up at his father, a look of innocence on his face. The hobbled spider flopping out of sight on the floor, struggling to right itself.

"Jimmy, we got a call from the school today. They said you weren't there. We got the same call last week, but your mother and I assumed it must have been incorrect. Why weren't you there?"

Jimmy's eyes narrowed as he looked at his father. For only a moment, Jimmy considered telling his father the whole truth. The awful truth. But only for a moment.

"Dad, I was there. I swear. See, the problem is, I was in the bathroom during homeroom. My stomach was really acting up this morning. Mom's cooking last night, probably." Jimmy winked at his dad and gave him a wry smile.

His father smiled and seemed to release the tension in his shoulders. He turned to walk out of the room but then stopped, remembering that was only half of the issue.

"And last week?"

Jimmy sighed heavily, buying him the moment he needed to quickly concoct a story.

"Okay, I admit, last week I was late to school one day. But it was for a good reason. You know I ride to school with the guys. Well, Adam had a really big test in social studies that day. You know that's my subject. He begged me to help him do some last-minute studying because he had a test second period. I didn't tell you guys because I didn't want you to get mad, but I thought me being late was for a good cause."

Jimmy's tongue spun such amazing stories so quickly that even he was impressed sometimes.

His dad sighed. "Alright, well, I certainly can't fault you for wanting to help out your friend. Adam's a good kid. I just wish he'd take his education as seriously as you. The boy needs to study on his own time."

"You're right, Dad. It won't happen again."

At that, Jimmy's dad nodded and turned. Jimmy's eyes lowered and burned a hole through his father's back. His father paused only for a moment in the doorway, hand pressed against the wall before he closed the door slightly and began to walk away from Jimmy's room.

Jimmy slithered over to the side of his bed and looked down to find his victim. The spider hadn't made it far. He sat up in his bed, eyes focused on his prey.

"Jimmy," his father said as he peaked his head in between the crack in the door.

Jimmy blinked and quickly snapped back to reality.

"Yeah, Dad?"

"How'd Adam do on the test?"

Jimmy blinked, having already dismissed his lie, hesitating for a moment.

"Oh, he passed. B-minus or something, but for Adam, that's pretty great."

Jimmy's father patted the wall, smiled, and closed the door entirely.

"Fucking guy needs to learn how to knock," Jimmy said quietly as he crouched down next to his bed. "Next time he comes in without knocking, maybe I'll knock my bat against his bald fucking head."

Jimmy flipped the spider over onto its back again and pressed his right index finger down on it. The crunch of its exoskeleton was satisfying.

And Jimmy smiled ear to ear.

Russ lay in bed with the manila envelope in his lap. He opened it up, curious as to what was within. When he pulled out the papers, his questions were answered. In bold letters on the top of the first page, read:

DNA Results-Russell Tolliver

Russ had forgotten all about this. About a month back, he and Marie had paid for a DNA testing kit, more for fun than extreme interest. Russ decided he'd wait for Marie before he looked at the results-it was her idea, after all.

Marie finished her shower and walked out of the bathroom. Her tank top clung to her breasts, the outline of her nipples showing just enough to catch Russell's gaze. As she walked past, Russell saw that her panties were riding up enough to make his mind wander to things outside of the papers in his lap.

"Can I help you, sir?" Marie said as she sat down on the bed and put her legs under the blanket.

"You look amazing," Russ said as he tried desperately to refocus his attention.

Marie leaned over and kissed him. "After all these years, you still think so, huh? That, Mr. Tolliver, is why I love you."

"Oh, I meant to ask you what happened earlier. To the car. With the craziness, it slipped my mind until now."

It took Marie a moment to figure out what he was talking about, but then she remembered the cracked windshield. She pushed the thought of the monster she thought she saw in the road from her mind. "Oh, a rock kicked up in the road. I'll get it to McNeil's as soon as I can."

She searched for a way to move off the subject when her eyes, seeing the papers in Russell's lap, lit up. "Is that the DNA test you did?" She grabbed the papers out of Russell's lap. "Have you looked at the results yet?" She glared at Russ, awaiting an answer.

"No, not yet. I was waiting for you. I figured I'd get the evil eye if I looked without you here. I guess I'll get it either way."

With a satisfied smile, Marie scanned the results. Russ leaned in toward her and looked as well.

"Mostly English, like I figured," Russ said, slightly disappointed.

"Yeah, but look, this is interesting. It says you're twenty percent Native American. It actually looks like part of your heritage stems from right around this area. The Wimpak."

"Let me see that," Russ said as he took the papers from Marie's hands. "Huh, I'll be damned. I never knew that. My parents always just talked about their English ancestors, especially when they were drinking."

"Hey, isn't Mitch Wimpak?"

"I think so, Native American for sure, but I think I remember him saying something about his tribe being historically from here. I don't remember him being too forthcoming."

Russ flipped through the papers a bit more and found himself deeply intrigued by this newly discovered news. It's strange. When you find a previously unknown fact out, curiosity tends to take over. But curiosity killed the cat, as the saying went.

Marie leaned over to Russ. "It must be where you get those gorgeous eyes."

Her hand crept below the covers of the bed and began to caress Russell's manhood. Suddenly he remembered why he had been so worked up a few minutes ago. Marie leaned in further and kissed Russell on his lips.

"It's been a really long day, Russ. Let's finish it right," she breathed as she started kissing her way down his chest.

When Marie's lips finally kissed the bulge that had grown large beneath the sheets, the only thing that mattered was the two of them. Thirty minutes later, they both lay naked in bed, sound asleep.

Sam's eyes snapped open. He sat up in his bed and looked around his room anxiously. He had heard a noise. A noise that had woken him up out of his sound sleep. It was the middle of the night, and Sam was not used to being up this late. Of course, he had been up this late before, but only if he had to pee. But even then, he went directly to the bathroom, peed mostly in the toilet, and went right back to bed; tonight, Sam did not have to pee, and he was wide awake.

He scanned the room, but there was nothing out of the ordinary. Moonlight shone through the bedroom window, illuminating the room enough for him to see his poster of the Flash, his clothes laying on the ground in the center of the room, and his reconstructed toy masterpiece sitting on his dresser. Fear of what he had seen at school threatened to rise again when he looked at the little house, but with the moon shining bright, he was able to push away the thoughts that tried to attack his mind.

Sam took a deep breath in and, feeling a bit braver, got up and walked to the window. He walked on cat's feet, careful not to make any loud noises, and peeled the curtain back. Outside was picturesque, even in the darkness. Sam opened his window to feel the cold chill hit his face. Leaves danced in the night; an owl hooted in the distance, and the earthy smell that he recognized from earlier that day attacked his nostrils.

The smell seemed to burn his nose, and worse, it made him think of what had happened in school. A shiver ran down his spine, whether from the cold or the smell. Sam was unsure. He was sure, though, that he needed his bed, his blanket-comfort. He closed the window and turned around to make his way back to the warmth and safety of his bed.

To Sam's horror, there was a person sitting on the end of his bed. He couldn't make out a face, but it looked like a boy, someone his own age. It sat frozen in place at the head of Sam's bed, criss-cross applesauce. The boy faced the door, and Sam wasn't sure if the figure even knew that Sam was there. He stifled a scream somehow, and curiosity began to take over. Ready to run and scream for his mom and dad at the slightest movement, Sam called out to the boy.

"Hello?"

There was no answer. Sam took one cautious, timid step closer.

"Hello? Why are you on my bed?"

The figure's head turned slowly. The neck muscles seemed to catch, making an unsteady, twisting motion. The boy straightened his legs in the same awkward manner as he turned to face Sam.

Sam recognized the face. He may not have been a friend, but Sam knew his classmates.

"Alex? W…why are you here? Mrs. Granger and everyone thought you were hurt. Are you okay?"

Alex stared blankly at Sam.

"Alex, you're scaring me. Are you okay? I'll get my mom and dad."

As Sam took a step toward the door, Alex's eyes widened. Sam froze in place as all his flesh broke out in goosebumps.

"Alex, what's wrong? You're scaring me. Tell me what's…"

Alex's arm raised jerkingly and pointed behind Sam. His mouth opened wide and hung there like a gaping maw. A blackened cave leading to unknown terrors.

Horrified, Sam glanced over his shoulder and saw a living nightmare staring at him from behind the pane of glass. It was darker than the street; it was darker than the night sky. Sam felt himself getting dizzy, and his stomach dropped like when he went on the kiddie roller coaster at Canobie Lake park. From Sam's bed came a voice that couldn't come from Alex's mouth. It was not that of a young boy, but of an other worldly thing.

"Ruuuuun!"

The creature outside let out a scream that cracked the glass. By the time the window had fully spider-webbed, Sam was in his parents' room, screaming in terror.

Tom opened his eyes and was utterly confused as to what he saw. There seemed to be a light somewhere in the distance. Tom squinted against the sharp pain stabbing at his eyeballs. A warm, sticky feeling pulled at his skin as he tried to move his head away from the harshness of the golden morning sun.

He realized he was lying on the kitchen floor, the small puddle of blood that had pooled around his face the cause of the pulling of his skin. He had obviously passed out, smacked his head on the cabinets or the floor, and been laying there for quite a while.

As Tom struggled to stand up, his back ached with stiffness, partially from exhaustion but more so, Tom thought, from laying on the hard kitchen floor for hours. As he made it to his feet, he realized his old bones didn't take to falls like they used to.

He took a step forward and nearly fell again, his head woozy, nausea beginning to creep up in his gut. Tom put his hand to his head and pulled away crusty red fingers. A groan escaped his lips.

Daring to test his legs again, he took another step toward the sink. The wooziness wasn't so bad this time, and Tom found that he was able to make it to the sink, grab a dish towel, and wet it. He wiped his forehead, the dish towel coming back a darkened red. He wondered what he had been doing before he blacked out. He shuffled over to the freezer for a couple ice cubes to help quell the knot that was forming. The coldness of the ice stung, and Tom breathed heavily through his teeth. As he headed for the living room couch, he noticed a book on the floor. He reached down (carefully, *very carefully* now), memories flooded back into Tom's mind.

He could recall what he had seen, or at least what he thought he had seen, in the woods (his head was still so damn foggy). The noise it made…and was there a finger? Grasping the book and turning it over, he realized that his memories must be real. He had come home after searching, with futility, the woods for hours. He had gone back to his office and rifled through his small library of books, searching for some idea as to what he had seen. When Tom found it, he had left the office in a rush, knocking over the desk lamp and finding himself feeling his way around the darkness for the door. He had tossed the book toward the couch and went into the kitchen. That's when it all got fuzzy.

The book Tom had found was *The Lore of The Great North Woods* by none other than local historian extraordinaire Bryce Callahan.

Tom sat down on the couch with the book and began to flip through. Drawings of all manner of creatures haunted page after page. Stories of lights in the sky following couples down darkened roads, tall, hairy creatures lurking in the thick forests, and ghosts of children crushed in landslides unfolded before him.

Tom's eyes began to get heavy. The throbbing in his head began to lull, and he found himself in a restless sleep as his head rested on the couch-the ice melting on the plush carpet of his living room floor.

CHAPTER 14

Tom awoke with a start as his doorbell echoed throughout the house. Groggy, Tom shook the cobwebs from his head and glanced at the clock that hung over the television set. He sat up slowly, still aching from his smacking against the kitchen floor. He rubbed his eyes and squinted at the clock: 9:15. *Christ*, Tom thought, *I haven't slept this late in years*. The doorbell rang throughout the house again.

"I'm cahmin', I'm cahmin,' Tom yelled toward the door.

As he stood up, the sharp pain in his head returned with a fury, and he wobbled, needing to grab the arm of the couch in order to steady himself. Tom paused for a moment, put his hand to his head, and pulled it away. No blood, but the large egg that had formed was throbbing. Tom was fairly certain there might be a small concussion that formed as well.

Another step forward, and his foot stepped in the icy puddle that had formed where the cloth had fallen. "Ah, Christ," he complained as he continued toward the door.

A knock, sounding much louder than Tom thought it was, greeted him as he reached for the handle.

Russ stood just outside, his face a bit ashen and his eyes slightly bloodshot. He looked exhausted.

"Heyah Russ, mahnin."

Russell's eyes shifted from Tom's forehead to the torn, dirty shirt that he had been wearing the previous day. "Jesus, Tom, what the hell happened to you?

Tom looked down, having not even realized he hadn't changed his shirt when he got home. His red flannel button-up was missing a button and had a tear down the seam of its breast pocket. Dirt encrusted it, and Tom realized his hands were caked in dirt as well. "Well, shit, Russ. You ain't exactly the picture of beauty this mahnin' neither." Tom looked Russ up and down, though he let a smile crest across his face to show no harm was intended. "I musta just passed out when I got home last night. Long day out theyah."

"Actually, Tom, that's what I wanted to talk to you about. I saw you when you got home, and you looked…I don't know…shaken. Then I saw you again when I went out to get the mail. Heard a bang and everything coming from over here. Then when you didn't answer the door right away this morning…"

Tom held up a hand. "Why don't you come on in heyah," Tom stood to the side and gestured for Russ to enter.

"That's one hell of an egg on your head, Tom. You okay?" Russ said as he entered the living room.

"I don't know Russ, ta be honest with ya." Tom closed the door and headed toward the kitchen. "Can I get ya some coffee?"

"No thanks. I only have a few minutes. Marie needs to head to work shortly, and there is obviously no school today for Sam, so I need to be getting home. I just wanted to come check on you." Russ looked down at the carpet and saw the darkened color of the soaked floor. "I couldn't shake the feeling that something was wrong."

Tom looked over at Russ, confused. "Why's the school closed?"

Russ looked shocked but realized that Tom had been out in the woods all day yesterday and had no idea what happened. "Oh shit Tom, I didn't even realize you wouldn't have known."

"Know what? Sam's okay, isn't he?"

"Well, he's shaken, but he's okay. A boy in his class was killed yesterday. Well, there is no body yet, but from the details I heard, there is no way he's alive."

Tom's knees began to buckle again, and he leaned against the counter. "Jesus, Russ. How? What happened?"

"That's the thing, no one really seems to know. The class was out at recess, and this boy, Dinsmore…Alex, I think, must have snuck off into the school again. No one even noticed until they came back inside. Fuck, Tom, they found the boy's boot at the back of the class in a puddle of blood. Sam said he saw his foot still in it."

Tom was horrified. Nothing like this happened in Isolation. Tom searched his foggy mind in an attempt to come up with some sort of logical explanation. "Bear maybe get into the class?"

"No way. There would have been tracks, scat even. There was no sign of anything out of place. The boy was just…gone."

"I'll be a sonofabitch," Tom said.

Russ looked at the clock on Tom's wall and said, "Shit, listen, I'd love to talk more about this with you, Tom. The whole town is in an uproar, but I have to get home, or Marie will have my head."

Tom nodded. "Ahyup, you get home to ya family, Russ. Hold that boy close."

Russ stood up and headed toward the door. "I'll check back in with you tonight if I can when Marie gets home. You rest. That knot looks like it is pretty painful."

Tom's hand instinctively went to his head. Just as Russ opened the front door, he said, "Oh heyah Russ, what about you? You doin' okay?

You look like the asshole side of a dead deyah this mahnin'. Looks like you were up all night."

Russ chuckled. He never could get enough of Tom's way with words. "Yeah, poor kid had a nightmare last night. Said he saw that dead boy in his room. Said there was a monster outside his window, too. Craziest shit though, Tom, when I went to go check his room, his window was cracked, and there was this strange smell. Almost like turned-up soil. Strangest damn thing. I stayed up with him all night so Marie could get a couple hours of sleep. Anyways, we'll talk later." He waved a quick goodbye and shut the door.

Tom stood by the couch, deep in thought. "Yeah, Russ, see you later," he muttered. As he sat down on the couch, his eyes caught the book he had been reading. He picked it up and began to read.

Eve lay in her hospital bed, broken. Her body would heal, but her mind, well, that would take more time.

She lay alone in a sterilized prison, unable to escape. It wasn't a true prison, of course. She was not being held for an indeterminate amount of time, unable to be out in the world-but she was alone. The hospital had tried to locate her husband, Jamison, but had, at present, no luck in finding him. She needed him with her. She needed his touch, his voice telling her it would be okay and that he wouldn't leave her side. Eve was beside herself with worry, but what kept crawling to the front of her thoughts was the figure that had caused her to drive off the road. The menacing, dark figure had stalked toward her car as she lay mangled in the driver's seat. But she had scared it away. Oh yes, Eve knew how to handle things that others knew nothing about. Dark things. Supernatural things.

Eve had heard the cruel rumors that spread around town about "the witch" that served breakfast at the cafe. *Probably putting spells on everyone that eats there*, she heard, or *I bet she takes the used silverware and uses it to do black magick*. Eve was familiar with the dark arts, but Eve made sure to toe the line, choosing to stay more in the light than in the shadows.

When that nightmare appeared on the road, after she had crashed her SUV and had her leg pinned painfully between the engine that had been pushed through the steering column, Eve instinctually closed her eyes and spoke. The words she spoke flowed naturally though she couldn't even be sure she could recall them now. As the beast came closer and the words flowed faster, the creature began to slow. It let out a scream, and it disappeared. Though the experience had been short-lived, she couldn't get the thing out of her head. It was darker than any force she had ever dealt with.

Eve's eyes began to droop as more pain medicine made its way through the intravenous line in her hand. Her head began to spin. Her vision faded to a pinpoint. Just before she lost consciousness, she had a fleeting vision. Just a momentary glimpse into another place, another time.

Jamison was there.

He lay prone.

Torn in half.

Marie met Russ at the door. She was frazzled, but she knew she had to go to work. She had several showings today, and it wouldn't do to cancel them all; besides, she already ran out on the one yesterday, and she was sure Barney would want to talk to her about that. Sam was on the couch watching cartoons and having some fruity cereal that was more sugar than nutrition.

"Oh Russ, I can't believe I have to go in today. Our little guy needs us."

"I know, Marie, but there isn't anything you can really do here. I know you want to be with him, but he'll be fine today. We'll watch some TV, maybe play that candy game he likes so much. And sooner than you think, you'll be home." Russ put his hand to his wife's face and pulled her in for a kiss.

"I know, you're right. Promise me, if he needs anything, you'll call."

"I promise," Russell said, a smile creeping across his face. "I've got this."

She gave him one more kiss and headed to her car, giving a wave and a honk as she pulled out of the driveway. Russ closed the door and walked over to the couch. Pulling the blanket on to the two of them, the Tolliver boys sat quietly and thought of nothing but the warmth that embraced them.

CHAPTER 15

Marie pulled up to the first showing, a small ranch-style home with two bedrooms, two bathrooms, and a quaint little yard. She met the young couple, standing by their car, hands in each other's hands, smiles of excitement on their faces, and greeted them warmly. A smile, a handshake, and a how-do-you-do. She had worked with this couple previously, with little success, but today seemed to be the day that the buyers would buy and the sellers would sell at any price (well, within reason, of course).

Marie was with the couple in the small ranch for only twenty minutes before they informed her that they were interested in putting in an offer. Marie made the appropriate phone calls and gave them the appropriate paperwork, and with a smile, a handshake, and a "we'll be in touch," she headed back toward her office.

Halfway there, her phone rang, and she was pleasantly surprised to see that it was Mandy, whose name greeted her on screen. She hadn't spoken to Mandy in months, but the greatest friendships tend to have staying power. You can go months without speaking, only to pick back up right where you were. Those friendships are rare, but when you find them, you cherish them.

"Oh my God, Mandy. I'm so glad to hear from you," Marie beamed as she answered the phone.

"Hey, girl! Guess where I am!" Mandy responded with her always bubbly personality. Mandy was always able to make the dark times seem sunny. Sure, she had her own issues, mostly with relationships that had come and gone with the seasons, but she always tried to keep a positive outlook.

The only time Marie had ever really seen Mandy down, truly down, was their senior year in college. Mandy had an exceptionally tough final coming up, and during finals week, her father died of a heart attack while driving to the grocery store. They needed a closed casket. Mandy flew home and attended the funeral. She had gotten an extension on her final, but her mind was elsewhere. She ended up turning in work that, while passing, pulled her gpa down quite a bit. That two-week span, and only that two-week span that Marie could recall, was the only time Mandy had ever seemed truly depressed.

"Wait, I'll tell you," Mandy cut in before Marie could formulate a thought. "I'm at your office! Surprise!"

"You're up here? Oh my God, I'm so excited! Mandy, that's a long drive. Is everything okay?"

"Absolutely! I just had some time off of work, we hadn't talked in a while, and I wanted to come surprise you! So where the hell are you?"

"Actually, I'm on my way back to the office right now. You know, I'm a real estate agent. I don't spend a lot of time there. I have another showing in a couple of hours and then one more later this afternoon, but I'll be free in between. Are you staying up here tonight?"

"I was hoping you'd be okay with that. Do you think Russ will mind?"

"Well, there was a really tough situation that happened at Sam's school yesterday."

Mandy paused, waiting for Marie to go on. After a few moments, Mandy's bubbly personality turned serious. "Is everything okay? Is Sam alright?"

"Yes, yes, Sam is fine. I'll tell you about it when I get there."

"Okay. You know, Marie, if now is a bad time to stay for the night…I should have called."

"Not at all. Your personality will light up the house. Russ won't mind at all. And Sam will be thrilled to see you."

"Alright, yay! Well, hurry up bitch. I want to see your pretty face!"

"Ha ha, I'm about fifteen minutes away."

"Okay. Hey, I think your boss is looking out the window. I'll go in and introduce myself and wait at your desk."

Marie's thoughts turned a little darker. "Just wait in your car. I'll be there soon."

Marie and Mandy went out to lunch and laughed and talked until Marie was forced to leave for her next appointment. Marie called Russ and told him that Mandy would be coming over for the night and to be expecting her. As Mandy hugged Marie a temporary good-bye, a familiar blue car passed by, and Barney reached a hand out of his window with a friendly wave and a hello.

He looked a little too long and smiled a little too wide for Marie, but Mandy didn't notice. Marie got in her car and told Mandy she would see her later. Mandy told Marie she couldn't wait, and they parted ways. Marie was just finishing up her second appointment when Mandy pulled into the Tolliver driveway. Sam came running out to greet her, at least temporarily forgetting the terrible thoughts that had clouded his head for the last day.

"Hi, sweetheart," Mandy beamed as Sam jumped into her arms. "Wow, you're getting heavy."

"Hi, Aunt Mandy. Mom says I'm as heavy as a ton of bricks," Sam laughed, his smile ear-to-ear.

"Hey, Mandy," Russ said as he came out to greet her. "We're so glad to see you. Unexpected, but glad." Russ gave Mandy a hug and picked up her bag. "Come on in."

"Thanks, Russ. You know me, always spontaneous."

They walked into the house, Sam laughing and smiling the whole way. For the next several hours, the three of them would share stories, share laughter, and (at least the adults) would share a glass of wine. For that afternoon, the Tolliver household was joyous.

When Marie arrived at her final appointment of the day, she showed up at an empty house. She liked to run early, so this wasn't entirely unexpected. She went inside and straightened up anything that appeared to be even slightly out of place. Her heart was happy. Mandy always seemed to know when Marie needed her. It was almost a psychic ability. With what happened at Sam's school, this visit was needed, and Marie couldn't wait to get home and have a bottle of wine with her husband and her best friend-make that several bottles of wine.

When Marie heard a car pull into the driveway, she took one quick look in the mirror to make sure she was presentable, brushed the hair back from her face, and walked over to the door to let her clients in.

She opened the door and was shocked to see Barney standing on the stoop. He looked slightly disheveled, his hair unkempt, sweat glistening on his forehead. He licked his lips, and his eyes darted from side to side. It was almost as if he had a plan, but the plan had left his mind as soon as she opened the door.

"Barney," Marie said, startled, "what are you doing here? I have clients that are on their way."

Barney wiped the sweat from his brow and stepped into the house, causing her to take several steps back. "Actually, Marie, I just wanted to stop by because I got a call at the office from your clients. They have to reschedule. Something with their kid." Barney closed the door behind himself.

Marie paused momentarily as she took stock of her current situation. She looked around the room that suddenly seemed to be closing in on her. "Well, thanks for letting me know, Barney. But, you know, you could have just given me a call. No need to drive all the way over here and inconvenience yourself."

"Oh, no inconvenience at all. Besides, you seem to be out of the office quite a bit lately. I thought it would be nice to catch up and have a conversation." Barney's eyes lowered, and he took a step toward Marie. His eyes leered upon her body. "Say, Marie, how's that husband of yours?"

Marie sensed the danger that was trying to sneak up on her from the shadows. Barney walked over to the windows by the door and closed the shades. "Russ, oh Russ is doing great. We're great, actually. In fact, we're supposed to meet for dinner right after this showing. Since they canceled, I should probably just head out and get to the restaurant." Marie took a few steps toward the door, but Barney stepped in front of her, blocking the path.

"Hey, hey," Barney said, as he reached out his lecherous hand and touched her shoulder, "what's the rush? If he is expecting you to be at your appointment, then we have a few minutes to talk." Sweat now beaded upon Barney's upper lip. As though he saw Marie looking at it, he wiped it away with the back of his hand. His breathing became heavier.

Marie took a step back. She unconsciously touched the shoulder that Barney had just grabbed. She could feel the touch still even though his hand was no longer there. It was like a burning sensation. Like when you grab a hot pot and quickly release it, the sensation remains. A violation. It turned her stomach, and she could feel her eyes welling up with tears.

"Hey, Marie, who was that hot piece of ass you were out to lunch with?"

The question hit Marie like a heavyweight boxer's punch. The sneaky threat that seemed to be hiding in the shadows showed itself. There was no question anymore. Marie saw and felt the danger. With the door shut and the windows drawn, she felt completely isolated. She stepped back again, her mind racing, her eyes darting around, looking for an escape route.

"Hey, Marie, did you hear me?" Barney stepped forward with every step back Marie took. Barney's legs longer than Marie's, he was closing the distance with each stride. "Marie, I want to know your friends. You're important to me. It would be great to get to know your friends."

"Barney, you're my boss. I don't think you need to know…"

"*Marie,*" Barney screamed suddenly, "why can't you answer a simple fucking question? What is it with you women and not being able to answer a simple goddamn question? Is it a lack of giving a shit, or is it that you are just too stupid?" Marie was backed up against the wall now. Barney was so close she could smell his lunch still stinking on his breath. Tuna salad, she thought as her stomach twisted. His pupils were large. So large his eyes appeared black. His tongue danced in his mouth as he licked his lips.

"Barney…stop. You're scaring me." The tears that Marie had fought to control finally spilled over. Her legs felt like she had just run a marathon, weak and shaky.

Barney saw the tears as they rolled down Marie's cheek. "Why are you scared? Oh, I know. I bet you're scared because that hot piece of ass must have gone back to your place. I'm glad to know that you and your husband are doing so well because, wow, Marie, let me tell you, it would be really hard to push a woman like that away. But, you know women. She'll try to get some anyway. There is no loyalty in women. She'll try to get him to relax and then make her move." Barney slammed his hand against the wall by Marie's head. "She probably pulled her thong up so he could get a look. She'll press against him as she walks by. Maybe let her hands caress him between his legs."

Barney's body pressed up against Marie now. Her head was down to avoid his eyes. She wouldn't allow him to see the fear in hers. She hid from his eyes but couldn't hide from his breath. That awful, rancid, sour breath. She suddenly couldn't concentrate on anything but the warmth of it against her neck.

"Women like her. They are just cock whores. You can't trust a woman like that. She only thinks about one thing. But not you, Marie. You're different," Barney's hand rested against her thigh. "You're an honest woman. A respectable woman. You're the type of woman that a gentleman deserves. A man like me." Barney's hand moved under her dress.

Marie's eyes happened upon the knife rack next to her. It would be a risk, it was just out of arm's reach, and Barney was stronger than her. "Barney, stop. Please."

Barney's breathing continued to speed up, and the sweat began to pour again as he inched his way up her thigh. "Marie, you're a great woman. Why don't you just forget that guy? He's probably balls-deep in your friend by now, anyways. Start fresh. We'll get away from here. Let them have each other. They deserve each other." He pulled her panties to the side and touched her. "Mmm, your warmth tells me you want this too."

Marie held her breath and made her move. She lunged at the knife and was able to grab it before Barney could react. She turned and slammed it into Barney's thigh. His scream resonated throughout the room, and his eyes, once scary, were now terrifying.

"You fucking bitch! You fucking stabbed me! You are just like them! Just like the others!" He lunged at her, but Marie ducked out of the way.

She ran to the door as Barney stumbled to follow her. She flung open the door and ran to the car, hearing Barney screaming behind her. Her hands were shaking, but she was able to get the keys in the ignition before Barney had even made it to the door. She reversed out of the driveway and hit the gas. The tires squealed before catching the pavement and launching the car down the road. As she looked in her rearview, she saw Barney bent over in the front yard, clutching the knife in his leg.

When Marie got home, she ran into the house, tears streaming down her face. Thankfully, Sam was playing in his room, but Russ and Mandy ran to her. Russ held her as she bawled. Mandy brought her to the couch and asked what happened. Marie told her the whole story. Mandy listened, Russell fumed.

"I'm so sorry, Russ," Marie turned to him and said with guilt in her voice.

Russell held her tightly. "You have nothing to be sorry for. You're okay now, Marie. I love you."

Marie and Russ went to the police station to file a report. Mandy stayed with Sam, so he did not have to be further upset. They filed the report at 6:00 PM. By 6:30 PM, the police were at the house in which the attack took place. A puddle of blood was found on the doorstep, but no Barney. By 7:30 PM, Berlin police were knocking on Barney's door. But there was no sign of him.

The following morning several police officers raided the real estate office that had once made Marie so happy. This, too, was empty.

There were no records of Barney having gone to the hospital and no sign of his car between Berlin and Isolation.

Barney was gone.

CHAPTER 16

The next morning Russell woke up with the sun. He had tossed and turned all night, and his head swam with grogginess as he tried to pry his eyes open. He rolled over and saw that Marie was still sound asleep, the blanket pulled up to her chin. Looking past Marie and out the window, he noticed a beautiful pink sky greeting him. A peaceful morning after a horrible night. Russell stood up and put on some sweatpants, a T-shirt, and his running shoes; as he leaned down to tie them, he stretched his hamstrings deeply, the loosening of which seemed to wake him up a bit. As he walked out of the bedroom, Sam opened his own bedroom door.

"Good morning, Dad. Where are you going?" Sam whispered.

"Morning, bud. I'm just going for my run. It's still super early. Go back to bed."

"Okay, Dad." Sam turned to walk back into his room before turning back toward his father, eyes wide with concern. "Hey, Dad? Is Mom okay?"

Russ looked at the innocence in his son's eyes. He had seen an awful tragedy two days ago, and though they had hidden from Sam his mother's fear and anger yesterday, children are very perceptive. He knew something bad had happened to his mom, and he was scared.

"Mom will be okay, buddy. Don't worry."

"You'll protect Mom, right, Dad?"

Russ smiled and rubbed Sam's hair. "I'll protect your mom. And I'll protect you too. From anything that thinks of sticking its mean little head into our lives." Sam giggled as Russ poked him in the belly. "Now go back to bed, handsome. Mom will be up in a little while, and I'll be home soon."

Sam smiled, gave his dad a kiss on the cheek, and climbed back into bed. Russ quietly walked to the front door, careful not to disturb Mandy, dead to the world on the couch. He stepped out into the crisp morning air and took a deep breath. The cold engulfed him, but it was soothing. Russ began to run toward downtown.

For Russell, running was very meditative. The stomping of his feet on the pavement and the blood pulsing in his head set the rhythm and pace that he would keep. Some of his best stories came to him in the pre-dawn hours with the wind stroking his face. He found that if he focused on his stories, he didn't focus on his strained, wheezy breathing.

However, this morning he used the running as an emotional release. He had so much anger inside, more anger than he had ever felt before. He couldn't get his mind off of Marie's experience. The images flashed in his mind, and his blood boiled. He had never met this…Barney, but Marie had told him enough stories. At first, she had found him charming, although strange. But Marie had been getting more and more concerned over the past few months.

Why didn't I just tell her to find a new job? We have enough in savings right now. She could have just found something new. There are plenty of real estate offices up here.

Russell chastised himself over and over again. When something happens to a loved one, you always wonder if there was any way it could have been avoided. Russell thought of countless times in which he could have asked Marie, hell if he knew it was going to amount to this, forced Marie to find something else.

He wanted to kill Barney. To wrap his hands around his throat and squeeze until he felt the tendons of his neck strain against his fingers. To watch the life leave his eyes.

He stopped about half way between his home and downtown, and screamed. His scream was one of anger, but it was also one of pain. Birds flew from the trees, startled at the agonizing noise coming from the man stopped on the road. He screamed a second time, releasing all the pent-up anger that he could. Tears stung his face as the wind blew against him. Russell wiped them away and inhaled deeply, trying to soothe himself from his wife's pain and fear.

An ambulance blared by, startling Russ out of his thoughts. His heart raced as he followed the red and white lights toward the center of town. The ambulance sped through the center and took a left onto one of the side roads just past *The Dusty Bookshelf*. As Russ approached the small grouping of shops, he saw Tom's truck outside of *The Back In Time Cafe*.

Russell jogged the rest of the way to the cafe. When he opened the door, he saw Tom, already sitting at the bar, sipping his coffee (black, anything else was for kids, Tom would say). Russ pulled up the stool next to him and sat down with a heavy sigh.

"Hey Tom, fancy meeting you here."

Tom looked over at Russ and gave a small smile, a nod, and a "mahning."

Russ ordered himself a coffee as well (two creams, two sugars because he's looking to wake up, not grow hair on his chest). "Tom, you still don't look too good. That knot on your head is as big as an apple. You feeling okay?"

"Ah, I'm alright, Russ. Just got somethin' on my mind lately. I'm tryin' to git some answers to it."

"Anything you wanna talk about?"

"Naht yet. Just waiting to see Bryce Callahan. He's usually heah about this time every mahning."

"The guy that is always hanging out here with the other older folks? Call themselves the professors or something like that?"

"Hey," Tom said with a serious tone, "you watch it with that age stuff. Bryce isn't much older than me." Tom smiled and continued, "Historians, Russ. He's a crotchety pain in the ass, but he knows what he's talking about in these heah pahts."

Russ took a sip of his coffee and thought for a moment. Solemnly he said, "Tom, I gotta tell you something. Marie was attacked yesterday at work."

Tom slowly put down his cup on the bar in front of him. "Attacked? What do you mean attacked?"

"Her boss. Creepy sonofabitch. He followed her to a showing and attacked her." Russ slammed his fist on the counter, shaking the two mugs that sat in front of them. Myrtle turned with a start and looked at Russ. "Sorry, Myrt," Russ said with his eyes lowered. Myrtle took his apology in stride and turned back to her work. Russ looked back to Tom and met his eyes. "We went to the police, but they couldn't find him. She's very shaken up."

"Jesus, Russ, I'm so sahrry. I hope they find the bastahd. Please give Marie my best. Tell her to keep her head up."

"I'll do that, Tom. She'll appreciate that."

"A bad run of it in this town the last couple days. Your boy's school, Marie, even the old campground had a big fire, took half of it to the ground in ashes." Tom took a long sip from his mug. "I'll make sure to keep an eye out on your place while you're not there. Marie and Sam deserve to feel safe. I mean, Christ, this is Isolation, not Boston."

The bell above the door tinged as Sarah Thornberg and Miles Gray walked in and pulled up a chair at their normal table by the window. Tom took the last sip of his coffee and stood up.

"I gotta go talk to them, Russ. I'll see you latah." Tom clapped Russ on the shoulder and walked over to two-thirds of the historians. He pulled up a seat and spoke quietly. Russ took another sip of his coffee and looked up at the news. The Patriots had a big game on Sunday that had been the talk of all the sports fans in the area. On television, they were replaying a section of Bill Belichick's interview with reporters the previous day. The news cut to the weather, and the radar, with ominous colors projected, showed a big snowstorm coming out of the north that was headed toward Isolation.

"Damn Canadians can keep their storms up there. Too early in the year for this shit," said one of the regulars of the cafe that Russ wasn't too familiar with.

Russ thought back to the sunrise this morning, *red sky at night sailor's delight, red sky in morning sailor's take warning.* He remembered hearing that as a kid, and it always stuck with him.

Tom got up from his seat and headed out the door and to his truck, passing Mitchell Freemore as he went. Mitchell walked in and stuck his baseball cap on the hanger by the door. As he turned, he caught Russell's eyes and smiled. He greeted him with a nod and approached. Mitchell and Russ weren't fast friends, but they were friendly, for sure. Having lived on the same road, they often shared pleasantries as they passed.

"Hey, Mitch. I was actually hoping to run into you." The waitress refilled Russell's cup as Mitchell pulled up to the stool next to Russ. His genuine smile greeted Myrtle as she walked over.

"Oh yeah, what's going on?" Mitchell placed his order and turned to face Russ.

"So Marie and I did one of those DNA testing kits. Turns out I'm twenty percent Wimpak. That's your heritage, right?"

"Hey, *BROTHER!*" Mitch exclaimed loudly as he slapped Russ on the back. He eyed Russ carefully for a moment. "You don't really look

Wimpak, though. Maybe the eyes," Mitchell laughed. "But a Wimpak is a Wimpak. Mitchell smiled and took a sip of his coffee.

Russ forced a little chuckle as he sat his mug back on the counter. "But listen, Mitch, I wanted to talk to you about it. I wanted to learn a little bit, you know, embrace my ancestry and all." Russ felt like an imposter, talking to a man about his ancestry and trying to claim it as his own. But Mitch didn't seem to take any offense, which put Russ at ease.

"Yeah, for sure. I don't have much time right now, but maybe come over after dinner Friday night. Couple beers? I'll tell you everything you want to know."

"Sounds great, Mitch," Russell said as he placed a few bucks on the counter. As Russ stood up to leave, an older woman that Russ faintly recognized from town came into the cafe in a panic. Wild-eyed and frantic, she ran in and right over to the two historians. As Russ passed by, he heard the conversation.

"The Dinsmores," the woman said in a panic, "they were found dead this morning. A complete mess in the house. They are saying murder/suicide, but I heard they had claw marks all over their bodies."

Russ stopped. "Did you say the Dinsmores? The family that just lost their son yesterday?"

The woman looked at Russ, tears welling in her eyes. "Yes. That poor family."

Mitchell came up next to Russ, apparently having overheard the conversation as well.

"What the fuck is going on in this town?" Mitchell asked Russ.

"I don't know, but there is definitely something foul in the air."

When Deputy Walker arrived at the Dinsmore residence shortly before dawn, he had been greeted by a crowd of neighbors gathered outside the home. All had attested to hearing loud screaming and a commotion inside the Dinsmore house about an hour before.

When the screaming first started, the neighbors closest to the home assumed it was the wailing of grieving parents, having just lost their child in a seemingly horrific way. The wails that they heard had transformed over the short time that they were audible, however. At first, the sounds of screaming-scared and shrill; then the sound of howling-painful and agonizing; and lastly, the sound of desperation and despair. Then nothing.

Several neighbors had called the police only a few minutes apart from each other. One of them, a young man named Tyler Merket, who worked part-time down at McNeil's Auto Body, had gathered enough courage to walk into the Dinsmores' yard and was heading toward the door when a shriek unlike the others ripped through the neighborhood. Tyler Merket decided to back up as quickly as possible and wait in his own yard for the police to arrive. By the time the blue lights were strobing against the houses on Pine Street, a group of about ten were milling around, whispering about what they thought happened.

As Deputy Walker had turned down the road, a sudden case of deja vu came over him. He had followed the Dinsmores home after the terrible incident at the school. The road had seemed relaxing yesterday afternoon, even in the midst of such a terrible event. This morning, the serenity was gone, taken over by the eerie feeling of being isolated in a maze, lost with no way out.

Deputy Walker stepped out of his patrol car and was approached by several of the neighbors, excited to tell their version of the events that took place. They told the deputy there had been no other sounds coming from the house since the last shriek that had scared Tyler Merket off the property. The deputy radioed for backup but sensed the importance of getting into the home for help even before the backup arrived. He knew this was a foolish move, but he believed time was of the essence.

The sun was just starting to peek over the horizon as Deputy Walker approached the home, hand on his holster. The pink clouds appearing in the windows of the home looked like cotton candy. The disjunction of his thoughts and what he suspected he was walking up to startled him. He knocked once, then twice; silence was the only response. Carefully, he looked through the windows and saw a house turned upside down. A lamp was broken on the floor, the couch overturned, a pool of blood lay next to it. The deputy strained his eyes against the dark home as the cotton candy threatened to obstruct his view. A pair of legs lay behind the couch on the blood-stained carpet.

Deputy Walker turned back to the door and kicked it in, announcing himself as he entered.

The scene inside the house was one that the deputy would remember until the day he died. The house was in complete disarray. The glass, the blood, the stench was everywhere. The smell, like dirt and stagnant water, hung in the air and threatened to choke him. He cautiously walked toward the legs that he had seen from the window, calling out, hoping for a response. When he could finally get a look at the body, he saw that the torso had been torn completely in half. The legs remained whole and together, although several deep claw marks tore through the meat above the knees, but the torso was torn almost perfectly in half. Mr. Dinsmore's head and neck twisted at an awful angle.

He backed up, bile sneaking its way into his throat, and bumped into something on the floor. He shone his flashlight down and saw Mrs. Dinsmore lying at his feet beneath the window, her head turned completely around. The deputy's breath caught in his throat, and he stumbled toward the door. When he reached the front yard, he dropped to his knees and vomited. He remained there until his backup arrived.

CHAPTER 17

Tom pulled up to the small blue house on the corner of Rainbow Road and Main Street. He paused for a moment and looked at the home. The windows were dark, and there seemed to be no movement in the house.

Just after seven in the morning, Tom thought, *he may not be used to visitors this early, but he's gotta be up.*

Tom waited another few minutes for any sign of movement in the home. He almost put the car in reverse to head back to the cafe when he noticed Bryce peeking through the shades of his living room window. Tom gave a small wave of acknowledgment, and Bryce did the same before heading over to the front door. Tom got out of his car, book in hand, and headed toward the door where Bryce was now standing, a note of cautiousness covering his face.

"Can I help you?" Bryce said as Tom approached.

"Mahnin. You're Bryce Callahan, ain'tcha?"

"I am," Bryce replied, still weary of the man that was on his walkway.

"Names Tom Richmond. I'm from the other side of town. Funny, we've both been around these pahts for yeeahs and never had the pleasure."

Bryce nodded. "Ah, Tom. Yes, I recognize you from Myrt's place, I think."

"I've been known to get me some of that liquid magic now and then." Tom chuckled slightly. Bryce waited for him to continue. "I was hoping I could ask ya a few questions about this heah book," Tom held up the book in his left hand and, as he approached, stuck his right hand out for a handshake.

Bryce looked down at Tom's hand but didn't accept it. "I mean no disrespect," Bryce said as he took a small step back toward the inside of his home. "I'm just not feeling very well today. Woke up with a real ass-kicker of a headache and been feeling sick to my stomach. Couldn't even get down to get my mornin' coffee, you know."

"Ahyup. Stopped at the diner this mahnin' to find ya. Talked to Sarah and Miles. They sent me this way. Listen, Bryce, I know you aren't too familiar with me, but I really need to talk to you 'bout some of ya research. Somethin' strange is goin' on 'round heah."

"Well, Tom, I think maybe another time, yes? As I said, I'm just not feeling well this morning and…"

"I saw something in the woods," Tom cut Bryce off. "I think it killed someone. It wasn't an animal. My God, it was…something else. I heard about the little boy at the school. The one who was attacked yesterday. I saw this…thing yesterday mahnin' myself. I can't shake the feelin' that it's related. I was reading ya book and was drawn to somethin' called," Tom flipped through the book, "the kee-wakw."

Bryce Callahan's face paled. "Kee-wakw, are you sure?"

"Well shit Bryce, no, I ain't shuwah. You're the expert. That's why I'm heyah."

Bryce stepped aside. "Please come in."

Tom stepped inside and moved toward the couch. The inside of Bryce's house was dark. *Probably the headache,* Tom thought. The sun, which had been so beautiful only, what, a half hour ago, an hour tops (Tom's mind was still so damn clouded from the fucking bump on the head), was now beginning to peek out only sporadically between the clouds.

The carpet on the floor of the living room was dark, maybe a dark brown, not quite black, and looked as though it had been vacuumed recently. On the walls hung paintings, mostly nature paintings and Native American artifacts that could have been real or could have been purchased down in Lincoln or North Conway at a local gift shop. Tom suspected at least some of them were authentic, maybe even acquired during the time Bryce was writing the book Tom now held in his hand.

The smell of the room was stale. The stench of sickness hung in the air, stifling the room like the humidity of a hot July afternoon. The house seemed well put together, though the stench seemed to counter what would have otherwise been a very welcoming ambiance. Tom decided it would be rude to say anything that might draw attention to it, instead simply saying, "This is a nice place ya got heah, Bryce."

Bryce gave a small smile and walked toward the kitchen, offering Tom anything to drink. Tom thanked him politely but declined and sat on the couch. Bryce grabbed a glass of water and made his way over to the chair across the room, making sure to keep his distance at the risk of giving Tom whatever was plaguing him.

Bryce sipped his water for a moment before he set it on the end table beside him. He slowly lifted his head, and his eyes met Tom's.

"Please, tell me what you saw."

Tom took a deep breath and said, "It was the damndest thing. I went up to the woods. Ya know, up by Wimpak Hill. There was an old pickup already up there."

"Old pickup? What kind?"

Tom scanned his memory. "Ah, Ford. Seventies. Late seventies. Little rusty."

Bryce nodded. "Jamison Crowley's sounds like. Police been searching for him since yesterday. His wife got in an accident. Strange for him to not show up to the hospital."

"Bryce, there was no reason for me to feel even a bit peculiar, but dammit, something just seemed wrong. Men out huntin' when the season is fresh, normal as kissin' ya wife. Normal as…as your mahnin' coffee, Bryce. But when I got out of the truck and heard a scream, a scream like I ain't nevah heard before…" Tom paused for a second. Bryce thought Tom must have been recalling those moments, pushing through the fear that threatened to choke off his words. "I ran to where I thought I heard it…"

Tom left out the part about how he almost shit himself and hid in his truck a bit to regain his nerves.

What a pussy, he thought before he was brought back to reality.

A low buzzing noise started in his ear. Tom shifted in his seat, his brow beginning to glisten with sweat. Whether from the recounting of the story or the staleness of the room, he wasn't sure, but he took out his handkerchief and dabbed his forehead dry. Bryce leaned forward in his seat and sipped his water again, waiting on bated breath for the rest of the story and wondering why Tom thought a kee-wakw was in the woods outside of Isolation.

"Bryce," Tom continued, "there was a finger layin' in the leaves. I thought it must have been an animal that got this poor bastahd. Then I saw…it."

Bryce looked at Tom engrossingly. "Saw what?"

"It was…it was a monstah, Bryce. It was a goddamn monstah. Black, utterly black. Its teeth, no, fangs, Bryce, they were stained red, probably from the poor bastard it had just attacked. But the worst part about it was how it moved. The speed, the speed was…I couldn't comprehend it. It was in one spot, and then it was in another instantly. It knew I saw it, but it tried to stay hidden behind the trees. God help me. I don't know why it didn't attack me, but as quickly as it had appeared, it disappeared. It gave a screeching, high-pitched awful scream and was just…gone. May the Lord strike me down, Bryce. I think it went to the school. I think it left me to go after that little boy."

Tom broke down, guilt overtaking him. He took his handkerchief out and wiped the tears from his eyes before they overflowed. Bryce leaned back in his chair, his look somewhere between incredulousness and shock. He finished the last of his water and cleared his throat.

"Tom, that's a…a hell of a story." Bryce took a deep breath and collected his thoughts. "I mean, the finger, did you bring it to the police? Did you even call the police to report it?"

"I…uh…I didn't, Bryce. I think I dropped the finger up theyah on the hill. I haven't gone to the police yet. It was a strange day yestuhday. I wanted to get home, I wanted to get in my car and drive away as fast as I could, but I just wandered, Bryce. I wandered in the woods. I don't know why. I couldn't pull myself out of tryin' to understand what I saw. I mean, I thought I was goin' crazy. It just don't make any sense what I saw. But then…when I heard about the boy…I just know it's the same thing that got him. I just know, Bryce."

"Okay, listen, Tom, first, you need to go to the police and report what you found. Maybe leave the scary monster stuff out, but report the scream and the finger. I admit, the description you're giving me does sound like the kee-wakw, but I'm not convinced."

"Well, what do you think it was then? Why not that kee-wackwaw?" Tom asked, a little more standoffish than he intended to be.

"Kee-wakw. Well, for one thing, the kee-wakw is from Abenaki lore. The Abenaki weren't from around here. Nearby, sure, but the Wimpak and Abenaki were bitter enemies and fought over that hill for decades. The Wimpak pushed the Abenaki east and north of here. That's why it's called 'Wimpak Hill' and not 'Abenaki Hill.'"

"Alright," Tom said matter-of-factly. "That makes sense. But they were still close-by right."

"Yes, as a matter of fact, they were in most locations around here. Just not there. But there are other things that make me wonder."

"Like?"

"Like the kee-wakw doesn't just disappear. It doesn't move with the kind of speed you're talking about."

"Bryce, I know you don't really know me, but I ain't no liar."

"Well, Tom, I'm not saying you're a liar, but…well, that's a hell of a story. You're right, I don't know you well, but I also don't think you'd drive out here and tell me some made-up tale just for shits and giggles." Bryce stood up, ran his hands through his hair, and went to go fill up his glass of water again.

"I know what I saw, and it was awful," Tom said, almost to himself.

"I believe you, Tom. Well, at least, I believe you enough to put some time into researching this a bit. Give me until tomorrow. Let me try to kick this headache before I go stuffing my nose into books and straining my eyes against the damn computer screen. Let's meet for lunch tomorrow at the cafe. Say eleven?"

"That sounds great to me," Tom stood up and went to shake Bryce's hand again before remembering not to. "Bryce, I want to thank you for this. I'm happy I made the trip over here. If theyah is somethin' to find, I'm sure you'll find it."

Bryce led Tom to the door and showed him out.

"Tomorrah at eleven. See ya then, Bryce."

"See you then, Tom."

As Tom sat back in his truck and started the engine, the first flake of snow fell from the sky and landed on the windshield, melting before Tom had even had a chance to register it there. By the time he was back to the center of Isolation, the snow was already covering the hoods of the idled cars in front of the cafe.

CHAPTER 18

Eve sat in her hospital bed down in Berlin, meditating on what she had seen, or thought she had seen, a few days before. Fear had begun to take hold of her. The police had found Jamison's truck out by Wimpak Hill, but there had been no sign of him. Something was definitely wrong.

Yesterday, Myrtle Beck had come to visit her, which was at least a temporary break from her frantic thoughts. Myrtle brought one of the cafe's famous coffees for Eve to enjoy. The sweet aroma caressed her nostrils with pleasure the moment she walked into the room.

They chatted for hours and even laughed a little bit, though it pained Eve to do so. When Eve told Myrtle the story of her crash, she kept away from recounting the monster she had seen-Myrtle likely would have chalked it up to the pain medication anyways. However, she did ask about Jamison. Myrtle confirmed that she had not seen him in the cafe lately, but she hadn't thought it strange since she assumed he had been with her. Jamison only loved one thing more than hunting and *The Back In Time Cafe's* coffee-Eve.

While this added to Eve's worry when Myrtle told her about the strange happenings in town, Eve's dread was heightened even more. Towns like Isolation don't have mysterious disappearances (the occasional hiker that might get lost in the woods for a few hours but nothing more), and they certainly don't have deaths that have been ruled foul play (and multiple at that). Concern spread across Eve's face as Myrtle told her everything (waitresses tend to hear a lot and share a lot of gossip). When Myrtle finally left Eve's bedside, Eve's mind was wracked with thoughts that she hoped weren't premonitions. She slept little that night.

The snow had been falling since yesterday morning. It had slowed overnight but picked back up in the morning, covering the branches of the trees outside her window. The storm created a winter wonderland landscape that, for Eve, helped to ease the pain in her aching body. The wind blowing the snow against the window made her happy to be inside, warm in bed. Even if it was a hospital bed.

Eve had always loved the winter. Its symbolization of all things coming to an end before starting anew gave her hope that every new year offered a chance of greatness-of happiness beyond imagining. *May the best of your today be the worst of your tomorrow*, rang true. It was the early, dark nights. It was the crisp night air. It was the thinning of the veil. The dampening silence that the falling snow brought; it helped to clear her mind completely.

As her mind drifted to the astral plane, the steady *whirring* of the machines around her helped her to focus on her intention-trying to find her Jamison. While she sat up in her bed, her energy traveled through space and time. She traveled in a void of shapes and colors, but she couldn't quite make out any individual thing. The colors swirled around her, searching for something that wouldn't present itself. Time had no meaning here. She could have been traveling for an hour, minutes, or a lifetime. It made no difference. Her mission was clear.

The tunnel of colors and shapes began to slow a bit; objects began to become distinct. When she was finally able to focus, she found herself in the middle of the woods. The leaves were turning, and the weather was cool, but there was no snow on the ground. She didn't know where her mystical travel had taken her, but she knew she wasn't in the present.

Her breath rose in front of her face; she held herself in an embrace, rubbing her hands up and down her arms to warm herself. Her physical form lay broken in the hospital bed, but her life energy roamed these woods. And though no more than energy here, she was connected to her body, allowing her to feel the world around her. To experience this place as though she was truly there. The leaves lightly crunched under the weight of the squirrels that were scurrying up the closest trees, shocked by the sudden appearance of something esoteric in their midst.

Eve's energy wandered forward up a steep rise where she thought she could hear voices. The leaves shuffled, and the fallen tree branches cracked under each step. She slowed her pace and crouched down, careful not to make herself known. She may not be seen in this strange place. Although she wasn't completely confident in that hypothesis, she could certainly interact with the environment, similar to the way a poltergeist can manipulate the furniture in a home. As she reached the top of the rise, she saw men in some sort of uniform standing over several men that appeared to be Native Americans-chained and on their knees.

Eve couldn't quite recognize the uniform, but the men seemed to be some sort of military or militia. Some, however, wore no more than torn shirts and pants with some sort of hide shoes. Screams rose from trees behind the gathered soldiers. One of the chained natives rose and was met with the butt of the closest soldier's gun. He collapsed on the ground, blood seeping from the fresh gash against the side of his head.

Eve gasped.

The native men looked beaten, miserable, and exhausted. Eve thought they must have been walking for days. One of the men shuffled next to the man who was just struck with the gun. He leaned down and appeared to be whispering into the other's ear. The militia men smiled.

A soldier appeared from the trees behind the gathered men, still pulling up his pants. He smiled and laughed with the others. Some patted him on his back, some asked for details. Another scream rang out, and the man with the gash on his head opened his eyes.

The man slowly tried to stagger to his feet. The blood still dripping from his wound and covering the leaves beneath him. The steady *pat, pat, pat* of the blood hitting the leaves was lost on the bloody man as he stared defiantly at the man that came from behind the trees. The native man who had shuffled over to his bloody friend stood with him, trying to help him stay upright. They were each met with a punch to the stomach, doubling them over.

The group of men laughed, and another scream rose from behind the trees. This was followed by several thumps of, what sounded like, something hitting wet clay; the screaming stopped. Seconds later, there was a gunshot. The man with the gash got to his feet once more, steadied himself, and though his hands were chained, ran forward toward the man that had struck him with his gun. The armed man stepped to the side, and the wounded man fell to the ground again.

The rest of the Native Americans seemed to have had enough at that point. They rose as one. The militia's rifles rose with them. Neither party was flinching until the man from behind the trees emerged.

He was naked and covered in dirt. Leaves were stuck in his hair, sweat covered his body. Flecks of blood added color to his dirt-covered body. A twisted smile appeared on his face as the native man's eyes found his.

"What's this?" he demanded. The man with the gash on his head squinted his eyes in an evil glare. The naked man reached down behind the fallen tree from which he arose. He grabbed something and dragged it along with him.

Horror passed over each of the native men's faces in kind as they realized what he was holding. The naked man was holding a girl's hair.

Her naked and battered body was dragged from behind the tree. One eye swollen shut, the other wide with shock. Her mouth hung open, and several of her teeth were broken. One of her nipples was cut off, and fresh blood stained her inner thighs. The chained man that had fallen to the ground wailed. He screamed to the heavens as only a father who has lost a child by the worst means possible could.

Gunshots rang out behind him as his men fell to the ground, blood spilling from smoking holes in their chests. The naked man dragged the wounded man's daughter by the hair closer, making sure he had a clear view of her lifeless body. Eve stood horrified above the scene, tears streaming down her face.

"Mr. Appleton, sir," one of the men with a smoking gun said, "what should we do with this one?"

Isaac Appleton dropped the girl's body just in front of the wailing father. He looked down upon the man and spat. Years of fighting between these indigenous men and his men had caused Appleton to become vile, hateful. When Appleton first came out to these woods and encountered these people, he found them to be nothing more than a nuisance, but his opinion changed quickly. As the raids on his camps continued and the furs that they worked so hard to get were taken, Appleton's hatred grew. He squatted down next to the broken man and took the man's chin in his hand.

"Chief," he said with a condescending tone, "I warned you what would happen."

Eve hazarded a step forward, wanting to hear what the man was saying more clearly. Still unsure if she could be seen, she was careful with her steps. As she snuck behind a tree a few yards in front of her, a squirrel darted out and caused her to stumble forward. Leaves were kicked in every direction as she braced herself against the tree. The soldiers turned and aimed their guns in the direction of the noise. Appleton took his eyes off the man in front of him and glanced in that direction as well. Cold, icy eyes scanned the area, then, satisfied it was just an animal, he returned his gaze to the shattered man that was before him.

"Do you see what you've caused, Chief?" Appleton hissed. "Do you see what you've done!" Appleton screamed in his face. Spittle flew from his mouth, and his wild eyes flickered from side to side. Finally, the broken, chained man stopped sobbing and turned to look directly into Isaac Appleton's eyes. He began to speak.

Eve could not make out what the man was saying, but she knew the tone in which he spoke. The men raised their guns and pointed them toward the man.

"Mr. Appleton, sir, he's trying to curse us," one of the younger men stammered.

Appleton continued to stare into the man's eyes, not flinching. "Williamson, calm the fuck down. The chief has no special powers. He's a broken man saying his final goodbyes to this world." The chained man continued to chant. "You were a worthy adversary, Chief, but in the end, your people will fall under my blade as quickly as an animal in my traps. The only difference is this isn't for profit. It's for fun." With that, Appleton's knife, which had been held in the hand out of Eve's line of sight, came up quick as a flash and sliced the throat of the Wimpak Chief.

The chained man knelt there for a few moments, blood pouring from his severed neck, and began to sway. All the while, his lips continued to move as though he was still speaking to something. Appleton stood up and walked back toward the tree he had been behind. The Native American, having finally lost his battle with death, fell next to his daughter's broken body.

Eve screamed.

The men turned.

And suddenly, she was back in the hospital room.

It was a few minutes before eleven when Tom walked through the cafe door. He glanced over to the table where The Historians usually sat, only to find it empty. In fact, the diner was surprisingly empty. It was snowing, and it was coming down pretty hard, but these were hearty New Englanders. Snowstorms didn't scare away most folks in Isolation.

"Hey, Myrt," Tom said as he approached the counter. "Quiet mahnin'?"

"Town seems to be going loony," Myrtle said as she poured Tom his usual cup of coffee.

"What do you mean?" Tom loved to keep his finger on the pulse of Isolation, but the last few days, he seemed to be in a bit of a haze. He couldn't seem to focus long on anything but Wimpak Hill and whatever he had seen up there. At dinner, while watching the news, in the shower, his thoughts continued to drift to the severed finger, the blackness of the creature.

"Seven more people dead, Tom. Overnight! Seven! The Wilsons out by the elementary, McNeil and his wife too. Found them in the snow by the garage early this morning. Then, on my way in here, Sheriff went like a bat-out-of-hell past me, heading out of town toward the hill. Sarah Thornberg came in about an hour ago and told me the Johnson kid was taking a walk with his girlfriend last night and was found by the side of the road heading out of town."

Tom's face paled. Had he been so out of touch with reality that he didn't realize what was happening in town? Tom scratched his head, again lost in thought. The finger in the woods was one thing, awful as it was. The boy at the school was a terrible thing, but if it had just ended there…

"Christ Myrtle, I had no idea."

"You're not looking too hot yourself, Tom. Is everything okay?"

"I'll be fine. I'm just lookin' inta somethin' that's been keepin' me up at night." Myrtle cast a curious gaze at Tom but left it at that. She turned and started wiping down the back counter just as Bryce walked through the door.

Bryce's face was a deep red-Tom thought from the cold but conceded that it could be the sickness that plagued him yesterday. He brushed the snow from his coat and greeted Tom with a wave.

"I'll talk to you later, Myrtle," Tom said as he headed toward the table in which Bryce was now pulling up a chair. Bryce placed his jacket on the back of the chair, closest to the window, and ran his hand through his hair. Tom sat down and waited for Bryce to say something.

"Tom, we might have a problem."

CHAPTER 19

By noon, it had already been snowing for more than a day, and there was a good foot and a half on the ground. A few cars slowly maneuvered their way down Main Street while Jimmy Delaney headed away from downtown on foot. He needed to clear his mind. Over the past few days, people seemed to be dropping like flies in town, and he couldn't imagine who could be doing it. In a town like Isolation, everyone that was anyone knew everyone, and Jimmy definitely considered himself someone.

He had gotten up early this morning, having tossed and turned all night, and decided to take a walk to clear his mind. The snow never really bothered Jimmy. He had heard some old woman talking about Evan Johnson and his girlfriend, Anna Park, as he walked past the cafe. She had said something about finding them half-covered in the snow, dead as dogs.

Evan was just some asshole that Jimmy occasionally saw when the thought of going to school moved him. As far as he was concerned, it wasn't that big of a loss. But Anna was different. Jimmy actually found himself drawn to her. She was always smiling and laughing, and while Jimmy typically found that behavior obnoxious and fake, he appreciated the genuine feel she exuded when she'd walk by. And did she ever have great tits?

Jimmy didn't look at many girls. They were all too high maintenance and holier-than-thou as far as he was concerned. Jimmy gave his love to two things, his bat and the flame. Even still, Anna had seemed different. Knowing she was gone set Jimmy's mood on an even darker path.

Even with the snow coming down heavily, Jimmy's ire kept him warm as he lowered his head against the blowing flakes. His beanie was covered, and some of the snow slipped off it and down the back of his shirt, but he took no notice. His dark thoughts brought darker images before his eyes. Panic was beginning to take hold, and Jimmy needed to find out who was causing it.

After he had heard the eccentric woman outside the diner, Jimmy had turned and headed back in the direction of his home; he had no particular destination in mind, he simply went where his feet took him. Jimmy walked past a group of kids from the elementary school building a snowman in one of their yards. He hardly noticed them as he passed, glancing over for just a moment, only just long enough to see one of the little boys staring at him. His friend, seizing the opportunity, threw a snowball at the staring boy, hitting him directly in the ear and sending him crying toward the house.

The snow crunched under his feet, the only sound that was heard as the snowfall muted everything around him. Occasionally the wind would pick up and blow a sheet of snow across his path, and when this happened, Jimmy would only pause momentarily to pull his jacket a little closer to himself before continuing on.

By the time he reached Allen Street, Jimmy's cheeks were bright red, and his eyes began to sting with tears. He looked up to take stock of where he had walked and noticed that the storm was a bit more than snowfall now. The wind had picked up, and, combined with the snow falling and the snow being blown around, it was almost white-out conditions. Jimmy was about to turn around when something caught his eye a few houses in front of him.

There was a car sitting idly in front of a house, the red brake lights shining through the blanket of white. *Isn't that the author's house?* This normally would not be anything that Jimmy would have paid any mind to, but it wasn't moving, and it wasn't parked. He stared at the car, unsure why it gave him pause. The wind blew at his back as though pushing him forward. Jimmy let the wind carry him but remained out of sight, or at least he thought he was out of sight in the storm. The brake lights went out, and the car door opened. Jimmy moved toward a tree that was by his side, curious as to what was happening but unsure of his camouflage now that this person was out of their car. He was a thin man, sickly really, but Jimmy couldn't make out many more details from where he stood.

The man looked around nervously. He made sharp, quick movements with his head. He reminded Jimmy of a bird looking from side to side, making sure there were no predators ready to swoop in. The man crept carefully around the side of the home, looking over his shoulder to make sure no one was watching. As he made his way closer, he faded away into the whiteness. Jimmy moved closer, compelled by the wind to keep an eye on him.

By the time Jimmy was in a better position, the strange man had made his way to the side of the house. He was ducked down low by a window near the back of the home. The man froze, and Jimmy thought he must have heard something, but after a few moments, he began to peer into the side window. A few moments later, the man stuck his gloved hand down the front of his pants.

Jimmy was disgusted. Perverts like this weren't allowed in this town, not in his town. *Maybe,* Jimmy thought, *this was the asshole causing all the panic in town. This was the person responsible for the people being found mutilated. For Anna. If he's sneaking around in this weather, something must be wrong with him.*

Jimmy stepped closer and yelled to the man, "Hey, pervert, what the fuck are you doing over there?"

The strange man froze but did not turn around.

"Hey asshole," Jimmy yelled as he bent down to pick up some snow, forming it into the tightest snowball he could manage, "I said, what the fuck are you doing over there?" Jimmy threw the snowball as hard as he could, missing to the left and smashing into the window at the corner of the house. The man took off running just as Russ opened the front door.

"Hey, what the hell are you doing?" Russell yelled in the direction of Jimmy, who had now taken a step or two into the front yard.

"There's some creepy dude staring in your windows," Jimmy said, pointing toward the side of the house. "He just took off that way."

"Look, kid, why don't you head home, huh? Why are you even out in this weather?" Russell yelled as the wind picked up and blew snow over most of the tracks that were leading to the side of the house.

"Look, man, there was some creepy dude staring in your windows. Christ, whose car do you think this is?" Jimmy raised his arm toward the parked car that was rapidly collecting snow. "Sure as shit isn't mine."

Russell looked over at the car. He hadn't seen it around here before, but it could just be a friend of one of the neighbors. With the weather being so bad, they could have had a hard time seeing where they were and decided to just pull over, knowing they were close enough to get inside quickly.

"Go home, kid," Russell yelled and shut the door.

Jimmy Delaney stood out in the blowing snow only a few moments longer. He contemplated going after the guy but figured he was long gone by now. So instead, Jimmy took his pocket knife out and stabbed it into the back passenger side tire. "Fucking pervert," he whispered. The wind howled, and Jimmy, now out of his thoughts, finally acknowledged the cold. He put the knife back into his pocket and started back home.

Marie came out of the bathroom, her hair still wet from the shower. She walked over to the front window and tried to peer through the blowing snow.

"What was that bang?"

Russell barely heard her question as he walked back to his office, anxious to continue his story. "Stupid kid throwing snowballs."

"Oh my God, Russ," Marie said as she pressed her face close to the window. Russ turned around and stared at his wife. "That's Barney's car. What the fuck is Barney's car doing here?"

Russell's heart sank, and his fists clenched. He turned back around and stood next to Marie, whose heavy breathing had begun to fog up the window. Marie stepped backward awkwardly and fell into the seat behind her. Russ checked the lock on the door and walked into the kitchen, where he stared out of the window. The shadow of Wimpak Hill was only a subconscious fabrication in Russell's mind, and he glowered.

Though the wind was continuing to blow, it hadn't yet completely covered the tracks heading through the backyard. The tracks that were near the kitchen window.

The tracks that led into the woods behind the home.

Barney's tracks.

Just after dinner, the snowfall began to taper off, and the people of Allen Street began to head outside to assess the damage. Tree branches had broken under the weight of the snow and littered the yards up and down the road, yet the street did not lose power. A small blessing, to be sure.

Russ walked over to the living room window and stared into the darkness that had overtaken the outside world. The snow drifts against the house rose well over a foot, but the street didn't seem too bad, all things considered. Russ looked down toward Mitchell's house and made the decision that he would brave the elements (now that they were far more dulled, that is) and have those beers he had been promised.

"Hey, hon," Russ called to Marie, who was down the hall in Sam's room, "I'm going to head over to Mitch's place for a bit."

Marie came out of Sam's room, her eyes betraying a sense of hesitation. She looked out the window Russ was standing in front of before meeting her husband's eyes.

"How long will you be gone for?" Anxiety rising in her voice.

Russ smiled and embraced her tightly. She sank into his body and exhaled deeply. Her shoulders relaxed, and she looked up, staring deep into his eyes. Russ could see she was still on edge, fearing Barney would come back for his car that was still parked out in front of the home; though it was hard to make out now with the snow drifts covering most of it.

"I won't be long, an hour or so." Russ kissed her forehead. "He's not coming back, Marie. He wouldn't be able to get the car out of that snow drift even if he tried. Plus, I'm only going to be a couple houses down, and Mandy is still here."

She smiled slightly and eased her hold on Russ. "Okay, but keep your phone handy."

"Yes, dear," Russ said sheepishly with a smirk on his face. As he walked to the front door, he called down the hall, "Sam, I'm heading over to Mr. Freemore's house for a little bit. I'll be home before bedtime."

Sam came running out of the room, followed closely by Mandy. Both had a smile on their faces from the conversation that was taking place between Sam's G.I. Joe character and Mandy's wrestling action figure. "Have a good time, Dad. Don't get stuck in the snow. I don't want to have to come dig you out."

"I'll be careful, buddy. You're in charge while I'm gone." Russ looked up at Mandy. "I won't be too long."

Mandy gave a tight smile and a slight nod to Russ before grabbing Marie's hand and guiding her back toward Sam's room.

"Hey Marie," Russ called as he put his hand on the front door knob, "I love you."

Marie turned around to face Russ and said, "For all time, you are forever mine," and disappeared into Sam's room.

As Russ opened the door and stepped into the brisk winter night, he smiled and thought nostalgically of the first time he had heard her say that. They had been celebrating their six-month anniversary at one of the fancy hotspots near Faneuil Hall in Boston. As Russ carefully picked his way through the snow, his mind drifted to that night.

Russ had told Marie that he wanted to take her out on the town to have her dress up. Hell, he'd even wear a tie. Marie was so excited that she squealed just slightly when he told her the plan. When he picked her up that night, she came to the door of her dorm in a tight red dress, with her hair cascading over her shoulders. Her eyes shone. Russell's heart had skipped a beat.

As they sat down in the restaurant, they took in the view, at the top of one of Boston's many skyscrapers, at the flickering lights and light snow that was falling just outside. The cold outside became a distant memory as the two melted into easy conversation. Warmth washed over them.

Russell couldn't take his eyes off Marie. The way her lips were wet each time she sipped her wine. The rosiness of her cheeks as she laughed. The way the strap of her dress fell off her shoulder, just briefly. The heave of her breasts as she talked excitedly of their future together.

"You are the most beautiful woman I've ever seen in my life," Russell could remember himself saying. "I'd fight until the end of time just to see your smile."

He remembered her pause. Her smile and the single tear that spilled from her right eye. The shimmer of the candle bouncing off of it as it caressed her cheek.

Marie smiled wider than she ever had in her life at that moment. "For all time, you are forever mine."

As Russ approached Mitchell's house, he could smell the sweet aroma of burning wood emanating from his chimney. Nostalgic memories of Christmas mornings and cold winter nights watching television with his parents as a child flooded his mind. The living room light was on, and he could see Mitch sitting in his chair, sipping a drink. Russ knocked on the door and heard Mitch's footsteps come closer. A moment later, the door swung open, and Russell was welcomed in out of the cold and ushered toward the raging fire.

"Jeez Russ, I didn't think you were gonna make it over here tonight. I was getting ready to give you a call."

"And lose out on some beers I didn't have to pay for? Not likely." Russ turned around and cast his arm back toward the street. "Besides, it's barely snowing anymore. We're hearty New Englanders, Freemore."

Russ' smile broke through as Mitchell clapped a hand on his back. "Let's get you that beer and get over by the fire. It's a cold one out there tonight."

Russell hadn't realized until then just how cold he actually was. His hands were like ice, and his ears burned as they began to warm up. Mitchell's house was only a couple down from his own, but he felt like the tips of his fingers and ears were moments away from frostbite. He rubbed his hands together and blew into them to warm them.

"Sure is," Russ said as he sat on the sofa cushion closest to the fire.

Mitchell came into the room with a beer for Russ, some local IPA that Russ didn't recognize. The beer tonight was not for the taste but rather the social convention that was expected. Nonetheless, Russell was glad to have it.

"What do you think about all these deaths going on around town, Russ? Craziest damn thing I've ever seen."

"I've only heard about the Dinsmore boy and his family. Terrible tragedy. Has there been more? Sorry, Mitch, I've been really caught up in my own world lately. Marie getting attacked at work, Sam has been having trouble sleeping…"

"Woah, woah. Marie was attacked?" Mitch interjected. "When the fuck did that happen?"

"The other day. She was showing a house, and her," Russell seemed to choose his words carefully, "piece of shit boss showed up and pinned her against the wall. Touched her all over."

"Christ on the cross," Mitch exhaled and put the beer bottle to his lips, taking a long gulp.

"She did stab him, though. Right in the leg. Too bad she didn't aim a little higher." Russ took his own long gulp from his beer. Hoppy but not unpleasant.

"Did she? That's great. Serves the bastard right. Where does someone get off doing something like that?" Mitch took another long swig before placing the beer on the end table next to himself. "But seriously though, Russ, is she alright?"

"She will be. It could have been a lot worse. At least, that's what she said. I think it's bad enough just how it went down. She's still pretty shaken up. She swears that the car that's outside our house is his. I don't know when it showed up. Sometime in the midst of the storm, I guess. We called the police, but, well, they have their hands full with the deaths, you know? Can't much be bothered with a broken down car on a side street at the moment." Russell turned toward the fire and stretched his hands out toward the flames. "You said 'all these deaths.' How many are we talking here, Mitch?"

"Fourteen now. In only a couple days. It's damn terrifying, is what it is. I've heard a few people talking about getting out of town once the storm stopped. I guess we'll see now."

Fourteen, how was that possible? Russ thought. Had he really been that disconnected from what was going on around him that fourteen people could have been killed in Isolation without so much as a passing acknowledgment of the news by him?

"Jesus, Mitch. I had no idea. Do they know who's doing it? I mean, Isolation isn't exactly the urban center of New England. People know when Myrt's coffee shop opens ten minutes late and why. Surely someone would have noticed if someone new was in town, or if someone was acting, I don't know…off."

"Mmhmm," Mitch mustered as he swallowed the last of the bottle. "I'd thought the same thing. But that's just it, Russ, there doesn't seem to be any rhyme or reason for who is getting it. No one has seen any new people milling around. No one has been witness to anything, at least as far as I've heard. People are just found…ripped apart, Russ." He rose from his seat to get another beer.

Russ' eyes caught the fire dancing next to him. He stared at the flames and watched as they lapped at the wood. He watched as the wood took on a red glow and ash began to fall beneath. The wood crackled as Russ searched his mind for some sort of rational thought. Something to give some explanation for so many deaths in such a short period of time.

"But there have been whispers among folks," Mitch said as he sat back down and opened his bottle.

Russ tore his eyes away from the fire. "Whispers?" he asked. "What about?"

"You know, I grew up in this town. I may have left for a little while, but Isolation is my home." Russ nodded as Mitch continued, "Do you know I'm the only full-blooded Wimpak left here? Maybe anywhere. All the others either died off or left for bigger and greener pastures. What few weren't killed off all those years ago. But I got drawn back here. I still talk to some of the elders, though. The world is a much smaller place now."

Russ sipped his beer as he took in Mitch's words. He knew that Mitch often got a sideways glance when he passed by or an occasional rumor told about him, but Russ always liked the man. He thought he was a good soul. An old soul is what Marie had said once, whatever that meant. If there was one thing that Russ didn't like about small-town living, it was the prejudices and rumor-mongering that still happened all too often.

Mitch continued, "When I was down at Myrt's the other day, the day we talked after you left, I started chatting with her. She told me that some folks had been talking about feeling an eerie sense in the town. Felt like they were being watched. Hell, she said one person even claimed they saw something in the woods watching them. After the Dinsmores got killed, I walked down to their road. I'll be damned if I didn't feel, I don't know Russ, something off over there. I didn't feel in danger, but something wasn't right. When I got to the Dinsmore's house, it was already roped off, but a couple of the neighbors were still outside in their yards, talking about what they saw or heard. Some were saying they heard a ruckus in the house. Some were saying that Mr. Dinsmore likely went crazy after what happened to his boy. But they were all saying that they heard a scream, unlike anything they'd ever heard before. Bone-chilling. Something from another place."

"Another place, Mitch? Are we talking geographically, not of this area? Are we talking about outer space? Are people suggesting aliens are coming down and massacring the people of small-town New Hampshire?"

Mitch stared at Russ for a moment, a smile threatening to appear. "No, I don't think anyone is talking about aliens." Mitch's expression turned darker as he leaned forward in his seat, looking into Russell's eyes. "I got the distinct impression that the 'other place' they were referring to was on the other side of the veil. The other side of the barrier between life and death."

Russ stared back at Mitch, his eyes watching for a sense of sarcasm or humor. There was none. "Mitch, really? Do you hear yourself?"

"Oh, I do. Russ, I get it. But there is a bit more."

Russell sat back in his seat, took the last bit of beer to his lips, and listened.

"When I was walking back from the Dinsmore's place, as I got closer to Myrt's, I saw it."

"Saw what?" Russ asked, now sitting forward again.

"I can't really explain it, Russ. It was…dark. I almost mistook it for a shadow in amongst the trees, but it moved. It moved so fast. I stopped to watch it. It saw me, and I couldn't help but feel like it was taking stock of me. It was terrifying the way it moved, but I never felt threatened by it, though I know I should have. It let out a shriek like I've never heard before. It had to be the same noise I heard the Dinsmore's neighbors talking about. Then, just like that, it was gone."

At that, Russell got up and walked to the kitchen slowly, without a word. His head swam. It felt...familiar. Like he knew what Mitch had seen. As though he had seen it himself, but he couldn't place where. He couldn't nail down why he felt like that. He reached into the fridge and grabbed another IPA for himself and Mitch, and made his way back to the couch.

As Russ began to sit back, a thought slammed into his mind, and he knew why it all sounded familiar. The Lego house that Sam had made. The...thing he thought he saw in there. Dark as pitch, vibrating. He didn't know how what Mitch saw in the woods and what he saw in the toy home could possibly be the same thing, but he knew. In fact, what Sam described the other night looking in his window sounded like the same thing too.

"Fuck, Mitch, I think I've seen it too. And Sam. It's been outside my house. In my house."

Mitch gaped at this, confused. "But you...it didn't attack you?"

"No. Scared the hell out of Sam, but it never attacked him either."

Mitch sat for a moment and then nodded. "You need to know what I think we're dealing with here."

"Go on, Mitch. What do you know?"

CHAPTER 20

"I started the conversation off mentioning the deaths that are occurring here because it all leads into why you've come over tonight. Wimpak tradition and culture." Mitch said in a deathly serious tone.

"Okay, Mitch, you've got my interest peaked. How does my coming over to ask questions about my heritage link with the deaths, no, murders that are taking place here?"

Mitch paused for only a moment, then began. "After I saw that…creature in the woods, my only thought was of my grandparents and the ghost stories they'd tell me before bed. Not the best time to tell a kid of monsters that could attack a person's soul, but the elders always needed to prepare us for our dreams." Mitch got up and put another log on the slowly dwindling fire.

"Prepare you for your dreams? How so?" Russ thought of the couple of times he told Sam a ghost story before bed. It had not gone well. It certainly didn't prepare him to sleep. If anything, it prepared him not to.

"These stories were often scary, Russ, but they were important. You see, culture is extremely important in a Wimpak's life. I suspect some part of you inherently felt that which is why you came to me in the first place. The stories they told may have been scary, but it's the lore of the Wimpak my grandparents would tell me about. Great victories in battle and creatures from the darkest part of oblivion all had a part to play in my understanding of where I came from." He paused a moment, and Russ got the distinct impression he was remembering a moment in time. A smile crept onto Mitch's face.

"The stories weren't all scary, mind you. They told me tales of the great chiefs of the past and their daughters that commanded respect and awe. They told me of the animals they befriended and the codependent relationships they had with them. Those were my favorite stories. The ones where man and animal would travel together through the unknown wilds of the northeast."

Russ could imagine the adventures Mitch was describing, though he had never heard the stories himself. It was strange. It was as though he could smell the grass and hear the birds chirping. He closed his eyes and felt himself raise his head toward the warmth of the sun on his face as he walked in an open field, a deer walking beside him only a few feet away. His head swam. Happiness swelled in his body, and a sense of peace overcame him. The vision was powerful. Russ truly felt that this could be a memory and not his imagination creating a scene at Mitchell's description. Russell opened his eyes and saw Mitchell staring at him, a smile wide on his face.

"You had a vision, didn't you?"

Russell sat up and stammered, "I-I wouldn't say it was a vision. Wait, how do you know?"

"A ghost just visited you. I saw him briefly behind you. They come when a Wimpak is traveling to his past."

"Traveling to my...what? Mitch, what's in these beers?" Russ sat forward, clearly uncomfortable. "And a ghost?"

"Most Wimpak believe they are ancestors, but I believe that they may be nature spirits. Wimpak were tightly connected to nature, maybe more so than many of the other nations. It obviously wasn't *you* that traveled, but your energy. I think they can bring our energy, your soul, whatever you want to call it, to a time and place. We live many lifetimes, Russ, and our energy remembers them." Mitch looked at Russ, who sat across from him, his face having gone ashen. "Then again, maybe they are ancestors. Not exactly a scientific experiment we can do to discover the truth." Mitch chuckled a bit but then saw the look of shock on Russell's face and realized how this must all sound to someone who knew very little of the Wimpak culture. "Sorry, Russ, maybe I should slow down a bit."

"Uh, yeah, maybe a little Mitch. I mean fuck me, you just dropped some crazy shit on me like it was…I don't know, normal." Russ stood up and paced a bit in front of the fire. Mitch let him collect his thoughts. "This would have made more sense if it was aliens."

"Okay, let's start fresh, Russ. Come, sit down. I'll start from the beginning. Well, at least what I know of the beginning."

Russ sighed deeply but seemed comforted that he'd find out everything he wanted to know in a more coherent way. Maybe he'd be able to process the information better now that he had been walloped with ghosts and some form of ancestral spirit craziness. He walked over to the refrigerator to get another beer, thought twice of it, and called back to Mitch.

"Got anything stronger than those beers?"

"Whiskey, cabinet above the stove."

Sounds good to me, Russ thought. He poured two glasses and headed back to the living room. He handed Mitch a glass, ice cubes clinking together in a rhythmic dance within the brown liquid, and took his spot back on the couch. Russ took a sip. It was strong but smooth. He smacked his lips together and, with a sigh, said, "I'm ready."

"Okay, so the Wimpak people were originally from southern Canada, really on either side of the border that now sits there. Our ancestors were one with nature. Now I know you hear that cliche all the time about native people, and there are studies that take place in academia today that question the impact Native Americans had on their respective environmental landscapes. Yes, we still needed to chop down trees for shelter, and yes, we still needed to hunt animals for food, but our connection was a bit deeper than most.

"We believed in the gods and goddesses of the forest. We communed with them. We spoke with the animals that shared our world, and they spoke back. For reasons I don't entirely understand, the gods and goddesses came to us with or without the use of ceremony. They imparted wisdom in the visions they gave us, but they could not, or at least would not, interfere directly in our world. Some of the elders believe that the entities in the forest were there to assist in the bond between man and animal. Animal recognized that man must survive and may hunt them when needed, but man recognized that animal must protect their own kind when in danger. Both knew that reverence must be given at all times, even in death. We shared the land. We did not try to conquer it."

Russell nodded in acknowledgment. "It sounds like, traditionally, the Wimpak lived a pretty peaceful existence. One with the land, peace, and harmony, and all that. So why did they leave that area? Why didn't they stay where they lived for so long?"

In this case, because the Wimpak weren't a very large tribe, to begin with, them progressively moving further south and so quickly might be considered unusual. But to answer your question directly, they got moved off their land much the same as many of the local tribes. The whites.

"Once the Europeans came here and found the forest full of furs and lumber to export, they began to take whatever they could. At first, they tried to make peace with the Wimpak, but considering the importance of nature to our culture, that was never going to happen." Mitchell shifted in his seat and took a gulp of his drink to wet his throat.

"So, the Wimpak wouldn't negotiate, even though they lived in relative peace. Didn't they know they'd be slaughtered?" Russ asked curiously, leaning forward in his seat. "It wasn't unusual for Europeans to war with the native tribes back then."

Mitch gave a slight snicker. "Oh, I'm sure they did. But when your lifestyle is being threatened, your culture, you don't just give it up willingly. Besides, the Wimpak didn't have great proficiency with swords and guns, but as I've said, they had power within the forest."

"What does that even mean, Mitch?"

"The gods and goddesses of the forest couldn't intervene directly, but they could teach the Wimpak to harness the power within themselves, the power of the forest. Some say the Wimpak could call upon the animals to fight for them and defend them. They say they could call on the trees to do the same. This was their defense. This was how they fought, but the Europeans ultimately were too much. They cut the trees and burned what wouldn't be cut. When the animals attacked, they killed them and used their pelts just as readily as if they had been hunting them. The Wimpak held them off for a while, but steadily they were pushed further and further south. By the time they got here, the Wimpak were all but wiped out."

Russell's head swam again as he imagined the horror, the tension, and the anxiety of these people losing their homeland and being pushed into the unknown. His eyes closed once again, and he could smell the smoke from the burning trees. He could hear the screams of women and the cries of children. His eyes fluttered, and suddenly he had another place in front of him.

A group of Native Americans on their knees, trees burning all around them. A man standing in front of them, a man he recognized but couldn't put a name to. The man punched one of the kneeling men repeatedly, screaming at him. Instinctively, Russ ran to stop the abuse but tripped over a rock, twisting his right knee. The noise caused the men to look up. The man punching the kneeled man stopped and turned.

"Who's there?" he called.

Though Russ was only a few yards in front of him, the man with the bloody knuckles could not see him. Russell's knee throbbed. Then suddenly, he was back in Mitch's house.

His heart felt for these people. He had heard these stories throughout his life of the native tribes of North America being brutalized by European weaponry and disease, but in this case, it felt closer to his heart. He had actually experienced…something.

"Welcome back," Mitch said, once again smirking. You were gone longer this time.

Russell looked at the clock. Twenty minutes had passed. "What the hell is going on, Mitch?"

"You're accessing parts of yourself that were locked away. Your ghost was more clear this time. He looked a lot like you. Like you do today. Better hair, though," Mitch said as he took another sip of his drink and smiled.

Russell instinctively ran his hand through his hair and glared at Mitch. He shook his head in disbelief. Something was happening. It scared him, but it made him want to know more. The smoke still burned his nostrils, and his knee was swollen and pained, but his mind wandered back to the murders in town. I don't know what's going on, and I don't want to sound insensitive at all, but what does this have to do with the murders going on in Isolation now?"

"I'm getting there." He looked at Russ, his hand rubbing his knee. "Are you okay?"

Russ had been unaware that he was rubbing his pained joint. His mind was trying to find understanding in what was happening. Ghosts, lost time, seemingly journeying to a different time and place…it was crazy.

"Yeah. Knee's just acting up. I twisted it on a run the other morning. Must be the weather," Russ said more to convince himself than Mitch. "Go on."

"When I came home, after seeing that…thing in the woods, I called an old Wimpak man my family used to be close with when I was a kid. He moved away many years ago, but he was the first person I thought of when I got home and started looking for answers. His family were leaders in the community dating back as far as most people could remember, so I knew he'd have an idea as to what I saw." Mitch leaned toward Russ and lowered his voice, almost as if he didn't want the universe to hear what he had to say next. "What I saw is called a Tul-chu-wa."

Russell looked at Mitch, confused. "A Tul-chu-wa? Is that supposed to mean something?"

Mitch's face grew red as excitement built up within. "A Tul-chu-wa. A forest demon. A devourer of men. As far as the old man knew, it was the purest form of myth. There had only ever been one account, and it was anecdotal at that, of one ever being called by the Wimpak tribe. But he was sure, from the description of what I had seen, from the details I gave him about what is going on in Isolation, that we have a Tul-chu-wa here."

Mitchell wiped his brow and rubbed his hands on the front of his jeans. Russ may not have understood what a Tul-chu-wa was, but he understood the words "demon" and "devourer of men," and neither word nor term filled him with anything but dread. They sat in silence for a moment before Russ cleared his throat.

"So, okay," Russell organized his thoughts the best he could, "why is it here? I mean, it wasn't always here, right? The deaths just started recently."

"That's the thing," Mitch said as he stood up and moved toward the living room window. "The only way in which a Tul-chu-wa can come to be is through a curse on the land, but he didn't know what the curse was. It's been lost to time."

"So I suppose the way in which it can be stopped is lost as well."

"Actually, no." Mitch put a hand against his forehead and leaned against the window, his breath fogging up the glass. "According to the old man, there are two ways a Tul-chu-wa can be banished. The first is to speak a banishing chant that destroys the curse, but since we don't know what the curse was and most of the old chants have been forgotten long ago, that isn't an option."

"Okay, so what's the other option?"

Mitch sighed and turned to Russ. "Someone with Wimpak blood must destroy the creature by stabbing it through the chest with a ceremonial dagger in the place it was created."

"Well, where the hell is that? And where the hell are we going to find a ceremonial dagger?" Russ asked, exasperated.

"I honestly don't know. As for where it was created, it seems to hold to the woods as often as it can. I figure it must be there. And if I was to guess, I'd say it is probably somewhere up on Wimpak Hill. That is where Isaac Appleton killed the last Wimpak Chief. But again, I'm guessing at this point."

"Well, at least it's an educated guess," Russ sighed and ran his fingers through his hair again. "It looks like we've got to come up with a plan as to how you can kill this thing and how to find a ceremonial dagger from a tribe that was all but extinguished a couple hundred years ago. No pressure."

Mitch smiled and looked at Russ. "Me, huh? Just remember why you came here tonight. You have Wimpak blood too."

Russ walked into his house a half hour later. Mandy was asleep on the couch with Sam in her arms, one of Sam's cartoons playing on the television. He walked down the hall toward the bedroom light that was shining through the barely open door. Marie was laying on her side, sleeping soundly. The door creaked slightly as Russ pushed it open and walked to the bed. He undressed quickly and climbed under the blankets. He turned off the light and lay facing her. Russell kissed her forehead, and in Marie's slumber, she smiled.

"You are the most beautiful woman I've ever known. I'm so glad I have you." He said before drifting off to sleep. Russell's sleep was filled with fields, sunshine, and warmth on his face. A deer ran next to him, and everything seemed right.

CHAPTER 21

It was the middle of the night when Eve's eyes snapped open. The steady beep of the machines she was plugged into droned monotonously as she sat up in bed slowly, careful to not send her knee screaming in pain once again. She looked from her bed to the window and was able to see the moon shining in the distance. Wind blew the trees rhythmically while the moon's white glow caused shadows to dance around her room. She could hear nurses walking around outside her door, talking quietly amongst themselves, but not quietly enough at this hour, in Eve's opinion.

Eve's eyes searched the room, curious about her sudden awakening when she remembered her dream. She was back in the woods where the man was being beaten. She watched in horror, but silent horror this time. She needed to know why she continued to be drawn to this tortuous scene.

She wished Jamison was with her, to hold her. She still had not seen him since he had gone out hunting several days ago. She had filed a missing persons report, but, other than locating his truck, the police had not turned up any leads. She knew something bad had happened, and she just wanted answers. Tears brimmed in her eyes as she thought of her husband, but her dream broke through her thoughts.

Something was different this time. Something, no, someone was there that didn't belong. She caught a glimpse of a man running toward the beating, yelling. Then he tripped and disappeared. She knew the man, at least she thought she did. He looked so familiar, but she couldn't get a clear look at his face. She strained her mind, trying to see what eluded her.

"Russ Tolliver?" she said out loud. She leaned forward with her head in her hands, trying to pull the dream closer so she could better analyze it. But it just wouldn't come back.

Eve looked at the clock on the wall, illuminated perfectly by the moonlight. Something out of a Hollywood noir film, she thought, and saw that it was almost 2:00 AM. The nurses wouldn't be in for another hour or so to check her vitals. She would have time. She raised her bed to a slight angle and laid back. She rested her head on the surprisingly comfortable hospital pillow and closed her eyes. As her mind drifted to nothingness, she felt herself slip out of her body and into a void. A darkness that fell into eternity. Eve would get to the bottom of this. She would know what this place was trying to show her. Tonight.

Adam Hunt and Forest Walker waited outside *The Back In Time Cafe* while Jimmy took a piss around back. The snow had stopped falling hours ago, but the silence that it brought remained heavy in downtown Isolation. Jimmy, Adam, and Forest had been walking around most of the night, throwing icy snowballs at parked cars, business windows, and each other. One particularly icy one, thrown by Forest, who always had the best arm of the three, broke a window at *McNeil's*. The boys quickly took off before the shattered glass had even stopped tinkling to the ground.

The two boys spoke concerned words about Jimmy. He was getting more intense. More violent. And for the two boys, neither of which had ever been accused of good behavior, Jimmy had become someone to fear. So when Jimmy called at midnight and said they were going to go look for some pervert that was peaking in houses, the boys jumped.

They had asked why, of course. It didn't make sense to them that they'd just find some pervert strolling along the streets of Isolation in the middle of the night, but Jimmy said that's when perverts are most active. When they can see inside homes the best. Adam hesitantly mentioned that Jimmy had seen this particular pervert during the day, but Jimmy simply countered with, "There was a snowstorm, dipshit. He was hidden from view just like he would be at night." The boys just shrugged and took their places behind him.

Jimmy came out from behind the building, still zipping his fly. "So fucking cold out here, my balls crawled back up into my body." He finished zipping and put his gloves back on, shaking his hands vigorously to warm them.

"Say, Jimmy," Forest said cautiously, "why don't we call it a night, huh? This guy isn't out here, and we're freezing to death. We can keep looking tomorrow."

"Forest, you're such a pussy. I just had my dick out in this damn weather. You can't handle a little cold air?" Jimmy said as he gave Forest a light shove that Forest wasn't sure was meant entirely jokingly.

"Hey, I'm with Forest, man. It's too fucking cold out here tonight. I want to head home. Plus, it's late. My folks will kill me if they find out I snuck out." Adam said as he put his gloves over his mouth and exhaled deeply to warm up his nose.

Jimmy rolled his eyes and sighed. "Fine, we'll call it a night. But I want to see you guys in the morning. I know this guy is still around here somewhere."

A piercing, horrible shriek ripped through the silence of the night, and suddenly Adam Hunt's head was rolling down the sidewalk, leaving a trail of red with each rotation. His body stayed upright for a few seconds, not realizing the warmth running down it was his own lifeblood. As the blood hit the snow, it hissed slightly and melted wherever it touched. Forest and Jimmy stared at the body as it collapsed under its own weight and landed chest-first in the snow in front of them. The head still rolled a few feet ahead before settling face up. The eyes blinked, a reflex from the firing sparks of life left lingering momentarily in Adam's brain.

Forest screamed. Jimmy froze and scanned the area, trying to figure out what happened. His eyes caught a shadow around the corner of the building where he had just been pissing. It vibrated, and a sneer crept across its face. Blood dripped from its claws and created a semi-circle of red around itself. Jimmy remained still and watched it. Forest ran past Jimmy screaming at the top of his lungs. The creature turned its head. Though it seemed to have no eyes, it followed Forest down the street. It looked to Jimmy and back to Forest as if contemplating what to do next.

In a blink, it was gone. Jimmy only knew where it went because of the wind rushing past him in the direction of Forest. He turned toward Forest's screams for help, and suddenly there were no screams, and Forest stopped dead in his tracks. For a moment, Jimmy thought that perhaps the monster had simply left, gone back to the depths of hell from whence it came. Then Forest's body came apart. Split in two from head to groin. The sticky, wet sound of flesh, muscle, and tendons coming apart as the two sides fell away from each other was sickening, even to Jimmy. A light turned on across from where Forest's body now lay. Then another. A third turned on as Jimmy wretched on the sidewalk in front of the cafe. He heard a man scream, "Call 911," and a woman scream into the night. Jimmy ran in the opposite direction.

When the darkness cleared, Eve was once again surrounded by colors flying past in a prismatic blur. She let her energy be carried where it would, confident that whatever was trying to be shown to her would be. Though she felt like she was moving incredibly fast, no wind rushed past her. No breeze caressed her face. She closed her eyes against the swirling array of colors and concentrated. When she opened them again, she was in a small village. It was night and a fire burned in the distance.

She walked toward the fire, careful not to make any noise as she knew, though she hadn't been seen in her journeys to this point, she could definitely be heard. Her feet were bare, and she walked on rain-soaked grass. The coolness of the water that soaked her feet was refreshing against the heat of the air. Whenever she had traveled before, it had always been cool autumn weather. This time it was most certainly deep within summer. The humidity was oppressive, and even with the night upon them, she could hear the mosquitos flying about.

As she continued her careful approach, she could hear singing in the distance. She followed the voices, and a drum joined the deep, soothing singing that was taking place in front of her. There were a dozen or so men sitting around the fire, eyes closed, in a trance-like state. The singing man was old. He looked almost ancient, with a long braid and a face that wore a lifetime of experience on it. He wore no shirt and tan pants that were loose on his thin body. His chest was marked with many tattoos, the meanings of which were lost to Eve. The singing man had such a hypnotic tone that Eve couldn't help but find herself lulled into listening as well.

The drum beat and singing suddenly stopped, and Eve was left in silence. She caught a glimpse of movement to her side and turned cautiously. There were animals ringed around the outside of the fire's glow that she had not seen before. Pheasants, foxes, deer, moose, even a couple bears stood silently, watching the scene. Closest to her was a moose, towering over Eve only a few feet away. As she continued to stare at the massive creature, it sniffed the air and pawed the ground, sensing something not easily seen. The great animal turned its head from the men and the fire and looked in Eve's direction. The mooses' eyes caught Eve's eyes and held them. It lowered its enormous head in what Eve could only describe as a bow. Eve was stunned to find that, as she looked past the giant beast, many of the animals near her had all done the same thing.

She chanced a step toward the animals and extended a hand. She placed it on the head of the moose and petted it. The hair was softer than she expected, and the hairs on her own neck stood at attention. The moose kept its head low in a sign of deference, yet Eve felt as though she should be paying homage to these creatures.

A scream of pain sent the moose, and Eve jumping backward. She turned to see one of the men sitting by the fire, convulsing and spasming on the ground. The man next to him suddenly fell onto his back and did the same, and down the line, they all fell into convulsions one by one. The singer and the drummer froze and watched. Eve instinctually began to run toward the men that were writhing on the ground but stopped, realizing she would be of no help. The animals all ran off back into the safety of the woods. Eve watched.

The screams began to die out, and the convulsions slowed. One by one, the men began to sit up and, looking dazed, taking in their surroundings. The man that had been singing knelt beside the confused men and spoke. Eve could understand their words. While she knew many native tribes knew the English language, she was highly doubtful they spoke it when they were amongst themselves.

This place, whatever this place is, she thought, *time means nothing here, neither does language, it seems.*

"What happened," asked the elder man as he placed his hand on the closest man's shoulder.

The man sat, shaken, then spoke, "A premonition, Chief. A group of white men came and destroyed our village. They killed the animals and burned the forest. They captured us and chained us. Tortured us. A few escaped, but most were taken."

The old man eyed the young one. Taking in his words and processing them. He knew that tribes had been warring with the white men all over the lands, but the Wimpak had kept their distance and had no encounters. He looked to the other men, who were all nodding their agreement at what they had seen. He didn't want to believe the story, but he knew the astral realm never lied. Sometimes it was misinterpreted, but it never lied, and this story seemed to lack the ability to be misinterpreted.

Eve listened from a distance when movement caught her eye just beyond the closest trees. She peered into the darkness and saw a man standing behind a large pine tree, looking out of place. He hadn't noticed her as she made her way as quietly as she could over to him.

"Russell?" Eve whispered as she approached him from behind.

Russell, startled by the approach and unexpectedly being seen, stumbled over a log that was laid out before him. As he fell, pine cones and needles were sent flying around him. "What the…Eve. Where the fuck are we?" He said louder than he intended.

Eve froze and looked toward the gathered tribe. They had stopped talking and looked in the direction of the commotion. Eve looked down at Russell and reached for his hand, her other with a finger pressed to her lips. The universal signal for "be quiet."

Russell turned to look behind him and saw the tribesman looking in his direction, yet none made a move toward him. Their eyes scanned the area, and Russell realized that he had not been seen. He reached for Eve's hand, confused as to why she was there and where he was, and raised himself back to his feet. The two made their way away from the fire and the men and into the woods. When they were far enough away that Eve dared make noise, she turned to Russell.

"How are you here?"

"How am I here? How are you here, Eve? Where even is here?"

Eve looked around, still hesitant to speak too loudly. "We are in the place between time. The astral plane. I've spent years of my life training myself to search this realm, but that doesn't explain how you got here. Astral travel isn't easily accessible, and it certainly isn't for an inexperienced mind."

"I don't know what astral travel is, Eve, but I think it happens when I sleep. I think I'm dreaming this now."

"No, Russ, you're not dreaming. Your body isn't here, but your soul is. I've been here before, to this place. I've seen some pretty terrible things and…I think they know we are here. We can interact with the environment, which makes me think the environment can interact with us."

Russell considered this for a moment. "I think I've been here before too. I saw a man being beaten. I thought it was just a dream, but…"

Eve nodded. "I thought I saw you before. Listen, Russ, whatever is happening here keeps drawing me to this place. I think I'm being called here for a reason, and now that you're here too, I'm sure of it." Eve's head began to swim, and by the look on Russ' face, she could tell his was as well. "I'm losing my grip on this place. We're going to go back to our time now. Come to the hospital. We'll talk more."

Russ began to fade from Eve's view, slowly at first but then with haste. He was gone before she was. Just before the forest around Eve faded from view, she heard a voice directly behind her. It was the old man who had been singing by the fire. He stood mere feet behind her, and he spoke, "I know you are here, traveler. Protect us from the evil that comes and the evil we bring."

The man spoke with tears in his eyes.

He faded from before Eve. Color swirled all around her, and suddenly Eve found herself back in the hospital bed, the image of the pained man burned into her memory.

CHAPTER 22

When the sun began to peak through the bedroom curtains, Russ had already been lying awake for about twenty minutes. The morning silence rang in his ears, but couldn't penetrate his thoughts. With one arm behind his head, he stared up at the ceiling, remembering where his dream had taken him, or at least where he thought he had gone.

Russ' thoughts were only broken when he heard Tom's truck start up and promptly pull out of the driveway, faster than Russ was accustomed to hearing his friend leave. *Wonder where he's going so early*, Russ thought, figuring the snow would still be too high and the weather too cold for Tom to walk into the woods on another hunting trip.

"Good morning, handsome," Marie said as she lay wiping the sleep from her eyes.

Russ pulled himself out of his thoughts and faced his wife. "Good morning, babe," he said as he leaned over and kissed her forehead.

When he pulled his lips away from her, he smiled, staring into her eyes. "Sorry, I was out so late last night."

Marie sat up in bed. "I was just so tired, I crashed shortly after you left. Mandy said she would watch Sam. You have a good time with Mitch?"

Russell scratched at the scruff on his neck and sighed. "It was interesting." At that, he got up and headed toward the bathroom door. "I'm going to jump in the shower."

"I'll join you," Marie said with a wry smile on her face. Russell turned and smiled back. As Marie got out of bed and headed toward the bathroom door, she began undressing. Russell watched her as she approached, and he forgot all about the strangeness that had happened at Mitch's. As she walked past Russ, she ran her hand over his chest and walked to the bathtub turning the shower on. "You can get in first," she said, rolling her eyes when she saw the smile that refused to leave his face. "I just have to pee."

Russell got in and let the hot water run over his body. The steady massaging of the water is cathartic, Russ always thought. As he put his head under the shower, he heard the curtain pulling back, and Marie stepped in.

As the bathroom began to steam up, Russ let Marie take the hot water to her body. She leaned her head back and wet her hair. Russell watched the water run down her body. The water flowing over her breasts and down her stomach, pooling only momentarily in her belly button. Russell leaned into her and kissed her neck, tasting the water and her skin together on his lips. Her breath caught in her throat.

Russell pulled away. He reached over to the shelf on the side of the shower, grabbed the sponge, and put Marie's body wash on it. It foamed, and the smell he was so familiar with flooded his nostrils, stiffening him almost as much as the kiss to her neck did. He placed the sponge against her collarbone and worked his way slowly down her body. He took her arm gently and raised it above her head, cleaning all of her. The soap dripped from her body and began to run down the drain as Russell carefully lifted her legs, one at a time, and rubbed the sponge from toe to inner thigh. Marie let a moan escape her lips as Russell's hand went higher against her.

"Turn around," Russ commanded. Marie did.

Russell pressed himself against Marie and placed the sponge back on the shelf. He ran his hands over her body and guided the water to the soap bubbles covering her in what Russ thought were all the right places. He found himself kissing her neck again but forced himself to stop in order to finish what he had started.

Marie put her arms against the walls of the shower as Russell took the sponge again and soaped up her back. He thought Marie's breath may have picked up a bit, but he was sure when she leaned forward further, pressing herself into him and whispering two words, "Take me."

Russell took Marie, and Marie willingly welcomed it. After both had climaxed, Marie returned the favor and soaped up Russell. Ecstasy had washed over them. He turned the shower off and kissed her. "I love you, Marie."

"I love you, Russ."

As Marie wrapped herself in her towel, Russ stood in the shower for a few moments longer. Something strange was happening in Isolation, and something strange was happening to Russ, but Russ thought *today is going to be one fine day.*

By the time the two emerged from the bedroom, Mandy and Sam were already up making breakfast. Marie walked over to Mandy and gave her a big hug. "Thanks for watching Sam last night."

"No problem, babe. You two having a good morning?" Mandy smiled knowingly.

Marie's eyes went wide, and she smiled, giving Mandy a playful slap on the arm. Russell pretended not to hear and gave Sam a hug before walking over to the television set and turning on the news.

"I was thinking about going down to the bookstore today. Nothing like a good book on a snowy day. Come with?" Marie asked Mandy expectantly.

"You guys have a bookstore in this little town? I didn't know books were appreciated way out here in the sticks." Mandy said jokingly.

"You stop it," Marie said with a feigned exasperation in her voice. "You're coming. You'll love it. It's totally quaint and rustic."

"Small and dusty, Marie. That's what you mean."

"Mandy," Marie pushed her softly against the counter.

"Okay, okay, I'll go," Mandy smiled.

"Can I come too, Mom? I want a new book," asked Sam as he ran to his mother's side.

"Oh, I suppose so." She leaned down and kissed his cheek. Sam went running back to the couch to sit with his dad. Sam jumped into Russ' lap, causing a momentary heart palpitation as Russ imagined where his son's knee would end up.

"How about you, babe? You want to come too?"

"No, not this time. I'm going to spend some time writing the book rather than reading one. But you all have fun."

Mandy finished making breakfast while Sam, having lost interest once his parents were awake and choosing to talk to them rather than help, snuck a slice of bacon into his mouth. The four sat around the table, laughing and joking and carrying on while the newscaster talked somewhere in the distance about the storm that had just passed. For that moment, Russell wished time would stop. He wondered if he had ever been happier.

Marie, Mandy, and Sam said goodbye to Russ, who had already taken his seat at the typewriter in his office. It had been several days since he last wrote a word, and he was anxious to get going. He looked over his shoulder as Marie was closing the door to his office. He stopped her just before it fully closed.

"I love you, Marie. Have fun."

"I love you, my handsome man. Get some writing done so I can harass you about the details you won't give me later."

The door closed, and Russ was left in silence as he heard the front door close and the car head out of the driveway toward the center of town.

In the glow of Marie's morning she didn't even notice the car that had been in front of their home was gone. Tire marks in the snow were the only evidence it had even been there.

Russell began typing.

Marie drove cautiously down the road toward *The Dusty Bookshelf*. It looked as though the plow trucks had done their job well overnight, black pavement leading the way into downtown. Still, Marie had seen too many drivers find themselves in a ditch because of black ice; caution was what was needed on a morning like this. As she neared the center of town, the lights on one of Isolation's two ambulances and its two police cars greeted her. Caution tape covered the sidewalk from the cafe to the residential homes a few hundred feet away.

"What in God's name?" Marie said more to herself than the other two in the car.

"Mom, what's going on?" Sam said with concern in his voice. Mandy stared out the passenger window in silence.

"I don't know, baby." As she slowed the car, she saw puddles of red on the sidewalk. One in front of the white home that bordered the commercial buildings, another in front of the cafe. People were milling around as some spoke to the police and others to their neighbors. All looked shaken.

Marie, afraid that the sight of blood would scare Sam, tried to distract him. "Hey, Sam, have you thought about what kind of book you'd like?"

The distraction worked, and Sam looked at his mom's eyes in the rearview mirror. "I want one about space."

Marie's eyes gave away the genuine smile she gave Sam as she said it was a great idea.

They drove past the crime scene and just down the road, parking in front of *The Dusty Bookshelf,* which was just opening for business. Open early, close early. That was the motto of Mike Walker, owner of the business. The three walked in, careful not to let Sam focus on the police just down the road.

Once inside, Sam ran off to the back of the store, where Mr. Walker kept all the children's books.

Mandy turned to Marie. "What the hell is happening in this town, Marie? I've only been here a couple days, and there's been how many deaths?"

Marie's face blanched. "I don't know. We've been here six months, and these past few days are the only time I've ever even heard the police cruisers. I don't understand it."

"It's scary, Marie. This would be crazy in Boston, but up here, it's…" Mandy's voice trailed off as Sam came running over to her and grabbed her by the hand. Sam dragged Mandy to the back of the store, space book in hand and chattering about the different planets. Marie stood in the middle of the small bookstore and looked around, suddenly remembering why they had come here in the first place.

She walked over to the thriller section, small as it was, and found a single copy of Russ' first book. She picked it up and turned it over, smiling at the photo of him that was on the back. The photo she took herself. She remembered that day as clearly as if it were yesterday. Russell had wanted to wear this pumpkin-colored button-up shirt that Marie had always hated; Russell had always held it close to his heart for reasons that never made sense to her. She insisted that if she were going to take the picture, and if he were going to be seen for all of time on the back of a book, he wear the blue button-up she had bought him for Christmas that past year. Russell acquiesced. The nostalgia made her smile. She placed the book back on the shelf and scanned the rest of the section, searching for the next world she would dive into.

Jimmy's head rose as he noticed a familiar car creeping down the road. He watched from beside a tree, just outside the crime scene tape, as it slowed by the ambulance, cautiously making its way past. Jimmy found it strange when the car stopped in the middle of the road in front of the little bookstore before pulling into a spot across the street.

A man stepped out.

Jimmy recognized the pervert the moment he saw him. The blood rushed to his face as he walked around the crime scene tape and toward the bookstore. The pervert walked cautiously and with a pronounced limp as he shuffled toward the shop's door. Jimmy walked a bit faster, hesitant to lose sight of him. Jimmy would watch him, and when the time came, he would have words with the sicko.

Barney opened the door to the little bookshop and could smell Marie's perfume in the air. He stood in the doorway and breathed in deeply as his eyes combed the shop. The hairs on his arms stood at attention, and so did the muscle in his pants as the anticipation of seeing his Marie took over.

In the back of the store, he saw a boy and a woman, Marie's friend, he thought, but not Marie. He stepped carefully, softly, not wanting to be seen too soon. He wanted to surprise her. To apologize for his forwardness the other day. He made his way past the register and to the left side of the store, where he saw her at the end of the aisle. He crept up slowly behind her, watching her subtle movements as she fingered through the books. He loved the way she moved her hair back from her face, tucking it behind her ear. Her scent overtook him as he slithered up behind her and whispered, "Hello, beautiful." Marie jumped back and turned. Her eyes widened as Barney closed the few feet between them.

Tom had been to Bryce Callahan's house before the sun had even finished rising. Bryce's call had woken Tom, but his tone had caused him to jump out of bed. Bryce had discovered something exciting about the creature Tom had seen. About what had been going on in Isolation. They had coffee, bacon, and french toast and sat around the coffee table, going over books and papers that Bryce had collected over the years. Bryce certainly knew how to research and research well.

"Christ, Tom, I think this is it. It's the only mention of it I can find in all my collection, but I think this is it."

Tom looked at the paperwork and the drawing that accompanied it. A rendering created by a Wimpak elder decades before, yet more than a hundred years since the Wimpak had been all but destroyed. The description, the drawing, it made Tom's blood run cold.

"I think you might be right," Tom said in wonderment as he let the implications wash over him. "I need to head home, put my thoughts together. Figure out what to do, what we can do. Come by for dinner? Bring this stuff."

"Be there by six," Bryce said, never lifting his eyes from the drawing.

Tom left Bryce's home and slowly made his way down Main Street. His tires slipped on the icy road, and he steered into the fishtail like an old sea captain maneuvering his ship against the waves that threatened to wreck it. Tom slapped himself across the cheek, refocusing his attention on the road in front of him.

As he got a few hundred yards from downtown, he slowed even further, acknowledging the police presence that continued working at what looked to be a still very active crime scene.

A commotion coming from the bookstore caught his eye. A woman came rushing out of the door, falling into a snow mound just outside. A man was looming menacingly over the woman. The man wasn't a large man, but the look on his face sent chills down Tom's spine, even at this distance. He realized he knew the woman. "Marie?" he said.

A woman, with Sam clutching her leg, was coming out of the store, yelling at the man standing over Marie. She struck the man in the back with her fists, but the man seemed to hardly notice and dismissed her with a push against the storefront that knocked her to the ground.

Sam sat down and cried.

Tom parked his car just across the street from the disturbance and stepped out. In a commanding voice that only an ex-military man can muster, Tom screamed, "Hey asshole, leave her alone."

Barney looked up for only a moment, which was all that Marie needed. She kicked out at him and caught Barney in the groin. His mouth watered with a mucusy liquid that made him feel as though he would wretch. He clutched his injured manhood and bent over at the waist, gasping. Rage boiled within him as he kept one hand cupping himself and the other reaching out toward Marie.

Marie got to her feet and ran toward the familiar voice that had called out to save her. She leaped over the snow mound and landed hard on a patch of ice that covered the street. Tom took a step forward to help her, but Marie was back on her feet before he could step further.

She was about half way across the street when Tom heard the tires screeching and the car horn blowing. Time slowed as he turned and saw a black sedan fishtailing, out of control, its brakes trying to grip the street unsuccessfully. Tom screamed out for Marie to stop, but terror had taken hold of her. Her eyes were wild with madness. The primal fight or flight instinct had kicked in, and flight had won out. Her eyes locked on Tom's, and somewhere in the deep recesses of her mind, she heard Tom's words, though she couldn't comprehend what they meant.

Marie never saw the car as it struck her with its passenger side door. Marie was knocked to the ground. The car's tires still spinning, trying to stop its slide. Marie's eyes never left Tom's. Not until her head bounced off the road and everything went dark did Marie's crazed expression change. Mercifully, Tom closed his own eyes only a moment before the tires drove over her body, twisting it in an ungodly way.

When Tom opened his eyes again, he stood frozen, his face paralyzed with horror. His eyes focused solely on the red that pooled under Marie's head as the car came to a rough stop against a snow mound several yards away. A roar of agony came from Mandy and Tom simultaneously. They rushed to Marie's twisted body and fell to their knees. Mandy pawed at Marie's hair, wiping it away from her face. Tom felt for a pulse, but it was an effort in futility as Marie's neck was twisted at such an angle there could be no confusion about her fate.

Barney took in the scene from the sidewalk, and his heart raced. His groin no longer hurt, but he was frozen nonetheless. His mind was trying to tell him something, to break through the paralysis of the moment. *Run, Barney. Go.* His mind commanded him, and he ran down the block, away from his parked car.

Jimmy Delaney had seen the whole scene. He watched from only a few yards away but remained still as he watched the pervert run. Even for Jimmy, the woman laying in the street was too much. He turned away and walked slowly back toward the crime scene where his friends had met their fate.

Sam Tolliver stood on the sidewalk, looking at the broken body of his mother, in silence.

Russell stopped typing and listened to the silence of the house. A chill ran through his body as he stood up and walked toward the living room. He looked at the red numbers of the clock on the cable box. Marie, Mandy, and Sam had not even been gone for an hour, but something felt very wrong.

A light crash came from down the hall. Russell's blood ran cold as he walked slowly toward his bedroom. He pushed the door open slowly and saw nothing out of the ordinary. He was about to close the door when his eyes caught the picture that was kept on their night table, laying face down. As Russell walked toward it, a cool breeze caressed his skin, and the sweet smell of Marie's shampoo filled his nose. As he righted the picture, he saw the red dress that Marie had worn the night he fell in love with her. Marie looked so happy but for the cracked glass that now cut through the purity of her smile.

He picked up his cell phone and called Marie.

Ring, Ring, Ring…

No answer.

Russell's heart sank.

CHAPTER 23

Most of the day was a complete blur to Russ. He remembered getting a call from Tom, telling him the broad strokes of what had happened. Tom told him that he should get down to the hospital immediately and that he and Mandy had Sam, and that he was safe. He remembered arriving at the hospital but not how he got there. He remembered being escorted not to a hospital room when he asked to see Marie Tolliver but to the basement. To a cold, metallic room lined with drawers. In front of the drawers lay a stretcher with a sheet covering a body. He didn't even remember seeing Marie under the sheet, just a scream coming out of him that ripped at his throat. He sat in the corner, rocking until everything went black.

It was just about dusk when Barney made his way slowly, cautiously toward his car. He had disappeared into the woods a half mile away from where his Marie's life had come to a violent and abrupt end. Barney had run (well, limped quickly, the stab wound and his balls had not fully healed yet), fear and adrenaline carrying him faster and faster away from the crime scene. He stood alone, his heart beating in his ears and sweat threatening to freeze on his forehead. His tracks in the snow stood out like flashing neon lights at first, but once Barney saw that no one was coming, at least not immediately after him, he became calmer.

As the sun began to set, Barney finally felt confident enough to sneak his way back toward his car. He had seen the ambulance and police cars leave much earlier, but he thought it better to wait; Barney was always cautious. Maybe today, his emotions had gotten the best of him in the bookstore, but now that he had time to calm down and take stock of the situation, he realized that caution was necessary again.

He needed to leave this town. Leave it and never look back. He was sad that his Marie had been killed, but then again, she had spurned him. Spurned him in public. They laughed at him. He couldn't see who, but he heard them. If he had seen them, he would have shut them up. Shut them up just like he shut up that bitch that was with Marie. They laughed and laughed, and he even heard one woman say, "See, Barney can't satisfy his wife or any other woman. Better get his brother up here. I bet Marie will get on her knees for him."

Barney was furious when he heard that. He looked around to see who had the audacity to call him out like this. In fact, how did they even know his brother? No matter, Barney would have Marie finally. Like he should have back at the open house. She wouldn't laugh at him again. And once he had her, she would realize what she had been missing. Realize that she hadn't known true happiness until that moment. And if she didn't realize that, well, he'd have to show her the error in her ways.

She had been scared. She fell to the floor when she saw him and crawled her way backward around the bookshelves and toward the front door. He couldn't understand her fear. Barney wanted to hold her and take her away. He followed her, smiling down at her as he approached. He reached out to her, but that seemed to only make her more afraid. The store clerk said he was going to call the police, but Barney didn't care. He just wanted to talk to Marie.

She had made her way to her feet, finally able to muster a scream. Her scream alerted her friend in the back of the store, the one with the big tits that Barney knew was a whore. Barney heard her call out something, but he couldn't make it out; he was utterly focused on Marie.

Marie turned and ran for the door. Barney was faster and caught her arm, only momentarily. She spun around and slapped him across the face in one motion. He released her arm when she struck, her off-balanced body falling directly out the door and landing in a heap on the snowy sidewalk.

That's when he heard the laughter. The taunts. He tried so hard to ignore them. To leave the store and show Marie how big of a mistake she had just made. But when the man yelled, when she got up and ran, everything slowed down; silence ruled Barney's world at that moment. Her body bent in an unnatural way. Barney could swear he heard the breaking of bones and cracking of her skull as it struck the ground. But the sound that Barney knew would stay with him the rest of his life was the tires going up and over her head and the twist of her neck as it broke.

His memories continued to play through his mind on repeat as he crept to the side of the building and stared across at his car. The flattened tire that he had not been able to change gave his car the look of a broken thing, limping to whatever destination Barney decided to go to next. A smile crept over his face as he realized the parallel of his limping car with his own damaged leg. He made a mental note to pull over and fix his tire once he was out of town. Who knew when the police would be back to look for him.

The sun had set behind the trees, and the streetlights had just turned on. The street was empty, and he knew it was time to go. Barney smiled and stepped out from the side of the building. The freedom of his car only feet away. That's when he felt the crack of something blunt strike the back of his head. The pain was only momentary before everything went black.

Tom and Mandy sat in Tom's living room watching Sam as he sat quietly, absentmindedly watching some cartoon. Sam hadn't spoken since Marie was killed, and fear of deep trauma was rooted in Tom and Mandy's minds, though neither wanted to voice it.

Sam had clung to Mandy tightly for most of the day, but within the last half hour, he had peeled himself away long enough for Tom to comfort Mandy as she wept silently in his kitchen. As the sunset sent purple hues across the sky, both Tom and Mandy confessed their concern that Russ wasn't home yet, but neither wanted to call and rush him tonight. Sam was safe, and there was no need to push the issue any further. He'd be home when he was home, and that was it.

Tom suggested taking Sam to the hospital to get checked out, but Mandy said she'd take responsibility for him. She said that taking him down there when Russ was already there identifying Marie would only further traumatize them both. She did agree, however, that if Sam wasn't better by the morning that she would bring him herself.

Tom walked over to the couch and placed a hand on Sam's shoulder. The boy breathed deeply and, after only a few seconds, placed his head on Tom's hand. Tom smiled as his eyes began to well. Sam would be okay.

It would take time, but he would be okay.

When Russ regained consciousness, a nurse was standing over him, looking down over her wide-rimmed glasses at the cardiac numbers on the screen in front of her. The steady beep rang in Russell's ears like the bell in a clock tower. When Russell groaned and rubbed his hand over his head, the nurse turned her gaze to him.

"Well, hello, Mr. Tolliver. You gave us a bit of a scare."

"How long was I out?" Russell asked as the fogginess began to clear from his head. The beeping on the machine seemed to pick up some.

"A couple hours," the nurse looked back at the machine. "Take some slow deep breaths, please. Your heart rate has been high since we brought you upstairs."

Russell sat up in his bed a bit, careful not to go too quickly. "My wife…"

The nurse frowned and took her glasses off as she sat on the corner of his bed. "Your wife passed away, Mr. Tolliver. I'm so sorry. When you came in to see her, you went into shock. You passed out, and we brought you up to this room. If we can make sure your heart rate stabilizes, you can most likely leave tonight."

Russell nodded slowly as realization washed over him. He forced the pain to some back room of his heart so he could begin trying to accept that Marie was gone. At least for the moment. To begin trying to accept that he'd never hold her again or hear her voice. Tears came to his eyes, and the monitor began to beep rapidly again. He took a deep calming breath, and the nurse put her hand on his shoulder. A comforting gesture.

"Thank you, nurse," Russ said with all the enthusiasm he could muster.

"You'll be okay, Mr. Tolliver. I know it seems like you won't be right now, but you will." The nurse stood up and grabbed Russell's chart. "I have to get to my other patients. You should just lay here and relax. Watch some TV. Try to take your mind off everything as much as you can for now. I'll be back in a few hours to hopefully discharge you." She smiled back at Russ as she approached the door and passed through it.

Russell lay in silent thought for what seemed like hours but was more likely only a few minutes. The sun had just dipped past the horizon, leaving a purplish hue that felt surreal. Russell saw the clock on the wall and was shocked to see that it was only just after five o'clock. He couldn't believe that only a few hours ago, he was having breakfast with Marie, that he was showering with Marie, that he had felt as happy as he ever had.

He reached for his cell phone that had been placed on his bedside table and pressed the button on the side, illuminating the family photo that Russell had as his background. He ran his thumb over the picture, desperately trying to feel the contours of Marie's face. He tapped his contacts and found Tom's name. As the phone began to ring, a pit settled into his stomach, and a sudden longing to see Sam threatened to overtake him.

"Heyah, Russ. Glad ta heah from ya. You still at tha hospital?"

"Hey, Tom. Yes. I've actually been admitted."

"Jesus! Are you okay? What happened?"

Russell closed his eyes tight as the images of Marie laying on the table attacked his memories. As the machine began to beep faster, Russell opened his eyes and inhaled slowly. "I passed out when I was identifying Marie. They said I went into shock. My heart rate has been off the charts for hours. They're keeping me for a while longer, but if I get it under control, they'll let me leave."

Tom was silent for a few moments. "Russ, I'm so sorry. This has been a shitty day. A damn shitty day." Tom cleared his throat as a lump began to rise. "Listen, you try ta calm down a bit. Mandy and I have Sam, and he's just fine." Tom hesitated. "Well…as fine as can be expected, I suppose."

"Thanks, Tom. I'll be back as soon as possible. Tell Mandy thank you for me as well."

"Will do. We'll see ya soon."

Russell hit the end button and placed the phone back on the end table, the beeping of the machine slowing slightly. He closed his eyes and laid his head on the pillow, allowing himself to sink into the bed. He dozed off, or so he assumed, and woke to hear his name being called gently from the hall.

"Russ," the voice called. "Are you awake?"

The brightness of the moon was slowly rising, and the lights in the main hallway had been dimmed. He turned his head to the door and saw Eve Crowley rolling into his room, maneuvering her wheelchair professionally. Or at least competently.

"Eve," Russell said, surprised to see her. "I completely forgot you asked me to come to see you." Russell squinted his eyes a bit and thought for a moment. "You did tell me that, right?"

Eve put the chair right next to Russell's bed and responded, "Yes, Russ. That really did happen. But I didn't mean you had to get admitted. Patients can have guests, you know?" She said with a whisper of a smile crossing her face before she turned serious. "What happened? Are you okay?"

Russell's breath caught in his throat, and his heart rate rose again. He looked at Eve, concern growing on her face. "Marie was hurt." He paused to regain some semblance of composure. "She died."

Eve's mouth dropped open, and she immediately covered it with a hand. The other gripping Russell's arm. "I'm so, so sorry, Russ. What happened?"

"She was out this morning with her friend and Sam in town. The way I hear it, her creepy psychopath of a boss followed her into the bookstore. There was some kind of altercation, and he hit her. Marie was scared and tried to get away. Tom, my neighbor, saw what was happening and yelled at the jerk to stop. She ran across the street to get to Tom, but…" he trailed off before taking a calming breath, "the car couldn't stop. It hit some black ice and couldn't stop." Tears flowed again from Russell's eyes, and the machine's beeping quickened anew. "If I had only gone with them…"

Eve's eyes also brimmed over, and they sat together crying, neither wanting to look at the other. Eve composed herself first and was able to speak, "I'm so sorry, Russ. Marie was my friend, a great friend. Knowing her made me a better person. If there is anything you need, anything at all, don't hesitate to reach out. Doctors say I won't be in here too much longer if you can believe it. They wanted me to try wheeling around in this thing for a while. Just to see how I do. As soon as I'm home, I'll stop by."

"Thanks, Eve," Russell said, wiping tears from his eyes and trying to force a smile.

Eve took Russell's hand and gave it a squeeze. She then turned her wheelchair around and started toward the door.

"Hey, Eve," Russell called. She stopped her chair and turned her head in his direction, not saying a word. "Where were we? You know, where was that place?"

Eve lowered her head and smiled. "I'm not sure exactly, but I think it's here, well, Isolation at least. Those people are Wimpak, and I think the white men are Isaac Appleton's people. I thought I overheard them call him by name during one of my visits."

"Isaac Appleton? Like the guy who created the town. Isn't he supposed to be some kind of legend around here?"

Eve shrugged. "Whatever he is, I don't think the stories we know now carry much truth with them. When you left last time, one of the Wimpak knew I was there. He spoke to me. He asked for forgiveness for the evil they will bring. I think that's the key to why I keep going back there. I need to know what the evil is. I think it has something to do with what's going on in Isolation now." Eve shrugged again. "At least that's what I'm guessing."

"So then why am I going there too? I don't even fully understand what I'm doing or how I'm doing it."

Eve sighed deeply. "Maybe you're there to help stop it." She rolled out of the room and down the hall.

Russell was left in his room alone, watching the sun fall beyond the horizon, isolated in his own mind.

CHAPTER 24

Barney woke up in the backseat of his car, hands tied behind his back and a cloth of some sort stuffed in his mouth. His head felt like it had been in a vice grip for the past hour, his eyes blurry as he squinted them open, trying to get his bearings. He shifted in a mild attempt to raise himself into a sitting position. After several attempts to right himself, he gave up and lay back down.

The sun had set, and the road outside, at least the bit Barney could see from his prone position, was utterly black. No street lights to illuminate the shadowy trees that stood sentry. As the car hit a hole in the road, it jostled him, and his head smacked against the door. His vision started to blur once more as he let out an agonized groan.

Jimmy looked into the rearview mirror and watched the struggling man. "Well, hello there, pervert. You woke up just in time."

Barney struggled against his bindings. The gag in his mouth threatened to choke him as he tried to speak. He focused, trying to recognize the voice in the front seat. Barney's head was far too foggy to recall the voice, but he was sure he had not recognized it.

The car turned on to what sounded like a dirt road, and Barney could see trees towering above the car, finally illuminated by the light of the moon. "Don't worry. You'll see where we are soon enough, pervert. Just you wait," Jimmy said as if sensing the bound man's thoughts.

The car drove on for another minute or so before coming to a stop. Fear overwhelmed Barney as terrified pallor overtook his face. The man in the front seat jumped out and ran around the car to the back door. He grabbed Barney by the shoulders and dragged him out of the car, landing him on his back with a loud thud that forced the air out of his lungs. Barney's eyes cleared, and he realized that this wasn't a man, not in the truest sense. He looked like he was barely old enough to shave.

Jimmy looked down upon the man and removed his gag roughly. "Jesus, man, all that mumbling is fucking annoying. What are you trying to say?"

"Who are you?" Barney asked as his eyes went blurry again, this time tears threatening to overflow as he looked around and saw the emptiness of the area that the kid had driven him to. Concern turned to panic as the kid squatted down next to Barney's splayed-out body.

"Oh, you don't know me, pervert. But you have seen me. Outside that writer's house the other day. When you were peeping in the house."

"Please, please, you don't understand," Barney stammered.

"What don't I understand, pervert. I watched you sneak up to the house and look in the windows. You trying to look at another man's wife? You hoping to get a quick peek at her getting out of the shower or something?"

"No, no, that was my Marie. She was mine."

"She was yours?" Jimmy looked down at the man curiously. Pity crossed Jimmy's face, but only for a moment. "You know, pervert, it's people like you that make me really sick. People that would pray on a woman, another man's woman at that. It's time you learned a lesson." Jimmy put the gag back into Barney's mouth and dragged him toward one of the cabins on the campground that had survived the blaze from several days before.

Barney flailed and kicked, but Jimmy was too strong, and Barney still too dizzy. Jimmy kicked in the door to the cabin and dragged the now hysterical man over to a chair waiting in the middle of the room. Jimmy dropped Barney next to the chair and grabbed some rope that was thrown into the corner. Barney screamed into his gag. Jimmy worked in stoic silence as he went back to Barney and lifted him into the seat. Barney struggled against the uncanny strength of his captor as Jimmy knotted the rope around his body.

Barney's struggles finally paid off as he was able to headbutt Jimmy in the chest, knocking himself to the ground in the process. For just a moment, Barney thought he might be able to make it to his feet and get away. He looked up just in time to catch Jimmy Delaney's foot connecting with his nose.

All went dark again.

When Barney finally opened his eyes, he was tied to the chair, and the boy was squatting in front of him, baseball bat between his legs.

"Who are you?" Barney choked out as blood continued to drip from his nose and into his mouth.

Jimmy smiled solemnly. "I'm the man that's going to show you not to fuck around in my town."

"P-please, I only wanted to see her. She worked for me. I was only going to check on her."

"During a snowstorm like that? You were just being a 'good guy' and checking on her. Don't you think she's safe at home with her family? You know, pervert, no one ever called me a perfect angel, but there still needs to be respect given to a person and their family."

Jimmy stood up and swung the bat just above Barney's head. Barney let out a squeal. Urine began to run down his leg and onto the floor. Jimmy looked at him in disgust.

"I meant no harm to her, I swear it."

Jimmy stopped and stared down at Barney, whose tears were flowing down his gaunt face. "Is that why you knocked her to the ground outside the bookstore? Caused her to run into the street. Get hit by that car. You didn't mean no harm?" Jimmy's face had become red; the tendons in his neck bulged out, snaking up towards his chin. He cocked the bat back and slammed it into Barney's knee, shattering it and bending the leg at an unusual angle. "I didn't mean no harm either."

Barney's scream tore through the silence of the night and his throat in kind, coating his mouth in a metallic taste that threatened vomit. Sweat dripped from his brow as he looked down at his mangled knee. Barney tried to beg, but no words would come out. He watched in horror as Jimmy cocked back the bat a second time and drove it into his other knee. Darkness tried to overtake him, but Jimmy ran outside and grabbed an armful of snow, and dumped it over Barney's head, shocking his system back to full consciousness.

"You see, pervert, I've always been interested in pain. What it does to a thing, you know, an animal, for example. But animals can't give you a proper verbal response to what they are feeling. Animals can't seem to take the level of pain that a human can. Then again, we're all just animals, aren't we?" Jimmy snickered. "Granted, I'm new to this whole human torture thing, so maybe I'm wrong about that. I guess we'll find out."

Barney's head wobbled, and Jimmy went back outside and grabbed more snow to dump atop him.

"Stay with me, pervert. I have faith that you can stay awake a bit longer." Jimmy grabbed Barney's hair and lifted his head up so he could look directly into his eyes. "It won't be too much longer."

Jimmy let Barney's head fall down to his chest again. Barney's legs had melted into a hot, throbbing ache. He was lucid enough to say a thank you in his mind for that little blessing.

As Jimmy spoke, he walked around the cabin, swinging the bat over his head. "You know, there is something strange going on in Isolation. People are dying all over the place. Kids. Adults. Sheriff can't seem to work hard enough. But you want to know a secret?" Jimmy got mere inches from Barney's drooping eyes. "I saw what's been doing it."

Barney's mind tried to put together what he was hearing. *This kid has to be insane*, Barney thought. The only lucid thought he could grab ahold of.

"I can't really explain it. It was like some sort of a monster. A demon, maybe. I never thought too much of demons, but, man, I can't explain it. It moved so fast." Jimmy's heart began to race with excitement as he thought about the previous night. The way the air seemed to vibrate around him when the demon-creature was close. His breathing became rapid, and his pants tightened as he continued.

"Forest and Adam." Jimmy looked over to Barney. "Those were the guys that used to follow me around. This thing…it got them. Took Adam's head right off his shoulders before we even saw it." Jimmy chuckled. "Split Forest right in two." He looked back at Barney. "That was even a bit much for me. But, I've been thinking about it and you know what I think? It was beautiful."

Barney's head had cleared some as Jimmy spoke, trying to make sense of the crazed boy's words. As he looked up from his seat and saw the look in Jimmy's eyes, his instincts sent adrenaline pumping through his system. He struggled with the restraints that bound his hands while Jimmy continued.

"I didn't get to actually see much; I was too far away. But it got me thinking all day, what makes a person…on the inside. The wet, slurping sound as Forest was torn apart. The blood squirting into the sky when Adam's head came off. I want to understand. I want to see more for myself." Jimmy turned to Barney again and raised his bat. Smiling, he said, "That's where you come in, pervert."

Barney's frantic cries were muffled as Jimmy turned his gaze back to him. His knotted hands were loosening behind the chair. Jimmy smiled. He walked behind Barney slowly, flipping the bat in the air and catching it before it hit the ground. Jimmy leaned in closer to Barney's hands and clucked his tongue.

"Wow, I'm impressed. A few more minutes and you might have been loose. Rubbed most of the skin right off your wrists. Reminds me of those wolverines I heard about that will bite their own leg off to get out of a trap. Impressive." Jimmy sighed and stepped back.

For a moment, Barney thought that the crazed boy might show mercy. Maybe his bloodlust had been satiated with the destruction of his knees. The cabin was silent. Then Barney heard the sound of the bat being dragged across the ground behind him.

"But not impressive enough." Jimmy touched the bat to the back of Barney's head lightly. Getting the angle correct. "Well, pervert, this is goodbye. But I do have to thank you for being my little experiment. For that, I salute you."

Jimmy cocked back the bat as far as he could and swung with all his might. Barney felt no pain as the bat connected against his skull. The blunt trauma instantly shut his brain off. Jimmy was splattered with blood, and his bat was dripping with gore. He raised the bat to eye level and, with his free hand, ran his fingers through the mess on his bat. He breathed in deeply and let his breath out slowly.

As Jimmy walked around to the front of Barney's slumped body, he was pleased to see one of Barney's eyes laying on the ground just in front of him, staring blankly at the ceiling.

Jimmy reached down and picked it up, all the while laughing softly.

Russell turned the knob on the front door of his house and entered for the first time as a widower. It was just before dawn, and the first sign of color was beginning to show on the horizon. He had been released an hour or so earlier, his heart rate having stabilized enough that the doctor felt comfortable letting him go and grieve in the privacy of his own home.

He walked toward the kitchen in a trance-like state, seeing but not truly. Instinctually, he grabbed a glass from the cabinet and ran the tap, filling it with water and taking a long gulp. He stared out the window and saw the looming presence of Wimpak Hill watching him. The dawn light was haunting as wispy clouds passed just over the summit. The silence of the house threatened to break him as his mind recreated the previous morning, sitting at the table as a family laughing and eating. Sharing in each other's presence. The whispers of yesterday called to him through the veil of time.

Tears came upon Russell quickly and suddenly. The smell of Marie's perfume wafted over to him as though she was standing directly behind him. He breathed in deeply, taking in every moment of this phantasmagorical encounter as though he may never experience it again.

His heart broke anew.

Russell finished his glass of water and walked down the hall to Sam's room. He touched the door gently, letting his hand rest upon the wood and taking a deep inhalation, careful to not wake his sleeping son. The door opened silently, and he saw Mandy laying in bed, Sam's head resting on her chest. He smiled and walked over to the sleeping pair.

Mandy's eyes opened slowly as she saw Russ enter the room. She smiled at him. Though her smile faltered after only a moment, Russell appreciated the attempt at normalcy. Mandy unwrapped her arm from around Sam and snuck out of bed. Russ pulled the blanket back over his son and kissed him on the head.

"Sleep tight, buddy," Russell whispered into Sam's ear.

Mandy signaled for Russ to come speak with her outside the room. Russell turned, and his eye caught the Lego house placed in the corner of the room, almost lost in the shadows. Russell shook his head and walked to the door.

He walked down the hall further and into his room. *Just his room now*, he thought. He sat on the end of the bed and stared at the floor. Mandy stood next to her friend and placed her hand on his shoulder, the only comfort she could think to offer. For a fleeting moment, he felt solace.

"She was my soul, Mandy," Russ said in a hoarse voice. "The moment I saw her, I knew I didn't want anyone else. That thought never faltered."

Mandy composed herself and spoke softly, " I remember the day you two met on the common at school. I could feel the connection myself. That first night she was dancing on clouds while she talked about you. You made an impact on her just as much as she made one on you."

Tears streamed again from Russell's eyes, but he looked at Mandy and forced a smile. "Thank you."

She sat next to Russ and hugged him from the side. "She was a great woman by herself. She was a better woman with you."

"And I have always been a better man with her." Russ wiped his eyes. "God, Mandy, what the fuck am I going to do now? How am I going to help Sam through this? I mean, he saw his mother die. Not to mention seeing the boy's shoe in the classroom a few days ago. How is he ever going to get by this?"

"You're right, Russ. It's going to be hard. He hasn't spoken all day. I don't know how much he saw, but it was enough. You just need to be there for him. You're a great dad. Just be with him. Don't force him to talk. Let him come to you. He will."

Russ shook his head and looked at the ground. His breath caught in his throat, and he began to weep. "I'd give anything to have her back."

Mandy sat next to Russ, holding his hand and listening to the wails of a broken soul.

Chapter 25

Tom lay in his bed staring at the ceiling. What he had seen today had pushed the creature that was stalking Isolation from his mind entirely. Flashbacks of his time in Vietnam had plagued him all afternoon and evening, though he had done his best to not show that to Mandy and Sam. But now that he lay in bed, by himself, in his own thoughts, he was having trouble keeping the ghosts at bay.

Visions of the horrors he saw played continually in his mind. The heat, the bugs, the stickiness. None of it compared to the armed kids killing soldiers. Soldiers killing kids. Rape, blood, torture. It all came back in the silent, lonely night.

Tom's palms were sweaty, and his eyes hyper-focused on nothing in particular, but they saw another place. He saw a little Vietnamese boy that he had saved from a fire fight that had broken out in his village, clutching to his pillow under the bed he had slept in for the last several years. His mother and father had been killed. Tom didn't know by which side. The village burned around him as the last of the Vietcong left the area, firing as they retreated.

He held the boy to his chest and ran back to the safety of his unit. The boy's bones felt brittle against Tom's arms as they plodded through the jungle. He stank of sweat and dirt, and Tom made a mental note to make sure he washed the boy when they got back.

As they approached the base, some of the men began to mock him for rescuing the boy. Some spit toward him, but when Tom sat the boy on a rock just outside the gates of relative safety and demanded they fall in line and respect him and the terrified child, most backed down, walking away and mumbling something disgusting under their breath. Tom spoke to the boy, unsure if he could even understand him but knowing the kindness of his voice would cross the language barrier.

He slept next to the boy each night as they camped, marching to their next camp. The days were brutal hikes through the thicket that would have been impossible to navigate if not for the machetes chopping a clear path. The insects bit the men and harassed their faces constantly, yet the boy seemed to take no notice. He kept up with the men, and for that, Tom was thankful. If he had fallen behind, the men would have demanded they leave him. There would be no way for Tom to carry him, so he'd have to choose to leave the boy or leave his men. Happily, the boy kept pace, and during the hottest parts of the day, it was Tom and his men that had to keep pace with him.

He watched over the boy, made sure the other men didn't get any ideas about hurting him. He couldn't explain why he took to the boy so much, but he knew it was right to bring the boy along. He could sleep better knowing he was doing something right here, on the other side of the world. It could have been the other side of the universe.

One night Tom woke up with a start, and the boy was standing over him with a knife clutched in his small right hand. For an instant, Tom thought he had made the wrong decision to bring the boy along, to let him sleep so close. The knife came down hard just above Tom's head. Tom twisted and saw that the blade had gone straight through a stalking cobra's head. He looked at the boy, who simply removed the knife, tossed the snake away from their sleeping arrangement, and laid back down to sleep.

The next morning Tom told all the soldiers in his squad what the boy had done. They mocked him again and said that the boy probably put the snake there in the first place. They said Tom was losing sight of why they were there. Killing gooks is all that Tom should be focused on, not saving them. Tom spat.

When they got to the next camp, Tom was sad to have to leave the boy. He had grown to feel comfort in seeing the boy's face. There was comfort in knowing that the boy was safe, that he was safe because of Tom. His sorrow was remedied only slightly when he was assured that he would be safe there until they could get him out of the warzone. Tom was reluctant but satisfied.

He kneeled down next to the boy and held him to his chest tightly. Tom noticed that his bones didn't seem so frail anymore. They'd only been together for two weeks, but the boy seemed stronger, calmer. Tom moved the boy out of his embrace and looked into his eyes; he told him to be safe and to be strong. The boy, who had spoken no words in all the time they had been together, smiled and said in his best English, "Thank you."

Tom hugged the boy again and left him in the care of the men that would be marching out of the jungle the next day. Tom turned away from the boy, and though he never turned back, he could feel the boy's eyes on him until he disappeared into the jungle. Though Tom considered himself a hardened soldier, as he fell back from his men, he allowed himself to cry.

Days passed, but miles did not. Shortly after leaving the area, no more than four clicks from where he left the boy, the skies opened up, and torrents rained down on the men around the clock. It just so happened that the VC had set up an ambush in the same area, pinning the squad down. The terrain did not allow for backtracking, and time was running out for Tom and his squad to make a safe retreat. A plan was made, and the men pushed the enemy back. Though years had passed and Tom could remember the horrors, the successes had faded from memory long ago. He remembered the ambush but none of the details about how they got themselves out of it. *Strange*, Tom thought.

As the men marched forward to where the VC had been, Tom saw a single body hanging from a tree. A small naked body, broken and disfigured, his hair matted to his head from the neverending cascade of water. The small boy was turned away from Tom and his men, but a sinking feeling washed over him. He stood at the feet of the boy, reached up, and touched his foot, turning him. Tom gasped as the bloated face of the boy he had spent those quiet nights with looked down upon him. His swollen tongue hung out of his mouth. The boy that he had saved from the burning village. The boy he had protected.

Tom collapsed to his knees and screamed. He reached up again and tenderly held the boy's feet, apologizing for having ever left him. A few of Tom's men stood around and watched their leader's display of emotion stoically. Many simply walked past the boy without a second glance. One man came over and put his hand on Tom's shoulder to offer condolences, but even he made his way past without so much as a word.

Tom's heartache changed to rage. His vision went red. Tom ran to each of the soldiers and demanded answers. "How could this be? He had left the poor boy only two days ago! He was told the boy would be safe; he'd be safe, dammit!" Tom screamed at each of the men.

Some of the men were shocked at the sudden outrage of their brother-in-arms. Some were angry as Tom grabbed them by their shirt collar and demanded answers. He got none. The men stood a few feet away and let Tom calm down as they made camp for the night. A few men talked about crazy Tom Richmond, how he'd finally gone nuts like the rest of them over here. As Tom sat with his knees pulled to his chest, even with the thunderous rain breaking through the canopy of trees, he heard their laughs. But most of the men kept their heads down and focused on staying alive. Living one moment at a time.

Days passed, and the rain slowed and then stopped as Tom's squad made it to the large encampment they had been marching toward. The men gathered in the mess hall and spoke loudly and joyfully, having made their way through the unforgiving jungle and to safety. Tom sat by himself, his mind a million miles away, wondering how he could have allowed himself to fail the boy.

When he heard the familiar voice of a soldier, he looked up and searched the mess hall until he found him. The man he had left the boy with was sitting on the other side of the room, smoking and laughing with a group of men. Tom's blood boiled, and he rose from his seat. His vision narrowed, and he could hear his heart thumping in his head. He approached the soldier from behind and threw him to the ground. The soldier never saw him coming, and after a few blows, Tom was pulled off by the men he had been sitting with.

The mess hall was silent.

The soldier stood up and screamed at Tom, but Tom heard none of it. Then he recognized who had attacked him. The soldier laughed at Tom. Asked him why he gave so much care to a kid gook. His comment was seconded and thirded by the men that had been sharing his table. To add insult to injury, the soldier that Tom had attacked punched him directly in the stomach, knocking the air out of him as the man's friends held Tom by the arms.

As he lay on the ground, the man knelt above him and told him that the night he left, he sent the kid out into the jungle, away from the barracks. He said they didn't have enough rations to help some gook that would probably grow up to hate Americans anyways. The men walked out of the mess hall laughing to each other.

Tom lay on the ground a few moments longer, crushed by the words of his brothers. No, not his brothers. Not truly. Tom wondered about the cruelty of people and was distraught. He only had a couple more weeks before he would be discharged and sent home. He had no idea how he would integrate back into the real world, none at all. But he would hold the boy's memory in his heart.

Tom spent the rest of his time in the jungle with his head down and his thoughts distant. Even in the hostile, unforgiving environment of Vietnam, Tom had always been able to find the beauty that was around him. Sometimes it was hard to find, but it was there if you looked hard enough. Now that beauty was gone. That beauty was destroyed by the swinging, tattered body of a boy that didn't even have a name to Tom.

When Tom got home, he was determined to get away from as many people as he could. Tom found Isolation and had lived there since his return back to the states. He loved the peace, the solace; the isolation calmed him. Flashes of what he had seen came back now and then, but for the most part, Tom lived a quiet and happy life. In his darkest moments, Tom would recall the little Vietnamese boy smiling genuinely and saying "thank you" with his thick accent. Even all these years later, Tom would revisit that moment and smile.

When Russ, Marie, and Sam moved across the street, the memories returned more often. The feeling of good, of doing something right. He felt that again when he looked at Sam. Sam had that same innocent quality of the boy thousands of miles away and dozens of years ago. They didn't look alike, but Tom was sure they shared the same essence. Tom was always willing to watch over Sam, even if from afar.

But today. What Sam had seen today, what Tom had seen today, brought all those bad memories back. Sam lost his innocence and his mother in one brief moment. Just like the boy in the jungle. The gore Tom saw today was more than he had seen since his days in fighting the VC. It rattled him. But what he saw in Sam's eyes shook him to his core.

Tom lay in bed, staring at the ceiling, sweating and shaking. Seeing ghosts dart around the room. Panic swelled within him. His eyes darted from side to side. He tried to remember the little boy. He saw the little boy's face, confused but grateful. But his mind slipped back not to his smile but to the boy hanging in the tree. But this time, when Tom walked over and turned the body, Sam's blank eyes stared back at him.

CHAPTER 26

Jimmy opened his eyes at the sound of a truck driving past his house. The tires bouncing in and out of a pothole, for just a moment, triggered the memory of the woman he saw struck yesterday. He pushed the memory away as he slowly sat up, his eyes darting back and forth, taking in his surroundings and calming at the familiar sight.

Jimmy swung his legs off his bed and stretched. His shoulders and back ached from the exertion of yesterday's activities. He looked down as his foot touched a shirt kicked half way under his bed. The shirt was covered in blood and dirt. *Shit*, he thought, *I meant to get rid of that last night. So stupid.*

A knock at his bedroom door came, startling Jimmy out of bed. He kicked the shirt fully under the bed and said, "Yeah?"

Jimmy's mother opened the door and poked her head in. "I thought I heard you. I'm making breakfast downstairs. You want some?"

Jimmy smiled at the offer. "Yeah, Mom, I'll be down in just a few minutes. Just waking up."

She smiled at him and closed the door. Jimmy sighed deeply and ran his fingers through his hair. His shirtless body looked normal, but the bottom of his pants were still covered in dirt from last night. Thankfully he had jumped up on the opposite side of the bed, furthest away from the door, so his mother hadn't noticed.

He undressed and put the pants underneath his bed with the bloodied shirt. He'd have to take care of that later when no one was around. He pulled on some jeans and a new shirt and made his way downstairs. The smell of bacon wafted up the stairs and attacked his nose in the most beautiful bombardment ever conceived.

It was Sunday morning, and Jimmy's sister, Sarah, was excited to see him up so early. She pushed away from her seat at the table and rushed to wrap her arms around him.

"Jimmy," she squealed exuberantly, "I never see you before we're back from church. I'm so excited. Are you going to come with us?"

He smiled and hugged her back. "Probably not today, Sarah."

Her disappointment was evident but lasted only a moment. She ran back toward the kitchen, calling over her shoulder to Jimmy about the bacon and french toast that Mom was making. Jimmy's morning only got better when he saw the freshly squeezed orange juice already set up at the table.

"Wow, Mom," he said. "What got into you this morning?"

His mother just smiled and said he should sit down and enjoy himself as she brought the plate of food over to the table. Jimmy put the first bacon slice into his mouth and let it sit on his tongue, taking in the salty, heavenly goodness. She sat at the table with Jimmy and Sarah, and the three laughed and talked about the past few days. They kept the conversation away from the strangeness that was taking place and the untimely loss of Jimmy's friends. Instead, the three talked about the upcoming holidays and the crazy, early snowstorm that had just hit. The Delaney household was full of laughter for the first time, in God only knew how long. The three didn't realize the fragility of the moment.

Jimmy was just finishing up his last slice of french toast when his father walked into the kitchen. He, like his mother, was in a joyous mood. He came over and tousled Jimmy's hair and gave Sarah a kiss on the head before giving his wife a soft kiss on the lips. Sarah smiled and laughed, looking away. Jimmy glared, anger in his eyes.

Don't touch my fucking hair, he thought. His eyes changed as his father looked up and faced him.

"Good morning, son. We didn't see much of you yesterday. How are you feeling?"

"I'm fine." *What are you getting at?*

"We heard about your friends, son. Just awful business. We're so sorry. If you need to talk, please know we're all here for you."

Jimmy looked around the table at everyone staring at him. Understanding dawned on him. He had always been close with his mother and sister, but he couldn't recall a single time, other than his birthday and maybe a holiday or two, where his mother had spent so much effort making breakfast. They pitied him. Forest and Adam had been brutally butchered, and his parents were trying to save Jimmy from going over the edge.

Pathetic, Jimmy thought. He looked directly into his father's eyes, *why don't you mind your fucking business*, and smiled. "Yeah, Dad, Mom, Sarah. I'm okay. I don't think it's truly registered yet that those guys are gone. I mean, I just hope the police find out what happened." Jimmy forced a pained expression. "They didn't deserve this."

Jimmy's mother and father went to each side of him and gave him a hug. He wrapped an arm around his mother and squeezed. He let his father squeeze him.

When he looked at Sarah, she simply smiled.

Russell was startled awake by the feeling of being watched. When his eyes adjusted to the light that was streaming through the window and directly into his eyes, he saw Sam standing next to him. He looked as though he hadn't slept too well the night before, but Russ forced a smile nevertheless.

"Hey buddy, good morning."

Sam looked past his dad toward the other side of the bed. "I miss Mom," he said, barely louder than a whisper.

Russ reached out and grabbed Sam, pulling him close to his body. He held him close and let his rhythmic breathing calm his son. Russ missed Marie terribly, but he needed to be strong for his son now.

"I know, bud. I miss her too. But you know what, it's going to be okay. We are going to get through this. It's going to be tough, and we are going to cry and miss Mom a lot. But we are going to get through this together as a team."

Sam looked up at his father, eyes glistening and red. "A team?"

"Just me and you, handsome. We still have each other. And Mom will stay in our hearts and our memories. We'll smile when we think of her, and we'll laugh at the silly things she did. We'll always remember her."

Sam started to cry at these words; Russ lost control as well. The two Tolliver boys lay in each other's arms and wept, both feeling like they lost a piece of themselves.

A knock on the door slowed their tears, and both looked to see Mandy standing in the door frame. "Good morning." She looked at Sam. "You want to come help me make coffee?"

Sam wiped his nose with his pajama top and looked at his dad. Russell nodded and kissed Sam on the forehead. Sam slid out from under the covers and walked toward Mandy. He paused and turned to his father. "A team, Dad. Always."

The two walked out of the room together, hand in hand. Russell lay in bed a few moments longer, his brain already spinning. He knew he had to get up, he had to start the day without Marie, but he had little desire to do so.

From the kitchen came the smell of his morning brew. He decided that was enough to at least get him through the next few hours. Russell got up and put clothes on, and made his way down the hall. Sam was sitting in the living room with a bowl of cereal, watching one of his favorite cartoons. Mandy was at the table sipping her coffee, a steaming mug sitting next to her, indicating where Russell should be.

"Thanks for making coffee this morning, Mandy. I don't know if I could have gotten out of bed without it." Russell sipped his coffee, and his features changed to a slightly more relaxed expression almost immediately.

"Not a problem, Russ." She sipped her own mug and contemplated how she was going to broach the next subject. "Listen, Russ. I'm going to stick around for the next few days, help out with Sam. But I'm going to have to leave after the burial. I've only been here a couple of days, and I mean, I've heard about and seen more deaths than I do down in the city in a year. And with Marie gone…" Mandy sipped her coffee, gathering her thoughts again. "Plus, I do have to go back to work and…"

Russell held his hand up to stop her. "Don't worry about it, Mandy. I totally get it. You've been an amazing help with Sam." Russ looked down at his mug. "With me too. I don't know what we would have done without you here. I mean, I haven't even had the chance to ask you if *you're* okay. Oh God, Mandy, how are you doing?"

Mandy forced a smile and nodded. "I'm just doing what I have to do for you two. I don't know that it's fully hit me yet, but I'm sure it will soon enough. Let's focus on you and that little boy in there right now. I'll have my own time to grieve."

Russell squeezed Mandy's hand as a sign of thanks and appreciation.

"I know you don't want to talk about this right now, but we're going to have to. We need to plan the funeral. I can watch Sam if you want to go out to make the arrangements. If you need me to go, though, maybe we can ask your neighbor to watch him."

"No, no. I don't want to put Tom out. Hell, he saw the whole thing happen as well. I can't imagine what he's feeling, either. I should stop over there later to check on him."

"Don't overdo it today, Russ. You've been through hell, and your body is probably running on adrenaline more than anything else. As for me, I'm going to try to get Sam to smile at least once today." Mandy stood up and walked toward the couch.

Russell heeded Mandy's words but knew that things needed to be done, emotionally exhausted or not. He finished his coffee and got ready to face the hardest day of his life.

CHAPTER 27

Several days had passed since Marie Toliver's life had been cut short underneath the screeching tires of a car futilely trying to stop on the icy roads of Isolation. She would be buried in the small, quiet cemetery just outside of town. The once underutilized cemetery that had suddenly become very busy.

Mitchell had tried to call Russ to offer his condolences, but he hadn't wanted to intrude by stopping by. Russell hadn't picked up the phone, so Mitchell made sure to see him at the burial. Most of the town showed up, the famous writer's wife killed in an awful accident right in broad daylight. For a few days, the town gossip was on the accident and not the mounting bodies that kept appearing.

Russell had looked better than Mitchell expected when he saw him sitting in the front row of chairs, head held high as the priest spoke beautiful words. Mitchell assumed it was a front put on to show strength in front of his young son. Even he almost believed the facade. When he spoke to Russ, the calm exterior Russ was presenting broke slightly, and Mitchell could see the damage that had been done by her death. He didn't take too much of Russell's time there. He wanted to let the man grieve.

Mitchell put an arm on Russ' shoulder and told him that if he needed anything, to please stop by. It wasn't lost on himself that this is what everyone says during times of crisis, and he wondered if it sounded genuine coming from his mouth. He thought Russ would appreciate the sentiment and know it was said from a place of caring and respect. He placed a hand on Sam's head as he stared blankly at the casket before moving away.

As he was approaching his car, Tom Richmond approached him with his arm extended. Unlike Russell's collected exterior, Tom looked like he hadn't slept in a week. His hair was a mess, and his beard seemed to be more white and gray than the last time Mitchell had seen the man. Black bags hung under his puffy eyes.

Tom wore a black shirt with the top button undone and a black loosened tie, as though he had wanted to dress for the sad occasion but simply lost the motivation to finish the ensemble. The man, once seeming so sturdy, looked like a shell of himself. Mitchell had heard that Tom had seen the accident happen first hand. He figured it must have shaken him deeply if his appearance was an indication.

"Heyah, Mitch. Was hopin' to maybe talk to ya 'bout something."

Mitch shook Tom's hand. "Yeah, sure, Tom. What's up?"

Tom looked over to where Russell stood, holding his son's hand, watching the coffin be lowered into the grave. "Not now, not heah. It's not the place. Think maybe we could meet at the cafe tomorrow mahnin?"

"Sure, Tom. What's this all about?"

"It's about what's goin' on in this damn town." Tom grabbed Mitch's hand and shook it before walking away without another word. He watched Tom walk over to Russ and put a hand on his shoulder. Mitchell's heart sank as he watched the terrible scene.

The next morning Mitchell was woken up by the flashing red and blue lights of a police car and ambulance parked just outside his bedroom window. He looked over at the clock next to his bed: 4:12 AM. He got up from his bed and made his way over to the window just in time to see a stretcher carrying a body being removed from the home.

"Jesus, Bryson Miller now?" Mitchell said as he stared in shock at the scene.

Bryson Miller had lived in the town since Mitchell was a kid. He was old then and even older now. He had lived alone since early 2005, when his wife passed away from pneumonia. He was a crotchety old coot, but he kept to himself and never paid any of the town gossip any mind. Mitchell figured all that was moot now.

Bryson wasn't in the best of health, but with all the deaths that had been happening in Isolation, Mitchell thought it best to go speak to Deputy Walker, who was standing by the ambulance looking exhausted and pale. Mitchell didn't want to get in the way, but these deaths were getting a bit too close for comfort, he thought.

The ambulance was just pulling away as Mitchell closed the front door. The cold morning air hit him like a sledgehammer and dismissed any remnants of lethargy that may have remained in his coffeeless morning. Deputy Walker hadn't noticed Mitchell walking over to him in the predawn darkness, and Mitchell could see he was talking to himself.

"Hey, Deputy," Mitchell called out, "everything okay over here?"

The Deputy froze, momentarily letting his eyes adjust to the darkness to see who had called out to him. "Oh, hey, Mitch. No, things are most certainly not okay."

"Yeah," Mitch said, blowing into his hands to keep them warm, "I saw the ambulance. Old man Miller finally passed away, huh? He had to have been ninety by now."

The deputy stared at Mitchell through bloodshot eyes. Mitchell didn't realize he had held his breath, awaiting a response until his lungs began burning, and he let out a long sigh. His breath steamed from his mouth. The deputy stared through Mitch.

"I don't know how much more of this I can handle."

Mitchell's heart sank, understanding the deeper meaning of what the deputy was trying to tell him. "His heart didn't just give out, did it?"

"No. Of fucking course not. No one dies naturally in this town lately. Every night, hell, every day at this point, we're getting calls of bodies being found. Sheriff had to hire a second secretary just to keep up with the calls. Some are cranks, asshole teenagers most likely, some are even people in a panic because they think they are seeing something out in the woods by their house. But more often than not, it's a body. It's complete fucking insanity, Mitch."

Mitchell probed the deputy, "Do you have any suspects here? I mean, no one has told me that they've seen any strangers around. Maybe an animal?" Mitch wanted to offer what he knew but was fully aware of how crazy it would sound.

"That's exactly what the goddamn F-B and I said when I called them to come in and help us out. This is too big for this little ass town. Shit, we only have five police officers employed as it is. And none of the volunteers want to help out anymore because they are getting burned out too. You can only see so many bodies torn apart before your mind starts to go, you know?"

Mitch blew into his hands again. The blood was pumping through his veins at such a rate that his body felt warm, but his extremities were freezing.

"A fucking bear, they said," the deputy muttered to himself more than to Mitch. He looked up and caught Mitch's eyes. "What kind of a bear can kill a person across town and another not an hour later? Not to mention there is no sign of any break-ins. A fucking bear…"

"Listen, deputy, I've got to head inside. It's freezing out here. I'll keep an ear to the ground as well. I think we all need to at this point."

Deputy Walker raised his hand in an awkward, quick motion indicating it was fine that Mitchell ended the conversation. "Thanks, Mitch. You be safe. Hey, mum's the word on this, okay? People are scared enough as it is."

Mitch gave a quick nod and, with that, walked back into his house and closed the door. He slumped down with his back pressed against it, fear coursing through his body. He realized that the shaking of his body wasn't entirely from the cold.

For the first time in days, Mitchell acknowledged the fear that he and the rest of Isolation had been living with for the past two weeks. He knew someone needed to figure out how to stop this nightmare before there was no more Isolation to save. If what Arthur Holt had told him was true, this all stemmed from Wimpak lore. He had to be the one to stop it; he had a responsibility. But he certainly couldn't do it alone. He couldn't go to Russell right now, but maybe Tom could help.

Maybe.

CHAPTER 28

Isaac Appleton came from humble beginnings. His father, John, was a blacksmith that decided to try his luck in America during the early days of the country. He was annoyed that the Americans had broken away from the monarchy like a rebellious child, but he wasn't having much financial success in London, and the "American dream" he was hearing so much about was too tempting to pass up. So in 1825, John Appleton packed up his belongings, along with his wife Elaine and his only son Isaac, and left London to seek fortune in the new world.

The Appletons settled in Boston in a small home by the harbor. Boston was a much smaller city than London, but that suited John just fine. John's blacksmithing shop was far more successful in his new, adopted home than it had been in London. Elaine was able to shop with the ladies of the growing city, and Isaac had to want for nothing.

As time passed and Isaac grew into his teenage years, his distaste for city life began to grow. Though he had friends and his family's success was known all around the city, Isaac had had enough of the gossip, the incessant need to always be on the go, and the smell. More than anything, the smell made his stomach turn.

Isaac apprenticed at his father's smithing shop and became a wonderful metal worker. Though *Appleton & Son Smithing* became a household name in Boston, and for sure around the entire state of Massachusetts as word spread to the more rural sections that needed to worry about Indian raids, Isaac found himself yearning for a more quiet life. The constant fear of Indian attacks didn't cross his mind. He figured if he left them alone, they'd leave him alone in return.

By the time Isaac was approaching his twentieth birthday, he had saved up enough money to set out on his own. He told his parents he would go north, to the great woods, and find his way with a trapping team. He would live on the land and satisfy his desires out there.

John and Elaine were horror-struck and insisted he stay, but Isaac would hear nothing of it. John chastised Isaac, demanding to know why he would give up a successful business, money, and a life of comfort to risk danger out in the savage's land. Isaac simply shrugged as he packed a few of his clothes into a bag, unsure or uninterested in answering and discussing the matter further. He kissed his mother on the cheek, shook his father's hand, and mounted his horse.

Isaac rode north that summer, uncertain of his destination but knowing that he must continue north. He rode through open fields and on dirt roads for what seemed like months. The bugs were constant, and the sun beating down upon him burned his skin. However, when he stopped to water his horse or find a tree to use as his bathroom, the silence overwhelmed him in the most magnificent way.

He sat and stared at the mountains cresting on the horizon one morning as he sipped at the coffee that he had purchased at a trading post. The cool summer breeze blew his hair lightly. The contrast of the breeze and the hot coffee blended into a perfect dance. The backdrop of the mountains framed the morning perfectly as he wrote in his journal, chronicling his adventure. He smiled and closed the book, replacing it in his pack, and mounted his horse once more.

As he continued north, signs of deer, moose, and bear began to appear often. Isaac read his book (the only one he was able to call his own) on the wildlife in the northeast and took note of all the minute details that were held within. With every passing deer track, Isaac was more sure he was making the right decision.

As the leaves slowly began to change color, he came across a valley in the midst of great mountains. On the summit to his left, he saw the unmistakable face of a man jutting out from the massive granite wall. Isaac knew this was a sign from the almighty that he was almost there. He ate the last of his rations and stared up at the face, sure he was about to discover success.

The night came upon him as he rode into a small village with a tavern illuminated by torches. He was exhausted, hungry, and weary after being on his horse for so long. Men's voices echoed from inside, and the smell of meat called to him. He tied up his horse and made his way inside.

As he entered, the voices became hushed, and the men (and a few women, too) stared in his direction. Isaac tipped his hat and made his way to the bar to order a nice hot meal. As he searched his satchel, he realized that he had spent almost all his money at the last trading outpost he had passed. Fear crossed his mind as he thought about what to do next.

A burly man sporting a handlebar mustache and a long scar that ran from above his right ear and down to his lips saddled up next to him, placed his beer on the bar top, and held Isaac's gaze as he chewed tobacco in a repulsive way. "Can I help you, friend?" The man asked Isaac in a gravelly, grating voice.

Isaac looked at the man and knew he was not someone to be on the wrong side of, especially after such a long ride. Isaac was having a tough time sitting up straight. He stood no chance fighting a man bigger and far more muscular than him.

"No, sir. I'm just on my way north. Gonna find me a trapping party so I can make my fortune."

The burly man looked over his shoulder and said, "You hear that, boys? This boy here is gonna be a trapper." The men in the bar laughed, and Isaac narrowed his eyes.

"I'd appreciate you and your lot not insulting me," Isaac said as another man moved next to him. Isaac, weary as he was, kept the burly man's gaze as the bartender came over and asked what he could get for the newcomer.

"Beer, please," Isaac said. The bartender promptly brought the drink back over, hoping to ease the tension at the bar if the men drank together. Isaac nodded to the bartender while continuing to hold the large man's gaze.

"What's your name, young buck?" asked the man.

"Isaac Appleton, and yours?"

"Desmond Mather. This slippery-looking son of a bitch, here's Rick Thomas," he said with a nod towards the man striding up behind Isaac. The men laughed softly at their tables as they drank and took in the sight.

"Pleasure to meet you," Isaac said in a firm but polite tone. He picked up his beer and offered a toast to Desmond Mather. The large man accepted and clinked glasses with Isaac before both took a long swig.

"So, you see, Isaac, there is a problem here that we haven't yet addressed."

Isaac lowered his mug slowly, trying to gauge what would happen next.

"This bar, well, it's a trappers bar. Well, what I mean is, it's our bar, seeing as we're the only trappers in the area. And you, Isaac Appleton, you are not a trapper."

Isaac sensed Rick Thomas' slight movement behind him, but he held Desmond's gaze. Isaac raised the mug again and finished his beer in one final gulp, and asked, "Well, how do I become a trapper with you fine gentlemen?"

"Oh, well, we don't have much room for someone with no experience, such as yourself. You'd need to pull your weight, and we don't like having extra weight on our team."

Just as Desmond finished speaking, Isaac saw the man's eyes glance past him. Instinctually, Isaac immediately slammed the mug on the bar, shattering it into a thousand pieces but keeping the base a jagged weapon in his hands. He spun on his barstool and slammed the glass into Rick Thomas' hand, pinning it to the bar. The knife Rick had been holding fell to the ground. As Rick screamed and blood pooled around his broken hand, Isaac turned back to Desmond, who had a look of wonder on his face.

"Now that, my boy, we can work with." Desmond stood up and clapped Isaac on the back, guiding him toward the table where the men sat. Rick's hand remained pinned as he writhed in pain. The bartender ran out of the tavern to fetch the town doctor while Isaac shared a beer with his new friends.

The next morning the men set out north once more. Desmond had hired Isaac to watch the team's back while they worked in the forest, to look out for Indians and maybe pick up a thing or two about trapping in the process. Rick rode alone for a long time with a bandaged hand and a look of disdain toward Isaac.

All was quiet as the men traveled. Days passing easily, nights passing quietly. Game was easy to come by, and dinners were filling and abundant. The men sat around the fire, laughing and telling tales that Isaac thought were probably exaggerations, but that was the fun part of being out in the country with the men. Tall tales made men larger than they were, and Isaac Appleton thought that was fine.

Desmond told the tallest tales of all, Isaac thought. He told tales of the native tribe just north of where they would be trapping, having the ability to communicate with the trees and the animals. He said he saw it first hand, a savage speaking to the creatures of the forest and the creatures responding to his words. The men all nodded in agreement that they had seen this too.

Isaac found these stories too far-fetched, even by the standards of the fireside tales. Far-fetched, and though he wouldn't admit it, a little alarming. Isaac was from the city, after all, London, then Boston, and he really had no idea what these savages were capable of out in the wild. *What if,* he thought, *these stories were true?* If they were able to communicate with nature in such a way, and they were going to be trapping the animals that they communicated with, that would put the men at a disadvantage, which made Isaac feel a bit too uncomfortable.

The men laughed at Isaac and told him not to worry. The savages were not to be feared. They said their war paint could be shocking when you first saw it, and Jesus, their whooping was ear-piercing, but they mostly kept to themselves. The few encounters the men had with them always worked out badly for the natives.

Isaac felt better knowing this, but his role as security for the group weighed on him more that night than the nights previous. Isaac sat by the fire and was certain he was seeing shadows darting around the men. He got his rifle, provided by Desmond and company, and walked the camp, never actually seeing anything. When the men rose the next morning and made breakfast, Isaac kept his eyes on the woods, barely touching his food.

The men rode for only a few short hours before they reached a beautiful lake situated amongst a vast rainbow of trees. Isaac had never seen such beauty before. The silence buzzed in his ears, and the smell of grass and trees and flowers danced to his nose. Desmond told him that this would be where they'd be setting up camp for the next few weeks. Isaac told the men he would be going down to the water to lay his head. It had been a long night.

As he lay a few feet away from the lapping water, Isaac looked at the cloudless sky and wondered about his parents. He wished they could have seen him at that moment. He had made the right decision, certainly. He would make his own fortune, live off the land, and find a home amidst the seclusion of the north country. Thoughts of a log cabin near a babbling brook played in his mind as he drifted off to sleep.

Isaac woke up to the sounds of whooping and hollering as rifles blasted and arrows whizzed past. He was completely discombobulated, and his mind swirled, trying to comprehend what was happening around him and where he was. The last he remembered was serenity, now chaos.

As he rose up and headed for the relative safety of a large rock a few yards away, a single arrow flew directly by his head. He could feel the wind and hear the *whizzing* noise as it zipped by. He scrambled to the rock on all fours and took in his surroundings. Men were firing into the wilderness, arrows flew back out. The clearing that the men were in was like shooting fish in a barrel.

To his right was his rifle; men were falling all around him. He grabbed his weapon, made sure it was loaded, and peeked around the rock. He saw Desmond on the ground, an arrow sticking from his back. His screams were being drowned out by the shouts of men running all around. Though he was crawling toward Isaac, he didn't look like he would make it much further.

Isaac fired his rifle and ran to Desmond. He grabbed him by his outstretched arm and dragged him behind the rock from which he ran and told him to stay there. He reloaded his weapon and made for the trees. He was a man possessed. The fear of the natives controlling the environment had left him, and bloodlust had taken over. When the men, many of whom were bloodied or doing their best to hide behind whatever obstacle they could, saw Isaac's charge, they were inspired. Even Rick Thomas charged forward after seeing him attack.

Isaac's senses seemed to be enhanced. He weaved from side to side as he ran, deftly avoiding arrows that were aimed directly at him. As he approached the tree line, he saw the first of the natives. Isaac lowered himself to a knee, aimed, and fired. He struck the native in the chest, tearing a hole in his flesh that burst through his back. Isaac continued his assault, sliding behind the tree where the Indian stood only moments before, and began loading his gun.

Another savage, perhaps the one that was shot's kin, charged forward as Isaac was reloading. Time slowed as he watched the man charge, his hatchet shining brightly against the sun. Isaac wasn't fast enough to reload but instead slammed the butt of the gun into the charging man's ribs. The native man fell forward, and though Isaac was sure he must have cracked a rib or two, the man seemed to feel little as his body was fueled by adrenaline and hatred.

He pushed the hatchet down toward Isaac's throat as he rose to a sitting position on his chest. Isaac pushed back against the man's powerful arms, though the hatchet slowly inched closer to his exposed neck. From the corner of his eye, he saw Rick watching from a few trees away. When their eyes met, Rick smiled toward him and ran after the now retreating native people.

Isaac's blood boiled. The hatchet nicked his throat, and he exploded. His knee came up into the man's groin and struck with full force. The man crumpled to his side and dropped the hatchet next to him, his face the picture of agony. His groin the embodiment of torment. Through watery eyes, he saw Isaac roll on top of him and raise up.

Isaac smashed his fists against the man repeatedly. He felt the man's facial bones break under the weight of his blows. Isaac saw red both figuratively and literally. The man's face softened, and the hard thumping sounds gave way to a wet, soft splattering with each consecutive strike. Isaac screamed with rage. A rage he didn't even know existed within him. A rage that was awoken at the sight of Rick Thomas' malicious actions.

When his fists stopped hitting anything that resembled a face, he stood up and looked around. He took in his surroundings, and what was once the manifestation of serenity and peace together had somehow…changed. He no longer saw a place of rest but a place to be feared. A place to never let one's guard down.

A scream rang out from behind him, and he turned just in time to see a man standing roughly twenty yards behind him with a bow drawn and an arrow nocked. The man stared at him and said something in his native tongue that was lost on Isaac. A shot rang out just as the arrow let loose. It struck Isaac in the left shoulder, sending him sprawling backward before he lost consciousness.

When he awoke, he found himself in a small tent of sorts. He thought he had heard the men call it a teepee during one of their many fireside talks. He had no idea how he got there, but he could hear his men outside. He tried to sit up and get dressed, but pain shot through his body as his shoulder pulsed. A groan escaped, and the men outside went silent.

A few moments later, one of the men, the youngest of the bunch, named Ben Williamson, poked his head inside. He came to Isaac's side and explained to him what had happened. He told Isaac that he had been shot by an arrow from a lone savage that didn't retreat with the rest of them. He apologized for not shooting sooner, but he insisted that the man that had shot the arrow had suffered for his crime. Ben explained that they had tracked the natives back to their camp, but by the time they got here, they had fled.

Desmond hadn't made it. After he was dragged behind the rock by Isaac, he bled out. They found him after the attack. The arrow pulled half way out of his back. Desmond had apparently fought until the end, but the damage had been done. Isaac's fury blazed again, but his body wouldn't let him release it in the way he wanted to. The men rested at their stolen camp for several days while Isaac healed, and then the men buried their dead.

He couldn't understand why the natives would have attacked them so fiercely. Ben explained to Isaac, one night around the fire, that the last time they had been in the region, one of the men had a run-in with one of the elderly of their tribe. Ben insisted that the man was no longer with them, but that he had simply asked the elderly man for directions when they found themselves lost. The elderly man struck at him, and he struck back in defense. But the elderly man was very old and weak, and the return strike was so strong that it stopped the native's heart. This must have been their revenge.

Isaac asked what happened to the man that was once in their troop. Rick spoke up that the natives had found him and killed him. Isaac wondered, if that were true, why they would attack again in a fit of revenge. It seemed as though they already had vengeance, but he kept that to himself. These savages had killed twelve of twenty-two men that were in the company, including their leader, a man Isaac had come to care for over the last few weeks. If the natives could take vengeance, they could receive it as well.

Weeks passed, and the men healed and mourned their friends. The woods provided more furs than the men had ever seen. When their time in the woods had come to an end, they almost had more than they could carry. No sign of any Indian was seen. The men marched back to the trading post south of the bar in which they met. They sold their furs, and each man received more money than he had seen before, largely because of the loss of life and not having to split the earnings as thin, though no man wanted to acknowledge that truth.

They all decided to head south, where they could enjoy their earnings on women and booze. Isaac told them he would stay and for them to return in one month for another round of furs. The men all nodded their agreement, except for Rick, who watched Isaac's movements and words with a hesitant curiosity. Isaac shook each of their hands and wished them well on their travels, all but Rick, to whom he simply said, "I'll see you soon."

Isaac watched the men on horseback as they faded into the distance. He took his earnings, bought supplies, and mounted his horse. He rode north with a supply of food, ammunition, his rifle, two changes of clothes, an ax, and his wits. He estimated that he may have just a few weeks before the first snows hit, but even that wasn't certain.

He rode his horse hard and decided on a spot a bit further south than they were before. The land was a bit flatter and the forest a little denser. A single large hill rose in the distance. He ate a good meal and rested that night. He lay out under the stars, in the darkness, just looking into eternity. He lay there as long as he could before it got too cold. He lit a fire and fell asleep by it.

In the morning, he got to work. He worked like a man crazed. First, he set traps. He scattered them all around in hopes of not only getting furs but, more importantly, food. Second, he began cutting down trees. He swung his ax until his arms were sore. Sweat glistened off his body, and his muscles grew. Each day he worked from sunrise to sunset. Blisters formed, broke, healed, and formed again, but Isaac kept working. He worked like this for four weeks until he needed to head south again to meet his crew.

To this point, Isaac had been lucky. No snow had fallen, though frost had covered his packs in the early morning hours. When he arrived at the tavern where he originally met the men, they were all overjoyed to see him. All but one man who sat in the corner watching. They asked where he had been. They asked how he had been. They commented on the way he had maintained his body during his time alone. Isaac thanked them and enjoyed several rounds of drinks bought by his men.

In the morning, Isaac was the first to rise. The men had rented rooms in the back of the bar for the evening, and Isaac went into each and woke the nine men. They grumbled and cursed, but they awoke. Some asked for coffee, some more asked for whiskey, but after a short time, all were ready to be on the trail.

They asked where they'd be setting their traps this time. Isaac simply told them to be patient. They would see soon enough. The men laughed and smoked as they enjoyed the cold, crisp air of the north woods. They told stories of how they had spent their money and how they couldn't wait to spend more. They spoke of the joy their wives and children showed when they finally made it home and their wonder at the beauty they described. The men left out the details of the Indian raid.

"We're here," Isaac said with a satisfied smile. As the trees parted, the men rode out into a clearing, where they saw their new home.

Isaac had spent the last month building cabins for the men. They'd have to pair up, he told them, and the homes were small, but still, it beat sleeping out in the cold nights. The homes were simple, no more than a one-room building, but each had its own fireplace to keep warm. The men had all brought sleeping bags to put down inside the homes, and each home had a large pile of chopped wood out front to use. The men were awed.

Isaac stood, smiling widely as he watched the men take in his hard work. He walked over to Ben and clapped him on the back. He asked him what he thought, and Ben replied with amazed thankfulness. Isaac said to the men that if they were going to be isolated in the middle of nowhere, they might as well be as comfortable as possible. The men cheered and ran to their cabins.

That night they all gathered in the middle of the small village and made a large fire. Some of the men were hesitant to light such a blaze, in fear that the Indians would attack them, but Isaac eased their fears by telling them he hadn't seen any of them since the attack that had left Desmond dead. Their fears somewhat alleviated, the men sat around smoking and drinking and celebrating Isaac. Most of the men agreed that they could make this place home with a little more work. The men with families vowed to write home and tell them to pack up the necessities from home and begin the trek north. The woods were prolific, and if they set down roots here, just think of the money they could make without having to lose time riding home.

Isaac arose just before dawn the next morning and walked outside, the silence deafening to his ears. He breathed deeply, and as he exhaled, the fog of his breath rose to the heavens. As the sun crested over the hill in the distance, he noticed two men on horseback watching him at the edge of the forest. They wore paint on their faces, *camouflage,* Isaac thought. They stared at each other, neither willing to take their eyes off the other. After what felt like minutes had passed, the two men turned their horses and rode off into the protection of the trees.

When the other men woke up, Isaac was already making coffee for each. The men slapped him on the back and welcomed the new day with some of the purest-tasting coffee any of them had had out in the backcountry. After the men had eaten their share of eggs and drank their share of coffee, they packed up their gear and headed toward the woods to set their traps and hunt their game. Isaac stopped them and guided them toward the woods on the opposite end of the clearing; the men nodded and made their way in.

Weeks passed, and the men worked tirelessly. The furs came in abundance, and the men spent their nights talking about what they were going to do with the money when their families arrived. Many talked of taking them on a trip north to Montreal once the warmer weather arrived again, of course. Others talked of bringing their wives to the small town just south of here, where they may be able to find a store with connections to some of the fancy clothing shops in Boston or New York. Others thought to spend it only on food and drink.

Some days the men spent hunting in the woods. Other days, men added on to their homes, building larger decks and adding rooms. One night Ben Williamson told Isaac that they should name this little slice of land. Isaac nodded and spoke a single word: Isolation.

Bryce closed the journal and looked across the table at Mitch and Tom. Both sat with their heads in their hands, having listened to Isaac Appleton's words. Bryce sat back in his seat and sipped at his coffee. He had been up most of the previous night going through the book and learning what he could of the man who settled the town.

"Where the hell did you come across this?" Mitch commented as he reached out to touch the delicate binding of Appleton's journal.

"Came across it one day in Mike's place. It was just sitting on a shelf, plain as day. Mike said he had never seen it before, but there it was. Sold it at a good price too." Bryce pulled the journal gently away from Mitchell's reach, fearful of another damaging it.

Tom leaned back finally and said, "So that's how this town came ta be?"

"Well, not exactly. The original Isolation was on the other side of the hill," Bryce said as he flipped through the book passively. "After those first few weeks in that small village, the Wimpak came back. They

attacked the village and burned it to the ground when the men were
out at their traps. Apparently, Appleton lost it at that point. His writing
gets more frantic, more odd."

"What do you mean," Mitch asked. "What ended up happening?"

Bryce exhaled deeply and tried to gather his thoughts. "Well, it
seems as though he and his men tracked the Wimpak south, past the
hill, and fell upon them. Several skirmishes broke out, a sort of guerilla
warfare, and finally, Appleton and his men captured the small
remaining band of natives and marched them here, to where Isolation
now stands."

"Why would they do that?" Mitch asked, hesitant to know the
answer.

"Appleton says that he had them rebuild the entire village and then
some. No more sharing cabins. No, he made them work day and night
until each was finished in order for the men's families to be
comfortable when they arrived. Once they were through rebuilding the
cabins, Appleton wrote that he marched them all to what we now call
Wimpak Hill. He made them build him a much larger cabin. One
where the men could go when they spent longer trips into the woods.

"The men seemed to have worked the Wimpak brutally hard,
beating them if they were to rest, feeding them no more than scraps
from their own plates," Bryce paused and looked away, "raping the
women that they had captured."

"Jesus," Tom and Mitch both said simultaneously.

"He wrote about all this in his book, Bryce? I mean, it's not like
you'd proudly be keeping a record of this stuff," Mitch said, leaning
back in his chair and taking a calming sip of his coffee.

"Well, in not so many words, yes, he did. Like I said, his words
become odd. These atrocious acts are discussed in such a matter-of-
fact way that it's almost as though he can't see them as wrong."

"He snapped," Tom said. "He had ta have been a wicked sick man
ta do that without a care. No conscience."

"Yes, I agree, it's awful, but what does any of this have to do with
what is happening now?" Mitch asked Bryce.

"After the men had completed Appleton's house on the hill, he led them away from it and killed the chief. But, before the chief died, Appleton says that his men believed the chief was cursing the land."

Mitch froze and thought of the monster he had seen. The shadow darting in the woods, the screams that had been heard tearing through the silence of the night for the past several weeks. "Holy shit, that's the curse." The men looked at him. "The Tul-chu-wa. The devourer of souls. I saw it the other day in the forest on my way home. That must be what the chief was cursing the land with."

Bryce nodded and was about to speak when Tom broke in.

"I saw it too," Tom said breathlessly. "It was up on tha hill. Never been so scared in all my life. I thought it was gonna come at me, but it ended up takin' off just before…" Tom paused and swallowed heavily. "Just before that poor kid at the school was killed."

Bryce nodded again while Mitch took in the information slowly, processing what it could mean before Tom once again spoke up.

"But this all happened a long time ago, Bryce. Why the hell is it here now?"

"Now that I don't have an answer for, Tom. Appleton did understand a little Wimpak, and he writes that, just before the chief was dying, he was mumbling something like, should a white man ever spill the blood of a Wimpak, death will be swift. Appleton wasn't super clear in the writing, but that was a close approximation, at least to Appleton's ears, as to what the curse was."

"Well, that doesn't make any goddamn sense," Tom spouted with frustration. "Ain't no war taking place around here anymore."

Tom and Bryce sipped at their coffee as they looked over to Mitch, who had not said a word for some time. His forehead glistened with sweat, and his eyes stood frozen in shock, staring at his hand. The hand that had been bandaged but now only held the faint scar from a wound having taken place only a few weeks ago.

"Mitch, you okay, buddy? You look like shit all of a sudden," Bryce said, a nervous snicker escaping him.

Mitch looked up at the men and finally blinked. "It's because of me."

The two men looked at each other in confusion. "What's because of you?" Tom asked incredulously.

"Holy shit, I can't fucking believe this," Mitch said, more to himself than to the men he shared a table with.

"Care to let us in on the secret?" Bryce asked, growing concern threatening to overtake him.

Mitch stood up and paced the small cafe. Myrtle stopped pouring her coffee, and the two men at the bar turned to see what the raucous was behind them. Tom and Bryce tensed as they watched Mitch's agitation grow.

"You okay, hon?" Myrtle called from behind the bar to Mitch. Mitch looked up and gave her a quick wave before taking his seat again and leaning into the men. The two at the bar took Mitchell's sitting as an indication that any potential excitement was lost.

"A couple weeks ago, just before the deaths started happening, I was up on the hill with Mike Walker."

Bryce and Tom both nodded and eagerly awaited more information.

"Mike shot this big buck, but the sonofabitch didn't go down right away. So he and I went off to go find it. It died a few hundred yards away from where it was shot, but tracking it was pretty easy. So anyways, we're down there, and we're dressing the deer, and Mike's knife slips and gets my hand. I mean gets it real good. I'm bleeding like a stuck pig. Hurt like a bastard too. That has to be it. Mike is as white as they come. I'm Wimpak. A white man spilled the blood of a Wimpak on the hill."

The two other men were shocked, but it made sense. It followed along with what Appleton had written, what he thought he had heard.

"So all this death is because of a fucking slip-up on a hunting trip?" Bryce asked with frustration in his voice. "You've got to be kidding me."

"It adds up, though, doesn't it?" Mitchell responded.

The men sat in silence for a moment, contemplating what this all meant. One of the town ambulances went down the road, sirens blazing. Tom's eyes followed it for the brief moment it was in front of the cafe.

"So how da we stahp it?" Tom asked the two, his northern New England accent emerging in full force again.

"I still have no idea, Tom. I've looked all through my collection of Wimpak material and couldn't find a word about how to stop this thing."

"I know," Mitch explained. "Little good it will do, though."

"Well, bettah tell us what you know anyways," Tom said as he picked up his mug to take another long sip of his now lukewarm coffee.

"After I saw the Tul-chu-wa in the woods, I called an elder of our community who used to live in the area, Arthur Holt. He said there are only two ways to end this curse. One is for a Wimpak to speak a banishing chant in the area in which the curse was created. He told me that the chants had been lost to time, so unless you have any information in your collection about that…" Mitch looked at Bryce hopefully.

Bryce shook his head slowly. "Sorry, Mitch. Those would have been oral traditions. Nothing that would have been written down."

Mitch nodded, expecting that answer. "The other option is that a Wimpak must use a ceremonial dagger to stab the monster in the chest in the area in which it was created."

Bryce's face lit up at this. "Now that I can help with."

"Jesus, Bryce," Tom said, "I don't know why I'm surprised. Where the hell do you get all this stuff."

Bryce simply shrugged. "What can I say? I'm a passionate collector."

Chapter 29

Eve's consciousness floated through the polychromatic array, searching for the right spot in time. She had learned to focus her attention so intently that she was able to pick out voices and glimpses of scenery as she passed.

Around her, she saw what appeared to be a present-day city covered in snow, laughing children and parents walking the sidewalks. She saw a man collapsing in the woods at the brink of a steep precipice, his dark green backpack with powerful red straps covering the dying man as if shading him from watching eyes. As she traveled deeper into the colorful abyss that beckoned her, she seemed to travel further back in time.

This place can't truly be chronological, she thought.

As she slowed herself, peering into the worlds she was passing by, she saw young girls helping their mothers in homes, men hunting and gathering furs, and finally, the place she needed to find again. She'd been here several times, and familiarity washed over her, though the feeling was not comforting. Foreboding clawed at her.

Her consciousness slowed to almost a stop, focusing only on that moment, letting the others wash away into the eternal abyss. She closed her eyes, allowing herself to be embraced by the uncomfortable feeling of being enveloped in a time and place not her own. When she opened her eyes, she found herself standing in a familiar place. The Wimpak Chief had just collapsed on the ground, blood still streaming from the gash on his neck where Appleton had sliced.

The men were on alert, searching the area with their guns raised, fingers on the trigger. Eve stood frozen, reluctant to move lest the men fire in her direction. She wasn't sure how getting hit with a bullet in this place would end, but she wasn't willing to find out. One of Appleton's men was mere feet from her as his wide eyes scanned the area to her left. She watched as sweat dripped from his forehead. His lips moved as though he was speaking to someone, but no words came out. A scar on his hand stood out as he looked down the sight line of his gun.

"Ahh, it's nothing," yelled Appleton to his men. "Let's get back."

The man closest to Eve paused and whispered what sounded like "fucking asshole" before turning back toward the other men and regrouping. They gathered in a tightly formed circle, Appleton in the middle, before walking down the trail and away from the carnage they had created.

For a while, Eve simply stood there, unsure of what to do. Her eyes kept flickering over to the torn, bloodied bodies that were strewn about the trail. Laughter, far off down the trail, snapped her back to reality if you could call this reality. She remembered why she was there and knew she needed to will her legs to move. To follow these men and discover what this place was trying to show her. With a deep breath, she ran down the trail toward the men that were fading from view.

Russell found himself among the bloodied men and one innocent girl, who had been alive only hours before, lifetimes ago. Now their skin color had faded; Russell thought they looked almost gray. He sat next to the man who had collapsed onto his daughter, the man he had seen get his throat sliced open by Isaac Appleton the last time he traveled here.

Why the fuck am I here again, he thought. It had been almost a week since Marie was buried. He remembered watching a movie with Sam and Mandy, putting Sam to bed, and drinking glass after glass of whiskey. He needed to numb the pain he felt. He didn't want to feel anything anymore. Now he was in these damned woods again, in a time not his own. *Why,* he asked himself again as he curled his knees up toward his chin.

The smell of smoke wafted from somewhere distant, the smell of an autumn evening. Russell raised his head in the direction of the approaching wind. He forced himself to stand, listening intently for something, anything. The woods were eerily quiet. No birds, no chirping insects, not even the sound of leaves rustling in the breeze, though he could see them blowing throughout the forest floor. He needed a plan. He knew there must be a reason he found himself back here again, and he couldn't sit amongst the dead until he found his way back to his body.

The wind carried the smoky air back toward him again, this time with the smell of some sort of meat cooking on the fire. The smell was captivating. *Just follow your nose,* he thought as the toucan from the "Froot Loops" commercials of his youth. Then, *Jesus, I'm really fucking losing it.*

His legs carried him down the trail toward whoever had killed those men and built the fire. As he made his way over a slight rise, he heard men swearing and laughing. The forest seemed to grow a bit darker. Dread carried over Russell's body, and as he approached the house the men sat in front of, recognition washed over him. He hid behind a tree, still unsure if he could be seen in this world, and stood in stunned horror as he looked at the house before him.

The house that Sam had built.

Eve had watched the men for what seemed like hours. She had become more brazen, knowing she couldn't be seen but cautious not to be heard. She slowly stepped closer to the men gathered around the fire, intent on knowing what they had to say, knowing why she was drawn to this place.

"That savage got nice and wet for me. I could tell she wanted it from the moment we tied her up," one of the men remarked to the man with the scarred hand.

The scarred-handed man scoffed and said, "Please, Jacobs, only way you ever turned a woman on was by shutting the fuck up."

The men gathered around the fire laughed loudly, all but Appleton, who stood by the front door of the house. Even Jacobs had himself a good laugh as the men tore into the cooked meat and drank from their flasks. Eve imagined the flasks were filled with anything but water.

The scarred man cleared his throat and turned to Appleton. "Hey, boss, why don't you come down here and give Jacobs a few tips as to how to get a woman's juices flowing. We all heard her moaning while you were with her."

Appleton's eyes flashed to the scarred man, and anger boiled over. "Shut the fuck up, Thomas. What I do with my dick is my business alone." Appleton nonetheless stepped away from the house and made his way toward the men. His clothes still bloodied from the killings. Appleton's muscular arms swung by his side, his body tense as he strode up to Rick.

Rick Thomas stood but didn't flinch. Instead, he stood bravely against Appleton, their eyes locked, neither man blinking. The men around the fire all watched in rapt anticipation. Eve wasn't sure why there was such aggression from Appleton regarding this man, but she could hardly breathe in herself as she watched what was to happen next.

A younger man finally stood up from his place around the fire and walked over to Appleton, and placed a hand on his shoulder. "Peace, Mr. Appleton. Peace. Let's not fight amongst ourselves. I believe we have bigger things to worry about."

Appleton turned and looked at the younger man. "What are you talking about, Williamson?"

Ben stammered a moment before composing himself. "The curse. The old man cursed us."

Appleton rolled his eyes and sighed heavily. "Not this shit again!"

Williamson stepped back at this affront. "Sir, it's true. Can't you feel the difference in the forest? The whole place is…dull. Even the sounds of the forest…the animals, it's all just…gone."

The men stopped what they were doing at this and listened. As if understanding had finally washed over them, the men began looking around, seeming to finally notice the hushed woods.

Eve stood breathless.

"What kind of witchcraft is this?" Appleton said to no one in particular. Goose flesh suddenly rose on his arms, a static charge seemed to be in the air. The men that were sitting around the fire all rose. Those who were already standing shuffled about in nervous anticipation.

A scream ripped through the air. Ungodly and awful. Like the souls from the darkest depths of hell having breached the earthen plane. The men all turned at once toward the sound and stumbled backward as one. A second scream pierced the silence of the forest, this time in the opposite direction. The men turned again.

Williamson closed the space between him and Appleton. "See. The chief did curse us. What are we going to do?"

Appleton and Thomas remained calm in front of the men, though panic within rose in each. They looked over the area, expecting to see some sign of what had made those awful screams. Sweat trickled down Thomas' brow, and his heart raced. A branch cracked off to his left. Rick Thomas turned just in time to see a black blur dart from the trees.

The pain didn't register right away. He felt the warmth of the blood spilling out of the wound first. He even heard the splat of his intestines hitting the ground before he felt an ounce of pain. A stench of earth and rot filled Rick, and his brain fired a memory of burying Desmond by the beautiful mountain lake that had once seemed so serene.

Before him towered a creature, immense in both height and girth. It looked down upon him with razor-sharp teeth, saliva dripping from its gaping maw. Where its eyes should have been lay nothing but flesh, no indents to indicate that there was ever any way for it to see. Its forked tongue caressed its teeth before it sprung from its mouth, flicking in the air as if tasting it.

As the first pangs of pain registered in Rick's mind, he looked down at the gaping hole that had once been his stomach. Blood poured, almost black, from his insides. He moved his hand to touch the wound, to check if what he was seeing was real. All movement had stopped but that of Rick's head, eyes looking down to the wound and back up to the creature above him. He dropped to his knees and let out a sound that only a dying man could conjure. A scream of pain. A scream from a man who's days had come to an end suddenly. The scream lasted only a moment before the creature reached out with one hand, placed it on top of Rick's head, and with one hard twist, turned his head around to face the men behind him.

Then there was chaos. Men began falling over themselves. Some running for their guns, some simply running. Appleton remained frozen in place, taking in the madness that was unfolding around him. He watched the creature dart from one man to the next in the blink of an eye. Men were falling all around him in pools of blood and gore. Appleton caught sight of a woman standing in strange clothes, watching with a horrified look on her face, only to disappear when Appleton turned briefly at the sound of a scream close by.

Gunshots fired at the creature, but none stood any chance of hitting it. The speed at which it moved was simply immeasurable. Appleton sensed a moment in which he could escape and ran toward the home. As the last man fell by the campfire, the creature raised its head as it sensed Appleton's futile attempt at escape. Within a fraction of a moment, the monster disappeared into the house. Eve heard screams and curses from the home. Sounds of death, wet, slapping, scraping sounds coming from within. And then there was silence.

Eve dared to step slightly closer to the house. She could feel the breeze against her back, but no sound passed through her ears. The house began to vibrate rapidly, and Eve stopped in her tracks. A deep reverberation passed through her body, making her breathing feel labored. As though she were trying to breathe with her hand covering her mouth. She watched as the house began to calm. The vibrations ceased from the top and made their way slowly to the front door. As they eased, the vibrations throughout her body eased as well.

As the shaking ended, a man walked slowly toward the front door and stepped out onto the porch. Jamison stood there looking strong and healthy, and when he caught Eve's eyes, he smiled. Eve's heart felt as though it would burst from her chest. She wanted to run to him, to wrap him up in her arms. She had been so afraid of what had happened to him, of where he'd been. She felt tears of joy rolling down her cheeks.

Russell had been silent, afraid to move for the length of this ordeal. Only now that he saw Jamison appear did he begin to slowly walk toward the strewn-about bodies in front of the home. Eve paid no notice to the bodies and was approaching the porch ahead of Russ. However, as he got closer, he noticed something horrible that Eve did not see. In Jamison's hand was the severed head of Isaac Appleton. The Jamison creature held the head by the hair as tendrils of muscles and veins hung below the torn patches of skin.

Eve didn't notice the danger. Her eyes focused only on his, and she stepped closer to her lover, smiling and drowning in his smile. Russell felt like he was moving through water in an attempt to get to her. He tried calling out to her, but his voice didn't seem to travel further than an inch from his lips.

Russell ran, and Eve stepped closer. The Jamison creature held her in its sight, hypnotically calling her forward. Russell knew he wouldn't make it, and so he stopped. He inhaled deeply and, with every ounce of energy that remained in this place, screamed out her name, "EVE!"

The scream seemed to break whatever hold this place had on their perception of sound. All at once the leaves could be heard blowing around them, the wind whistled through their ears, and Eve turned to Russ.

Her eyes, first confused, then scared as she saw the fear in Russell's eyes. "RUN!" he exclaimed.

Eve turned back to Jamison, who was now vibrating so quickly that the head of Appleton was shaking back and forth, splashing droplets of blood on the door frame. Understanding washed over Eve in a sudden flood of terror.

"No," she whispered just as the Jamison imposter darted forward. The creature hit Eve so hard that she was knocked back a dozen feet. She lay on the ground, sprawled out, her still beating heart throbbing in Jamison's hand.

She gasped for breath, an instinctive reflex taking place because her brain had not yet realized her life was ending in this place. The monster shifted back to its true form in front of her.

Russell screamed again and vanished.

Miles away from Isolation, a long, monotone beep could be heard next to Eve Crowley.

Russell woke with a start, covered in sweat and dread.

Sam slept soundly in his bed.

It was five in the morning, and Allen Street was silent.

CHAPTER 30

Russell sprang from his bed, and a wave of nausea cascaded over him. He forgot how much whiskey he had drunk. His stomach did not. He put his hand against the window sill and another on his knee as he bent over at the waist, waiting for the wave to pass. His mouth filled with saliva, saliva so viscous he knew that if he swallowed it, vomit would follow it back up. His head spun, and his knees buckled, but after a few minutes, the sick feeling did pass, and he hurried to put on his clothes. He needed to get to the hospital.

Russell ran from his room and woke Mandy, telling her he had to leave quickly but that he would return as soon as possible. Startled awake, Mandy only had time to simply acknowledge him as he rushed out the door. He got in his car and sped toward the hospital in Berlin.

That can't have been real, he thought. *She's fine. She's totally fine.*

The rows of trees went by in a blur of white, brown, and green. Russell's mind raced as he thought about everything he had seen in his dream. *That was the creature Mitch was talking about; that had to be it.*

He pulled up to the hospital and found the closest spot he could, jumped out of the car, and sprinted toward the front door. His foot hit some ice, and his heart sank as he skidded several feet forward, twisting his right knee slightly. No matter, he continued into the hospital and to the front desk.

"Hi," Russell breathlessly said to the front desk clerk, "I'm here to see Eve. Eve Crowley. She has a room upstairs."

"What is her room number, sir?" The aging woman with thick-rimmed glasses asked in her overly exaggerated customer service voice.

Russell scanned his mind. He hadn't gone to see her. She had come to his room. He had no idea. "Um, I'm sorry, I don't know. Eve Crowley, could you please look her up in the system."

The woman exhaled deeply and began typing away at her computer screen. She then picked up the phone and punched in several numbers. *An extension*, Russell thought.

"Hello, yes, it's the front desk. I have a man here looking to see Ms. Eve Crowley. Can I send him up?" The woman paused momentarily, then her eyes bounced back and forth. "Oh, oh my," she said into the phone. "Yes, yes, I'll send him up."

The woman hung up the phone and said to him, "Please, go on up. Second floor. A nurse will be waiting for you." She touched his arm as he walked past, delicate and caring.

Russell's stomach dropped as he walked toward the elevator. He pressed the up button and waited for the doors to ding open. *No way*, he thought. *This can't be happening.* He got into the elevator and took the short ride up to the second floor. When the doors opened, a woman in blue scrubs stood there looking just a bit pale.

"Are you here for Ms. Crowley?"

"I am, yes. I'm Russell Tolliver. I'm here to see Eve. I'm a friend," Russell said as he approached the nurse.

The woman guided Russell to a chair that was only a few feet away and spoke, "I'm so sorry, Mr. Tolliver."

It was midday, and Mitchell felt compelled to take a drive out to Wimpak Hill for reasons that he didn't quite understand. He had been sitting in front of the fire with a book in hand, a hot coffee on the table beside him when he had the urge to get up and leave the warmth and comfort of his home and step into the frigid northern New England morning.

Cold as it was, there was hardly a cloud in the sky. The sun reflected off the snow causing it to be much brighter than it otherwise would have been. Mitchell had bundled up and gotten into his truck, turned on the music, and cruised to the sounds of John Lennon as he sang, "Born a poor young country boy, Mother Nature's son. All day long, I'm sitting singing songs for everyone." The happy melody of the tune seemed to go along with the feelings that had overcome Mitchell this morning. He tapped his fingers on the wheel as he sang along.

He pulled along the side of the road that ran parallel to the mountain and put his car in park. He sat there for a moment, wondering why he was drawn to this spot. He looked around as he stepped out of the car and saw no signs of man nor animal having been by in quite some time. The snow drifts on the side of the road rose as high as Mitch's chest, so he walked down the road a bit, looking for an entry into the woods.

A few hundred yards from his parked car there was a break in the snow drifts. It almost appeared as though there was a trail there, yet no trailhead sign or blazing could be found and no footprints led their way into the forest. Mitchell paused and listened.

The wind was blowing, yet barely audible. Snow splashed across Mitchell's face as the wind kicked it up against him. He turned his head against the pelting of icy snow and looked down the road. It was almost completely flat, and as it faded farther from view, it appeared as though the trees were closing in around it, choking the road from existence.

The wind subsided, and Mitchell found himself thinking that he must be here for a reason. Intuition guiding him to the place of his ancestors, perhaps. He stepped off the road and onto the path that was seemingly made just for him. The snow crunched under his boot in a rhythmic song that only those that lived in cold weather climates could truly understand the words to. His breath rose to the heavens as he exhaled deeply, sending a part of him into the ether, giving more of himself to the world.

Mitchell had never been to this part of the woods before. He found this odd, that he would have stopped his car where he had, considering the time he had spent up here hunting and walking. Why stop in an unfamiliar area? He contemplated this while he walked, ultimately satisfied that there must be a reason for this adventure. He hiked for what seemed like miles on this strange path, climbing in elevation at a gradual pace. Eventually, he came upon a large rock, strangely clear of snow. He walked over and took his gloves off, placing his hands upon it.

The rock was cold, but not uncomfortably so, warmer than the air around him he thought. He ran his fingers over the grooves and indentations that decorated it. The rock stood almost perfectly to Mitchell's waist, a perfect sitting rock as he called this type of granite when he came upon its like while hiking. Mitchell harkened back to his roots and mentally thanked the rock for being placed in his path as he sat down upon it, taking, what he thought, was a well deserved break.

Thoughts passed through his mind as he sat. Thoughts that felt like memories, perhaps memories of his ancestors, danced in his mind. He closed his eyes and let his mind wander where it would. He listened. He focused on the environment and what it was trying to tell him. He could hear his ancestors speaking amongst the trees. He could smell their cooking fires and hear their laughter. He remembered their lives as the spirits of the past visited him.

A cracking stick and a loud grunt from behind him stirred him from his thoughts. He turned slowly, sure he recognized the sound but unwilling to allow fear to creep into his body yet. A few yards behind where Mitchell sat, walked a large black bear, sniffing the air and breathing heavily as it approached.

Mitchell froze. He had been in the woods plenty of times, and seen bears from a distance, but never one so close, let alone one that was approaching him. When the bear was no more than six feet away, it rose and stood on its hind legs. The creature was immense. Mitchell guessed that it was at least seven feet tall and had to weigh five hundred pounds. Its fur glistened in the sunlight and the claws at the end of its paws looked like no less than steak knives.

Mitchell unfroze long enough to let his mind run through all the wildlife survival scenarios he had read, watched, or heard about. His eyes flicked side to side as he searched his memory for some thought as to how to get out of this alive.

Suddenly, he remembered. He needed to get as big as he could and be as ferocious as the bear. It was the only chance he had to show no fear. He stepped upon his sitting rock and raised his arms high above his head. Standing on the rock made him taller than the bear. His arms being raised simply enhanced the facade. The bear locked eyes with Mitchell, and if for only a moment, he was convinced that the bear had a look of confusion across its face.

Mitchell's courage grew and he steeled his will. He filled his lungs and lurched forward, eyes closed, as he screamed as loudly as he could at the massive animal in front of him. He screamed until his lungs were empty and his diaphragm muscles ached. He heard nothing, not the bear walking away, not a roar in response, and certainly no paw slicing through the air and striking him down from atop this rock. When he finally got enough courage to open his eyes he saw the bear on all four legs, staring up at him. No fear or aggression appeared from the creature, only a look of curiosity.

Why did you do that? A voice came.

Mitchell spun around, but no one was there. Nothing but rows of trees and deep snow all around. Trees, snow, and the bear.

What are you looking for? The voice came again.

Mitchell turned back around and looked down to the black bear, still looking up at him, calmly sitting before the rock.

"No way," Mitchell said.

From within his mind, Mitchell heard the voice again, *You are Wimpak. I have not seen one of your kind in many, many years.*

Mitchell laughed. The crazy laugh of a madman, momentarily. He sat down upon the rock once more and curled his knees to his chest. Fear washed over his body. *I must be going crazy,* he thought.

The voice within him spoke again, *You are not going crazy. You are Wimpak. We can communicate in this way. Your kind must have told you about this.*

Mitchell nodded, unsure if he should speak aloud or simply think about what he was to say.

Either way works, came the response from the bear. *The animals can understand your language. We have just not mastered speaking it. Men tend to communicate with their minds. It makes others uncomfortable when they see one talking to the animals.*

Mitchell snickered. *I imagine it does.*

Ah, the voice spoke again. *You are understanding now. I am fascinated to see one such as you again. It has been so long. Now I know why I was awoken from my slumber.*

You're slumber, Mitchell thought hesitantly.

Yes, I am a bear, after all. I was sleeping, what you humans call hibernating when I was awoken by a powerful force. I was called here. I did not know why until now.

Mitchell thought about what this all meant. He had heard the stories from his youth, but he had never experienced anything like this. He could communicate with the animals, just as his grandparents had said the Wimpak could do.

The universe seems to have conspired to get us to meet, Mitchell thought. *I am glad that it did.*

As am I, human. What can I tell the others to call you?

Others?

Yes, human. I am not the only animal in these woods.

No…no, of course not. My name is Mitchell. Um, what can I call you?

Humans have trouble with our names as we have trouble with speaking human language. But a simple version of my name is Enok. This is what you may call me.

Pleasure to meet you, Enok.

The giant bear bowed its massive head in the direction of Mitchell.

And you as well, Mitchell. How is it…

A deep rumble reverberated through the forest, and the shrill shriek that had been heard around Isolation for weeks split through the silence of the forest. Enok rose on his hind legs, fur standing on end.

You must go now, Mitchell. It awakens to claim more lives. You know of which I speak.

Mitchell's heart sank, and dread slowly crept over his body. If a bear the size of Enok was fearful, Mitchell knew to be as well.

You are safer than I, Mitchell. I must go back to sleep. The massive bear came down on its four legs and began to move away, though its thoughts remained as clear in Mitchell's head as they had when he was only feet away. *We met for a reason. When the universe conspires again to bring us together, we will know why. Now go!*

Enok disappeared through the thick trees to the north of where they had stood conversing. Away from the shrieking creature that was claiming so many lives in Isolation. The dampened silence of the forest remained, but the air felt charged with energy. Somewhere in the distance, a reverberation began. It felt as though Mitchell was standing too close to a speaker at a concert.

Another ear-splitting shriek came closer this time, though not significantly so. Mitchell jumped off the rock and ran down the path toward his car. As he looked over his shoulder, he was sure the forest was getting darker behind him. Relief washed over him as he came to the road and ran as hard as he could toward his car. His hands fumbled with the handle, and the frigid cold had frozen the door shut in just the short time he had been gone. Finally, he controlled his shaking hands and opened the door, flinging himself into the front seat.

The dark shadow of death suddenly appeared at his driver's side window. One hand pressed against the glass. It took Mitchell in, seeming to look him up and down, though he didn't know how as it had no eyes. A wave of nausea came over him, and a tribal song echoed throughout his mind. Once again, he could hear the men singing and see the men dancing. He could smell the burning wood of the fire. The nausea subsided, and his head swam in the most peaceful swaying motion he had ever experienced. Pure euphoria.

The creature at his door recoiled and shook its head. Mitchell watched as it began to vibrate its entire body at such a speed that it looked as though it may split in two. In the blink of an eye, it was gone.

Headed in the direction of Isolation.

CHAPTER 31

Days passed since Eve's death and the doctor's were still in shock about the suddenness of it. They were calling it a heart attack, but Russ knew better. He had watched that creature rip her open. He had watched Eve die. What Russell couldn't understand was how what happened in that place could affect here. After days worth of researching astral projection and reading stories from purported astral projectionists, the best understanding he could come up with was that your energy was still tied to this reality, even when traveling. It seemed as though that connection to the physical body, even through time and space, was enough to affect the projectionist.

Over the last few nights, he had not traveled much to his easement. He had been living in a state of disquietude since Eve's death, fearful of going to sleep and seeing the creature, yet equally fearful of seeing his nightmare in his reality. Instead, Russell remained awake most nights, listening to the sound of the ambulances off in the distance. The silence of Isolation allowed for noises to travel over great distances, just not in those damned woods.

The vision of what he had seen had not left his mind, and he found that it was beginning to affect his demeanor, especially toward his son.

It wasn't that he held any sort of anger toward Sam. He had no reason to be angry. He just wasn't as present as he once was.

The death of Marie, seeing Eve get murdered by a creature from the darkest depths of imagination, this ability to project his consciousness to another place and time; it was all just too much. What might have been gnawing at him the most, however, was the house he had seen. The Lego house that Sam had built. How was that possible?

One thought kept replaying in his mind, *I need to find that house. That's where it comes from. That's where we find it.*

Russ decided to go talk with Mitchell. It had been a while since that night by the fire, drinking and talking...when everything had been okay. Well, everything at home, at least. They needed to make a plan and fast.

He knocked on Mitchell's door only once before it swung open. They stared at each other for a moment before Mitchell stepped to the side and said, "Come on in, Russ."

Russell walked to the living room and took a seat in the same spot he had sat the last time he was in Mitch's home.

"Drink?" Mitch offered.

Russell held a hand up in front of him and shook his head. "It's a bit early, and I'm trying to cool it with the booze. Since...well, you know. I've been hitting the bottle, well, bottles, pretty hard."

Mitch nodded and sat down across from Russ. Unsure of exactly why Russ came, Mitch simply asked, "What's up?"

"I've been thinking," Russ started, "this thing with Marie...it kind of put a stop to our plan. You know, to take care of this fucking...thing." Russ paused and looked deep in thought. "I don't know that we are going to be able to stop it, but what if we can. How many more people have died in this town because we've waited? Because I decided to drown my sorrows in a bottle. Marie wouldn't have wanted that."

"Russ, you can't blame yourself for that. Your wife died. No one would blame you even if they knew anything about what was going on. Panic has taken over. Most of the younger people have left, headed down to the city most likely. Getting away from the chaos and death up here. Ironic, isn't it? But the older people and those that have nowhere else to go are all staying, hoping someone comes up with a plan. They don't know we've already started to. So don't go blaming yourself."

Russ was calmed a bit by Mitch's words. At least he appreciated the effort. He choked back tears and simply looked at Mitch and nodded.

"I saw something in my dreams. I think I know where it lives," Russ told Mitch.

"You do? What did you see? Where?

"Isaac Appleton's house. It's in the middle of the woods somewhere. Up on Wimpak Hill. I just have no idea where."

Mitch smiled at the thought of the path that he had been on recently. The path that seemed to serendipitously be placed in his way. It all seemed to come together. That had to be where to go. Then, he thought of the creature that had followed him out of the woods, and his smile faded.

"I think I know where to go."

Though Russ was shocked to hear Mitch's words, he trusted his friend. "Well, let's go check it out," he said with grim determination and then added, "carefully."

The pair grabbed their jackets and went out into the seasonally cool air, got into Russell's car before heading toward Wimpak Hill. Russell called Mandy to ask if she would be okay with Sam for a few hours. He told her that he needed to look for something out on Wimpak Hill, but he promised he would be home soon and he would treat them both to a great dinner and ice cream.

Just like Marie would want, he thought and smiled.

CHAPTER 32

Bryce stood in the study at the back of his house. In contrast to the rest of the house, the room was well-lit. The heat from the fireplace was enough to keep the small room warm. He walked over to the safe that was placed under his desk and spun the lock, looking for the ceremonial dagger that he had received from an elder years before.

Normally, the Wimpak were very hesitant to give a non-Wimpak access to personal or traditional artifacts. But the Wimpak that had remained in the area knew of Bryce Callahan and his fascination with and respect for their tradition. So when the last of the Wimpak elders decided to leave the area, he told Bryce that he wanted to donate to his collection. The man had said he didn't need it anymore and, "You never know. One day you might." Bryce thought this a cryptic message but was so thrilled to receive such a piece that he soon forgot the ominous words.

As the last number clicked and the safe swung open, Bryce reached in and grabbed the ancient dagger. He had been told that this dagger had been passed down for untold generations and used countless times, though the elder man was unwilling to share the details of the use. Some things weren't for outsiders, even respected ones like Bryce.

It gleaned in the light, the blade so sharp to the touch that he was unsure how the sheath wasn't split as he removed it. Even after all these untold years, it somehow held its point. The hilt was brown and plain, yet if one looked close enough, one could see images and words etched into it. Bryce was unsure if they had been etched so lightly purposely or if it was simply time taking its toll.

Bryce had received a phone call from Mitchell Freemore only a half hour before. He had explained to him that they were heading out to Wimpak Hill to try to figure out where this creature was hiding. He said that Russ had come by his place and told him he was confident that he had seen a house in the woods where the creature resided and not to ask how or where he had seen it. Mitch told Bryce that if all went well, they would be back for the dagger later that day, and they would finish this once and for all.

After hanging up, Bryce contemplated the past few weeks. How many people had died? How many people had simply left? It seemed an unimaginable number. The town had always been so quiet, so quaint. But history seems to have a way of remembering. Of holding on to past grievances and enacting revenge when all seems to have been forgotten. Bryce guessed this was the best explanation there was for what had been happening. If it was going to end, it was better to end it now. There hadn't been a day in weeks that hadn't kept the small police department busy.

Bryce walked into his living room with the dagger in hand. He sat on the plush couch that he had owned for the past several years and picked up the book that sat on the coffee table, the new Stephen King best seller. He flipped through the pages and waited for a phone call from Mitch, telling him they'd be by for the dagger.

The silence buzzed in his ears like a million mosquitos.

The men hadn't been walking for too long, maybe a mile, Russ thought, when the mood of the forest seemed to change. Mitch pointed out where he had the run-in with a giant bear. A run-in that Russ found hard to believe, but Mitch seemed to believe what he was saying, and that was good enough for him.

The ground had been almost entirely flat with a few moments of gradual elevation gain, nothing that was too strenuous by any means. The path had been just where Mitch had said it would be. Strangely located away from any trailhead sign but along the same road where many of the hunters would park their cars and trudge into the woods. It seemed so out of place, yet it felt like the right way. Russ felt it instinctually.

The path was easy enough to follow, with only one set of footprints in and one set out. It was as though someone had shoveled out the way; Russ was slightly disquieted by this. However, once they passed Mitch's sitting rock, the path dissipated, and they found themselves creating their own trail, which further enhanced his unease. As they made their way further into the woods, Russell regained his sense of familiarity.

The pair passed several large maple trees and came upon the home Russell had seen in his ethereal travel. The place that Sam had somehow seen in his dreams. And dread passed over him, as though looking into the gaping maw of a blackened cave, never knowing what the depths held. Mitch stood in shocked silence, unsure what to make of the house.

"There it is," Russ said quietly. "This is where that creature lives."

The house appeared old to the men, yet the condition was almost immaculate. The porch in which the Jamison creature had stood called back visions to Russ. Visions he had tried very hard to suppress. Though the sun shone through the trees, none of the rays appeared to brighten the house, leaving it in a gloomy shadow that raised the hair on the men's necks.

Mitch looked from Russ to the house and back again. "It doesn't look like anyone has been here in a long time. There are no footprints leading in or out." Mitch found himself doubting Russell's assurance but nonetheless kept his voice low and edged slightly closer to him. "Maybe this is just an old hunter's cabin or something."

Russ looked over to Mitch, a look of annoyance on his face. "Does that look like a little hunter's cabin to you? On top of that, how the hell would I have known how to get here? It's in the middle of nowhere." He looked back to the house. "I'm telling you, this is it."

Mitch looked back to the house and nodded. "Okay, Russ, I believe you. Let's go see Bryce and be done with this."

The pair turned and began their trek back to the car, each in deep thought, unsure of what lay ahead but knowing they needed to keep putting one foot in front of the other. Snow crunched underfoot as the sound helped the men slip into a meditative pace, saving their town, their livelihood foremost in their minds.

Their contemplative state was suddenly jarred back into reality with the sounds of laughter, a child's laughter, coming from somewhere further ahead of them. It was a flat, dull sound characterized by the muted environment of the woods, but it had joy to it. Russell thought he recognized it and glanced at Mitch, who had seemed to hear the noise as well.

Russ picked up his pace until he was running, Mitch followed closely behind. As the two rounded a turn on the path, a woman and a boy stood before them. Russell was horrified.

"Mandy, Sam, what are you two doing here?"

The two beamed back at Russ. "There you are. I feel like we've been walking forever. Sam was starting to get tired."

Russ stood statuesque. "Y-You two can't be here. It's not safe."

Mandy chuckled softly and looked down at Sam, who was seemingly unaware of his father's strange reaction. "What are you talking about? It's just a quiet trail. Sam was sad that you weren't coming right home, so he said he wanted to go into the woods too. He's been in the house for too long, Russ. We drove out toward the trailhead and saw the car. We figured we'd walk a while and see if we could find you."

"Yeah, Dad," Sam spoke happily. "I was almost ready to turn around, but here you are."

Russell's heart broke at the sound of his happy voice. Sam hadn't been happy since Marie's death and Russell ached for more happiness to come to Sam's days. But now wasn't the time. "We need to go," Mitch said to Russ.

"What's gotten into you guys?" Mandy asked, frustration rising in her voice.

Just as the words left Mandy's lips, a buzzing began to pick up pitch in their ears. Not high pitched enough to hurt, but recognizable. Much like standing too close to an electrical tower. A deep concussive blast struck next, making the trees sway, though no explosive sound followed. Lastly, the shriek of the creature split the quietness of the forest.

"We need to go, NOW!" Mitch screamed, and he ran forward.

Russell, one step ahead, picked up Sam and ran.

Mandy looked over her shoulder as she ran with the others. Nothing was back there, but the forest seemed to be closing in on itself. She had heard that scream before in town and knew what it meant. Death was coming. She pumped her legs as fast as she could but couldn't keep up with the men. Tears streamed down her eyes as the second scream came from behind her, closer this time.

The men ran ahead and called back to her to move faster, but she could not. When her legs tangled beneath her, she collapsed to the ground, slamming her shoulder hard into the packed snow of the trail. She lay there, sure the creature would claim her life next. Too afraid to look up, she sobbed into the snow.

The men had heard her fall and stopped some feet away. The deep vibrational sound bellowed again, followed by a third scream right upon them this time. Though Mandy could not be sure, it sounded as though it was in front of her now, not behind.

She kept her head low, awaiting the strike that would surely take her life. She just hoped that it would be quick. Soon she would see Marie again, and they would keep each other company in eternity as they watched their loved ones live their lives, learn their lessons, and, hopefully, always be in search of "the good," as she had read from the philosopher Plato in her college days.

It was funny, Mandy thought, of the strange things that come into one's mind as they are approaching death. She had thought of Marie, which had triggered a memory of college and that damn philosophy class they had taken together. Mandy hoped that she had made Plato proud and that her soul would reach whatever awaited her at the moment of death.

A cry of anguish and pain ripped through the forest. A scream unlike the one that had been coming closer to the terrified group. For only a moment, Mandy thought it was coming from her. That she had disassociated herself so much that she was unconsciously letting out her death cry. But when she took stock of herself, and she realized she was not injured, no more than the fall had caused her at least, she was confused.

Until she looked at Russell.

Russ was on his knees, covered in blood. Mitch stood back with his hand covering his mouth. His face had paled so much that he looked like a ghost. Mandy stared at Russ as tears poured down his face, his head tilted to the sky, wailing. Mandy wanted to rush to him and find his wound, somehow stop the bleeding. But it wasn't Russ who was bleeding.

Laying on the ground, just in front of Russell's kneeled body, was the small body of little Sam Tolliver. He was on his side facing his father. He was still and, from this angle, looked simply like a child taking a nap after a walk in the woods with family. From where Mandy sat, little Sam looked peaceful. Maybe he was, now that he was with his mom again.

Russell looked down at Sam and screamed a horrified scream. The scream of a madman.

Russell Tolliver's mind had finally broken. The death of Marie was painful, awful. The loss of his son, whom he had just been carrying only moments before, was too much. In fact, it was too much for Mandy to even comprehend.

Mitch lowered his hand from his face and composed himself. What Mitch had seen, he would never be able to unsee. He started toward Russ slowly, not wanting to see what Russell could and Mandy could not.

Mitchell placed a hand on Russell's shoulder and started to say words of comfort. Something, anything to soothe the pain his friend was experiencing. But Mitch could not get a single word of comfort out. As his hand touched his shoulder, Russell turned to face him and screamed. He screamed so loudly that spots of blood flew from his mouth and painted his lips.

Then he fell to the ground. His eyes open, his mind lost.

Mandy ran to the road to call for help. Mitchell stayed with Russ.

By the time the medics got to Russell, he had been mumbling to himself for many minutes.

"I'm so sorry," Russell spoke into the ether. "Oh, my boy, I'm so sorry."

CHAPTER 33

Mandy rode with Russell, in the back of the ambulance, to the hospital while Mitch stayed at the scene answering the questions that Deputy Walker had. He was admitted to the psych unit of Berlin's hospital for an undetermined amount of time. The police conducted their investigation into the death of Sam Tolliver, but they saw no evidence that the wounds on Sam's broken body were caused by his father. Furthermore, the questioning of both Mitchell Freemore and Tom Richmond, though odd to say the least, confirmed much of the stories that had been told in the past few weeks to the sheriff. A strange creature, a terrifying scream, almost a shrieking, just before a body was found. Usually butchered in some way.

Mitchell went home that night, turned the lights off in his home, poured himself several glasses of whiskey, sat by the fire, and drank until he passed out.

Mandy returned to the Tolliver home later that evening, well after Mitch was snoring on his couch, and sat in the living room.

She wept silently at first. But as the tears flowed and her breathing became irregular, the moans of sorrow grew. Mandy cried herself to sleep that night on the couch where she had spent many nights those past few weeks, comforting a little boy who was no longer there.

Tom lay in bed again that night, haunted by the vision of the dead boy dangling from the tree. Haunted by the vision of Sam hanging from the tree. Haunted by the memories he hoped to keep buried.

Bryce had called Mitchell's phone several times that day while waiting for the men's arrival. Each time it had gone to voicemail, and each time, the dread within him grew. Now he sat in his office once more, pouring over books of the past.

Isolation, on this night, held true to its name.

Mitchell, Mandy, Tom, and Bryce all sat alone, victims of their thoughts and memories. The emotional toll wore heavy on each, yet they remained in the silence of their homes with chaos in their minds.

On this night, their isolation was eternal.

The next morning Mandy woke up, stiff from a poor night of sleep on the couch, and packed her bags. She needed to return to her life. To mourn in her home. To be here was just too much.

As she walked out of the Tolliver home, careful to lock up, Tom was walking out of his own house. He offered a warm wave as Mandy walked past her car and to the gentleman she had gotten to know over her time here.

"Hey, Tom. I'm glad we ran into each other."

"Ahyup. Mahnin' ta ya, Mandy. You thinking 'bout heading outta heah?"

Mandy looked away from Tom, sad to leave but knowing she had to get away from this place. The darkness that held sway over this little town was suffocating her. "I have to, Tom. I mean, first Marie, now…" she trailed off.

Tom went to speak and then paused and thought about what the right thing to say would be. Sometimes, Tom thought, silence is the best thing. He placed a hand on Mandy's shoulder and let the quiet hold the moment.

"What were they doing out there, Tom? That thing, it was out there. They knew it, didn't they? They were acting so weird when they saw us."

"I can't say for shuah why they were out theah, but I reckon they were out theah tryin' a stahp what's been going on heah. One of the old town historians and me, well, we've been speakin' with Russ and Mitch 'bout what we think is going on. I think they were aimin' to put an end ta it."

Mandy couldn't even begin to comprehend the explanation as to what had been going on in this town, but she accepted Tom's words as truth. Suddenly, horror-struck her. "Oh no, Tom. It's my fault. I knew what was going on in this town. I knew. But I thought…I thought out in the woods, away from people…"

Tom placed a hand gently under Mandy's chin and raised her head to look into her eyes and spoke. "Now, you don't go blamin' yourself. This is not your fault. Hell, none of this is anyone's fault, but it's certainly not yours. What you've done foah that family across the road theah, well, a man couldn't ask foah a better friend." Tom removed his hand from under Mandy's chin. "You did nuthin' wrong."

Mandy smiled at Tom as she stared into his gentle eyes. He meant it. And that made Mandy feel much better about leaving. "You're a good man Tom. I hope we meet again someday."

Tom smiled back. "I'm shuah we will, Mandy. You be safe now. I'll watch ovah Russ when he gets home."

Mandy embraced Tom, and the man's arms wrapped her up tightly. When they released from each other's arms, Mandy walked back to her car without a second glance. Tom watched her leave and sent her a silent wish for happiness and good fortune. Despite his words to Mandy, he suspected he'd never see her again. And he was right.

When Tom walked into *The Back In Time Cafe* a few days later, Mitch and Bryce were already sitting at the historian's usual table by the window. The pair seemed to be animated in their discussion, and Tom was sure he knew what it was about.

The cafe was empty except for the three of them and, of course, the ever-present Myrtle Cuthbert, manning her place behind the bar. So many had died at this point, so many had left, that Tom wondered why she kept showing up for work. He suspected for the same reason the three continued to meet in the cafe-normalcy.

"Hello honey," Myrtle said to Tom as she saw him walk in and place his hat on the rack by the door. "Can I get you some coffee this morning?"

"Please," is all Tom said as he smiled back toward her and made his way to the pair by the window.

As he approached, Bryce turned and welcomed him. Mitch gave a hello and a nod. Tom pulled up a seat next to Bryce, and Myrtle set his coffee down in front of him.

Myrtle paused and looked out the window. "God, this is just so awful. What's going on here?"

Bryce looked at her with care in his eyes. He had come here for as long as this place had been open and he had gotten to know Myrtle very well in that time. Even had her over for dinner a few times. She had always been a steadfast member of Isolation, but as Bryce looked at her, he had an overwhelming sense of dread. He wanted her to be safe. To make it through this nightmare. Myrtle was Isolation. If she died, Bryce was afraid Isolation would as well.

"Myrt, why don't you get the hell out of town? Go somewhere, anywhere, until this, whatever this is, settles up here."

Myrtle looked down at him and turned her head to the side slightly, seemingly confused by the question. "Same reason you haven't left, I suppose. This is home, Bryce. Maybe I'm a foolish old woman for staying, but this town is my home. I can't just leave it when things fall apart. Besides, I really would have nowhere else to go."

Myrtle looked out the window and saw the same teenager walking by that she had seen for days now. He seemed odd. Myrtle got a real bad feeling about him. When he raised his eyes and met hers, she broke her gaze and looked back to the three at the table. "If I can just do my small part to bring a sense of calm, of normal life, to this town, well…I'm gonna do it." With that, she turned and walked back behind the bar.

Mitch sipped his coffee and said to the others, "I suppose we're all like those people you see on the news during a hurricane."

"Whaddaya mean?" asked Tom

"You know, they warn you for days to get out of your homes. Seek higher ground. But inevitably, there are plenty of people who stay in their homes and endure the storm. Sometimes they live, sometimes they die. Some people call them brave, but more call them idiots." Mitch contemplated his next question. "What do you think they'll call us?"

"Heroically ignorant, I suppose," Bryce quipped.

The three laughed, the first laugh any of them had in days. Then they began to discuss the exacting task that lay before them.

Russell was in a psych unit. Mitch could not seem to find the house that he and Russ had been to only days before. It was as if it had just vanished. And the killings hadn't stopped.

It seemed an effort in futility. But the men had no choice. They had to stop this evil.

Jimmy felt drawn to the area between the bookstore and the cafe. Ever since his friends had been killed by that monster, he had the urge to spend much of his time there, looking for signs of its return. Looking for a reason it didn't attack him.

He thought he could feel understanding trying to creep into his mind, but it stayed just on the edge. Comprehension fell just out of reach. It scared him, true, but it captivated him. He wanted to see it again. To feel the energy it brought with it. To feel the power.

He used this time to contemplate his next move, also. His family wanted to leave. They wanted to cut loose and go down to the city. Jimmy thought he'd be fine if they went (well, he'd miss his sister and mother, but at least he knew they'd be safe), but he couldn't leave with questions like this searing into his mind. He thought, maybe, he'd just leave a letter and tell them to go. That he'd be okay. But he knew they wouldn't leave without him.

He had snapped out of his thoughts when he felt someone watching him. For a moment, his heart raced, thinking maybe it was the monster he was looking for. But when he looked up and saw the woman from the diner staring at him through the window, he sighed and stuffed his hands in his pockets. Three men sat around a table in front of her, not noticing him, but she averted her eyes right away and walked toward the back of the bar.

Jimmy's blood began to boil. What did he ever do to her to get that sort of reaction? For only a moment, Jimmy wished the monster would come back and take her like it did Adam and Forest.

He walked a bit further down the road, toward the bookstore, but the look in the woman's eyes dug deeper into his mind. He needed an answer as to why she felt like she had to avert her eyes from him. Did he disgust her? Did he scare her? Jimmy decided to turn back and make his way into the diner.

The bell above the door jingled as he stepped foot inside. His wet boots squeaked as he walked slowly inside, taking in his surroundings with a dark glare. The warmth of the building rushed against him. His face seemed to flush with the blast of air, and a shiver passed over his body as it tried to expel the cold winter air from its bones. Jimmy had never set foot in here, not once, but he could see why it was the place most people in town frequented. That is, when they weren't too busy running away or dying.

It smelled of coffee. The thick, sweet smell permeated every inch of the room. It was appealing, though Jimmy had yet to understand the appeal of the drink. The New Hampshire news station was on the television over the bar. A somber-looking reporter was describing a fire down in Manchester that had burned two homes to the charred frames. The reporter on scene told viewers that an electrical outlet was likely the cause of the blaze. Immediately after the report, the screen changed to sports. As though the fire never happened.

The fire should have got a lot more air time, Jimmy thought.

Myrtle looked up from her newspaper and coffee and stepped back slightly when she saw Jimmy standing a few steps from the doorway. The men at the table were deep in conversation and seemed not to notice the new customer.

Myrtle cleared her throat. "W-Welcome young man. I don't believe you've come in before."

Jimmy stared at her. He hadn't moved since the warm blast of air.

Myrtle tried again. "Why don't you come away from the door? Let me get you something warm to drink."

Jimmy stood still, staring through Myrtle. She seemed friendly enough now. The men at the table stopped their conversation and looked at him. An awkward silence building into tension that threatened to inundate the entire cafe at any moment.

Tom spoke up, "Heyuh, why don't ya come have a drink with us ovah heah, son."

Jimmy turned his gaze to the men. "I'm not your son."

Tom let out a nervous laugh and looked at the other men. He met Mitch's eyes and gave an "it's your turn" look.

Mitch acknowledged Tom's request silently and spoke next, "Yeah, man, come on over. It's too damn cold to be outside walking around."

Jimmy's gaze centered on Mitch, and his face flushed again. This time not because of the warm air pumping through the room. "The fuck you say to me, Indian?"

The men stopped moving at once. Myrtle gasped from behind the bar and sat down on the stool at her side. Jimmy walked over to the men but didn't take his eyes off Mitch. He stood over Mitch and looked down upon him, waiting to see what he'd do next.

Bryce broke the silence, "Woah, woah friend. We meant no harm here. We're all a bit on edge nowadays. Let's start over. I'm Bryce Callahan," He held out his hand to Jimmy.

"I know who you are, old man. You're the one that sits in here all the time with those other two geezers, ain't you?" Jimmy didn't take his eyes off Mitch as he spoke.

Bryce retracted his hand and spoke again, "Friend, I think it might be time that you head on down the road. We don't want any trouble in here. Frankly, we have bigger things to worry about. So why don't you just head back on out that door."

Jimmy smiled as he looked down at Mitch. "I kind of like it in here. It's warm. It smells nice. And besides, I can't leave until this red-skin tells me why he thinks he can speak to me."

"Now that's about enough," Tom broke his silence. "It's time for you ta get the fuck outta heah. Understand?" Tom pushed his seat out, and he stood. "Son," he added.

Jimmy finally broke his eyes away from Mitch and refocused on Tom. Bryce, sitting between the two standing men, pushed himself away from the table and stood by his chair a few feet away.

Jimmy turned to Tom and took a step forward. Though standing several inches shorter than him, Jimmy stared at him unafraid. "Old man, you do not want any part of me."

Tom looked down on him. "Little boy, I'll take a chunk larger than your scrawny ass can handle."

Jimmy snickered and looked Tom up and down. They stood in silence for a few long moments before Jimmy spoke again. "You know what I think? I think it's time that you and your boys head out. I think me and the old lady over there are going to have a nice conversation over some hot cocoa." Jimmy looked over to Myrtle and smiled. "Ain't that right, doll?"

Myrtle recoiled. And Tom stood his ground.

Mitch finally spoke again, "Tom, maybe we should…"

Jimmy spun around to Mitch before he could finish his sentence. Hate flew into his eyes as he lunged toward Mitch, determined to choke the words from his mouth.

Faster than Jimmy could have believed possible, Tom lunged forward as well. Before Jimmy could round the table to Mitch, Tom had him by the throat. He drove Jimmy back from their table at breakneck speed. Jimmy's feet slipped from beneath him, and with Tom's hand still wrapped around his throat, the pair crashed through the table adjacent to them. Chairs flew from underneath, and the table flipped to its side, sending the two slamming to the linoleum floor.

Tom held the boy down for a few moments longer, his eyes distant. Bryce and Mitch both ran to him and pulled him off.

Jimmy's head reeled from the collision. He had smacked it on the table as it had flipped, and he was having trouble focusing. After a few tense seconds, Jimmy rolled to his side and saw Myrtle now standing behind her stool, eyes wide with fright. He pushed himself up and turned to the men. A metallic taste attacked his tongue, and Jimmy realized he was bleeding.

He had to give the man credit. He hadn't expected him to be such a tough bastard. But he was, and he had caught Jimmy off guard. That wouldn't happen again. The metallic taste grew. Jimmy walked over to the mirror that was to his left. He stuck his tongue out to survey the damage and was shocked to see that he had bitten off the tip. He turned to the men and smiled.

"Time to go," Bryce told Jimmy.

"I think it is," Jimmy said through the blood that was rapidly filling his mouth.

His eyes darted back and forth between MItch and Tom, a coldness in them that gave both men pause. As he walked toward the door, he turned one last time. "I'll be seeing you soon."

CHAPTER 34

Bryce found himself once again in his office, slumped over a book on the history of Isolation, a dull yellow glow from his desk lamp illuminating just enough for reading.

Two days had passed since the boy in the cafe had been put through a table, and the men were no closer to being able to figure out where this creature was located than they had been.

The three had gone out into the woods each day with no success. And each day had returned home to find another body or two strewn about town. Frustration, futility, and exhaustion were constants in the men's lives.

The police department was crippled when Deputy Walker's body was found in his driveway, half outside the still-open door of his idling car. He was face down, but his body was being held up slightly by the seat belt that had wrapped around his arm. His slumped body was raised to a full sitting position by the two remaining officers and the sheriff. They were shocked to see the look of horror that was forever frozen on Deputy Walker's face. A look that would haunt their dreams that night and for many nights in the future.

Bryce had got a call early in the morning from his old friend Miles whom he hadn't spoken with in weeks. Miles' voice was quiet and sullen as he told him that Sarah Thornberg was found dead inside her home late last night. In this case, it appeared she died of heart failure and not the gruesome death that had taken so many others. For this, Bryce supposed, he was grateful.

What seemed to shock Bryce the most about this entire situation was that there was no news coverage. There were no reporters asking questions. There were no investigators (outside of the local police, that is) investigating any of the deaths or claims of a monster roaming the town. There was nothing. Surely the people that had left had spread word of the events taking place in northern New Hampshire, but it was as though no one cared. Small-town business was no business of the federal government, it seemed. They were on their own.

Bryce flipped through the book absentmindedly. He had read it countless times before and didn't really know why he was sitting there with it now. He tossed it to the side and rubbed his face. Exhaustion threatening to take over. He glanced at the clock on the wall and saw that it was just after noon, yet it was dark enough outside to be dusk. Bryce clicked off the desk lamp and made his way to the living room.

Rain fell in a steady, rhythmic stream. A low rumble of thunder sounded somewhere far off in the distance. *Strange weather to have this time of year*, Bryce thought. Nothing was a surprise anymore.

Thanksgiving had come and gone without so much as a passing thought given by most of the people left in town. No Christmas lights decorated any of the homes, no gaudy front lawn decorations lit up the night. When the sun went down, it was just…dark. He reckoned if this didn't come to an end soon, darkness would permeate the land permanently.

Bryce's phone rang again just as he sat down on the couch. It was Mitchell on the other end, sounding drained and melancholic. He told

Bryce that his friend Michael Walker, the one who had cut him in the woods accidentally and seemingly set this whole mess into action, had just been found in the middle of the road in front of his bookstore. The two hung up shortly thereafter.

Bryce was convinced at that moment that they would all die in this town. There was nothing left to do but fight. If they were going to die, they would go down swinging. He picked the phone back up and called Mitchell back.

"Tomorrow, after the rain stops, we pack our bags and go out into those damned woods and don't come back until it's dead. Either that, or we don't come back at all."

Mitchell agreed and said he would call Tom and report their plan. Tom was an outdoorsman himself. Whatever he could offer certainly wouldn't hurt their chances.

Bryce flicked on the television and turned to one of his old favorite movies that happened to be playing on the local station. He had a sense of calm wash over him. He smiled as he remembered watching the movie as a child, and he felt at peace. The rain pattered outside, and a low rumble of thunder sounded once more. He wondered if the rain would take care of most of the snow but realized that it would likely just lead to slush and ice. More misery in Isolation.

As the commercial cut into the movie, he thought, *this must be what it's like when you've resigned yourself to your fate. This is what it is like when you are prepared to die.*

On the other side of the town center, Jimmy Delaney was sitting with his mother and sister at the kitchen table, having a hot bowl of soup and grilled cheese for lunch. Mrs. Delaney had just informed the children that she and their father had decided to move out of Isolation. To head to the city where there are more job opportunities and, well, less death.

Sarah calmly asked questions about where she would go to school and did she think there would be new kids for her to play with when they got there.

Jimmy sat in silent contemplation.

Mrs. Delaney answered her daughter's questions enthusiastically. She watched Jimmy from the corner of her eye, unsure of what he was thinking. He seemed distant these last few days. He had kept to himself mostly, which in and of itself wasn't unusual, but he would hardly speak a word to Sarah, and that was strange.

"Jimmy," she said softly, "Jimmy, are you okay?"

He calmly placed the spoon back in his bowl and looked up at her. "Yeah, Mom, I'm fine. But is there any way we can wait a few days before we leave? I have to say bye to a few people."

Mrs. Delaney smiled. "Of course, honey. We still have to pack. Your father says we should plan on being gone by the weekend. You still have a few days."

A cold smile crossed Jimmy's face. "That will be plenty of time."

CHAPTER 35

Russell's mind ran almost as fast as his legs would take him.

Panic-stricken, his mind is plagued by what he's done. The only coherent thought he has repeats itself, screaming in his head: "Run. It's coming."

The path in these woods is littered with snow-covered rocks, making his escape more difficult. The only sounds he hears are his feet crunching the snow that covers the rocks and his heart pounding within his head.

Just as Russ turns around to locate his pursuer, surely mere feet behind him, the inevitable happens as he slips on a patch of ice, falling in a heap and smashing his knee on the rocks below. Pain, pure agony, washes over him as he screams at the top of his lungs. He struggles to roll onto his back, grasping his leg in his hands just above the knee, fearful to look down.

A thought crept into his head, one that he had not dared let his mind accept until that moment. There is nothing there. No pursuer. No dark, unholy thing chasing him through the night. It's all just his imagination. Through the pain, he allowed himself a laugh. The laugh of a man losing his mind.

He laughed, but a moment before, his nerves reminded his brain that his leg was mangled. Russell hesitantly looked down to inspect the damage and saw that his knee was twisted in a horrible manner. The kneecap, having shifted to the far right of his deformed leg, throbbed uncontrollably. Russell turned his head and threw up all over the rocks and snow that had caused this predicament. When the retching stopped, he attempted, foolishly, to flex his leg, testing its strength. The pain washed over him so quickly that he had only the quickest glimpse of a shadow standing next to a tree, not ten yards off, before his world was covered in darkness.

A shrill, awful scream startled him from his unconscious state. He sat up quickly, too quickly, and nausea washed over him once more. His eyes began to flutter back and forth as he remembers, at least he thought he remembered, his pursuer watching him just off in the distance. No figure remained hiding in the shadows. His heart began to slow its rapid beating.

Slowly, ever so slowly, Russell surveyed the area, looking for a stick, anything that would help him walk out of these anathematized woods. Behind him, just out of reach of his outstretched arms, lay a branch almost as long as a man and half as thick as his mangled leg, the perfect walking stick.

Cautiously, he began to drag himself back toward the branch. However, having never been capable of delaying satisfaction comfortably, he reached back far quicker and less cautiously than he should have. His body failed him again, and his balance gave way. Russell fell to his side again, smacking his useless leg against yet another rock. If he were taken that instant by the horror that chased him that night, he would have considered it a mercy that only a benevolent God could offer.

Tears streamed down his face as he sobbed heavily into the darkness and silence of the woods.

As the pain finally subsided and his courage began to creep back within him, he reached back again, this time grabbing the branch firmly, and hoisted himself up. The blood left his head, and he swayed, only remaining standing with the help of the branch.

Each step was agony. He had to remind himself to breathe as he inched forward toward the road from which he had come. After a while, he began to feel as though maybe the horror that he tried to escape was simply a figment of his imagination, nothing more than a hallucination caused by exhaustion and the eerie feeling of being alone in the dark woods at night.

However, just as he began to allow himself a moment of comfort, the evil shrill scream of the pursuer echoed all around him. Horror gripped him as he realized that he was falling, the branch having slipped out of his grasp at the sound of the shriek. An awful, twisting sound of bone scraping against bone echoed throughout his head as he fell to the ground.

He lay there, his leg now limp and extending at an unnatural angle, as he thought of nothing more than getting out of these woods. He had to get back to the road where he might find a traveler who could offer help. At this hour, he couldn't imagine who would be out here, but he had to hope. He had to move. Russell began dragging himself, inch by agonizing inch, away from the soulless creature that threatened his life.

He was making progress, slow progress, but nonetheless getting closer to the road when he permitted himself a glance over his shoulder. To his shock, the nightmare that had chased him from these unholy woods was just behind him.

It stood there, darker than the woods that surrounded him, a shadow of pure hatred and evil. All that Russell could see was the hulking form of a beast from hell, nothing more. It opened its mouth into an evil sneer as it stood looming over him. Saliva dripped from its razor-sharp teeth while it's tongue, split like a serpent's, licked each of them in kind.

Russell lost all control of his body as his bladder let loose, and warmth ran down his pant leg toward the destroyed knee that hobbled him. The nightmare let out its terrible scream again and walked slowly toward him. It began vibrating so fast that Russell could feel the reverberations in his chest.

Terrified, he disregarded all pain in his leg and crawled as fast as he could toward the road, now agonizingly close. As he dragged his body out of the woods and onto the road, he heard the monster scream one last time. The air around him began to settle, and soon Russell lay in the road silently. The frozen asphalt beneath him dug into his deformed leg.

Hesitantly, Russell turned back to the woods to see…nothing. A choked sob escaped his mouth as he pressed his head back against the road. He cursed the woods, cursed the God that would allow his life to come to such calamity, and cursed the evil that ruined the lives of so many people. That ruined his life.

As time passed, his bawling began to slow. Russell rotated his body carefully, trying to take pressure off his leg. Suddenly, he could sense a presence standing over him. Slowly, he looked up to see a little boy standing in the road. A little boy he recognized and knew. His son stood there in his winter cap and pants, wearing the same shirt and jacket that he had been wearing the day he died. His mind swirled. *How?* He wondered.

Sam did not stare at him so much as stare through him. As Russell's mind slowed, he realized he could hear his son's thoughts. He could feel his emotion, his pain. His son's words bombarded his mind. Horrific sadness washed over him as he lay in the road, pleading with his eyes for Sam's pain to stop.

That horrible day flashed through his mind. He and Mitch hiking through the woods looking for that damned cabin, hearing Sam's laughter around the bend as he walked with Mandy, then the dread as they saw the dark figure dart between the trees. He was reliving it all. Every moment was endlessly long. Every moment eternal.

Russ could feel the terror again as he saw the figure flash toward him and his boy. The torture of seeing Sam's lifeless body in his blood-stained arms. His face was frozen in a mask of confusion, pain, and fear. Sam's eyes stared up at him, searching for understanding.

His son's voice broke through the madness in his head. "It's all your fault."

Russ continued to lie on the ground, unable to move. Frozen in sorrow, his heart more pained than his mangled leg. He looked up at his son and cried out, "I'm so sorry."

Sam stared at him and stepped toward his father. Russell continued to cry out, "I'm so sorry. Oh, my little boy."

Sam stood directly over him and looked down, a blank expression on his face. As Russell looked at him and wept, Sam began to shake. He began to disappear in front of him. No, not disappear, but darken. He grew larger and wider before him.

Russell's eyes opened wide with terror as the nightmare that had taken his son's life, and so many others stood before him. The monster opened its mouth, and his son's voice came out. "It's all your fault." The monster's mouth opened wider and closed around Russell's head.

Russell was startled awake. As he looked around the room, he realized it had been a dream. A trick that the mind plays in the darkest hours of the night when the world is at its quietest. He could see the table that kept his writings in the corner of the room, the typewriter he'd sit at as he created his work, and the window he spent countless hours staring out of.

His heart was still racing as he lay in bed, the nightmare still fresh in his mind. He needed to get up and look outside; the trees and the stars would calm his nerves.

But as Russell tried to stand, the room faded to a different place, and he noticed the straps that covered his chest and legs. He was unable to move, and his heart began to race once again. He thrashed his body against his constraints and began to scream. He screamed at the ceiling, he screamed at his restraints, but he screamed most of all when he looked into the corner of the room and saw the dark figure standing there, watching him.

When the nurses came running into the room, the thrashing had shifted his bed a few inches from its original position. Russell's eyes were wide with fright. The nurses assured him he'd be okay.

As one of the nurses passed between him and the creature that haunted him, the figure in the corner disappeared. Russell looked down and watched as the Thorazine needle pierced his skin. He laid back and stared at the ceiling, feeling the effects of the medicine almost immediately. As he began to drift into unconsciousness, he kept repeating the same words, the words that had passed his lips that horrible day.

"I'm so sorry."

CHAPTER 36

The next morning Mitchell was up early. Anxiety caused him to toss and turn all night. He knew their plan was flawed. He knew it had almost no chance of succeeding since they couldn't even find the damn house anymore, but he knew they had to try something. Sitting at home and wondering who would be next to die was enough to make a man go crazy.

He sat by the fire and sipped his coffee as he had so many mornings over the years. The wood crackled and popped as the fire turned to ash. He sat in deep thought, feeling as though his ancestors would be with him this day.

For so long, he had disregarded his heritage. It wasn't as though he turned away from it intentionally. He just forgot what it was to truly be a Wimpak. Now he was almost certain his Wimpak blood was what caused all the death in the town.

He refused to blame himself. He couldn't, or he would drive himself mad. But he wondered if he had remembered the lore, if he hadn't spent so long away from home, if he wouldn't have been so careless when hunting with Mike…*Mike was a good man,* he thought. *He deserved better than what he got.*

Mitchell knew this was his own self-doubt and anxiety twisting its way into his head, but with everything that had happened, he thought he could allow himself a little self-pity this morning.

A cardinal flew onto the branch outside his living room window. The bright red bird looked so beautiful, contrasting with the snow that still covered most of the trees. *A sign,* he thought, *someone is watching out for me today.* The bird tweeted several times before flying off above the house. The snow fell from the branch as it took off, causing a mystical scene outside of his home.

Comforted by the belief that he was not alone in spirit today, Mitchell finished his coffee and rose to pack his bag. Any hearty New Englander had plenty of winter gear. One never risked being caught out in the cold (*pardon the pun*, Mitch thought) without some of the key essentials.

He went to his closet and found his backpack. He loaded it with everything he thought he'd need on the likely chance that he wouldn't be home for a night or two. A heavy sleeping bag, several pairs of long underwear, several pairs of socks, and other various layers, his portable stove, matches, a knife, some water purification tablets, and several other things he deemed necessary. He placed the bag by the door and ran back to his bedroom. He took his rifle with several rounds of bullets as well and placed it next to the pack.

As he was about to walk out the door, his phone rang. He looked at the caller id and saw that it was Arthur Holt. Mitch thought this fortuitous and sat once again to take the call.

"Hey, Arthur. Funny you should call this morning."

A moment's hesitation on the other end was broken when Arthur said, "What is it you're going to do?"

It was now Mitchell's turn to hesitate. "W-what do you mean?"

"You're about to do something very stupid, and I'm calling to find out why."

"How do you know that?" Mitchell asked, stunned by the accuracy of Arthur's words.

"Our ancestors spoke to me last night while I was traveling. They spoke of the land being covered in darkness there. And that the one full-blooded Wimpak in the entire area thought it was his duty to cleanse the land."

"It is my duty," Mitchell said sternly. Then added, "I'm not doing it alone. I have several men that have bore witness to the atrocities that are happening here. We can't just sit back anymore and watch everyone we know die, Arthur. We may not stand much of a chance, but the small chance we do have is better than just sitting here with our heads in the sand."

Silence greeted Mitchell for several long seconds. "Is Bryce Callahan still alive?"

"Y-yes, he is. In fact, he'll be with me today. Tom Richmond as well. He's an old-timer from around here too. Do you remember him?"

"I believe I met Tom many years ago, though I'm not too familiar with the man. Bryce, however, has something that you will need if you plan on returning alive."

"The dagger?" Mitch asked knowingly.

"Yes, Mitchell. The dagger of our people. I gave it to him before I left all those years ago. I sensed it might come in handy one day. I'm glad that I had the foresight."

Mitchell chuckled. "Yeah, me too."

Mitchell heard Arthur take a deep breath into the phone. "Listen, Mitchell, the Tul-chu-wa is no weak foe, as I'm sure you've seen at this point. It has few weaknesses. It was created as a protection against the worst kind of evil. The men who created it thought the only way to defeat the men that plagued them and the land was to create something even more evil. Oh, the simple minds of men," Arthur lamented.

The men sat in silence, contemplating the words that hung in the air thick and heavy. Finally, Arthur spoke again. "For all of recorded history, and likely longer than that, men have always felt the need to one-up each other. If a man does well, his neighbor must do better. If a man is harmed, he must seek to avenge the wrong done to him. Fighting begets nothing but more fighting. Violence is a never-ending cycle. No matter your race, background, or gender, the human condition can be awful.

"But there is good on this earth too, Mitchell. There are those that sacrifice for the greater good. The men that believe planting trees that they will never sit under is of the most importance. Perhaps you and your friends are planting those trees today. I just pray the price of your sacrifice is not too great."

Arthur's words struck home with Mitchell as his resolve grew. "Thank you, Arthur. Thank you for your prayers."

"Tell me what has been happening. Do you have any questions before you go battle this creature? Whether you are victorious or not, I can't let you go without knowing I gave you as much knowledge as I can."

Mitchell smiled at this. He was glad that he had reached out to him when he first saw the monster. For as far away from the area as Arthur Holt had migrated, there was still no one as knowledgeable or thoughtful on the culture and folklore of the Wimpak.

"Well, I mean, it just makes no sense, Arthur. It seems to kill at random. There is no pattern. No way to determine who will be next or where it will strike."

"Yes," Arthur said mindfully, "this is something inherent to the creature to spark fear into the men who had slaughtered us. Our ancestors believed that if the men could not anticipate its movements, then their fear would be that much greater. Destroy the mind before you destroy the body."

Mitchell couldn't believe the simplicity of it. Or the horror of it. He had hoped that Arthur could give him insight as to how they could be proactive in their approach, not reactive. His heart sank as the futility of the task in front of them.

"Okay, well, as terrifying as that is, maybe you can shed some light on this." Mitchell paused for a moment to make sure Arthur was listening. "A few days ago, we went into the woods to locate a cabin that one of the local men, a friend of mine named Russell Tolliver, said he saw in his dreams. A cabin where he assured me the creature dwelled."

"How did Russell have access to this dream? To the creature."

"Russell discovered he is part Wimpak. One of those DNA testing services. It said he was only about a quarter Wimpak, but it seems to be enough. I saw an ancestor visit him when he was here one night, asking questions about our ancestry."

Arthur mumbled something to himself that Mitchell couldn't make out but then said, "Go on."

So we went out, just the two of us, to the place he saw in his dreams. There it was, Arthur. Clear as day. Isaac Appleton's cabin, so Russ said. We left to go see Bryce, to get the dagger, and take care of this thing once and for all. On the way back, though, something awful happened."

"Tell me," Arthur said in sullen anticipation.

"Russ has a kid, had a kid, named Sam. Young boy but a great kid. Russ had left him with his wife's friend while we went out. They followed us. Russ' kid wanted to see his dad. There was no sign of the damn Tul-chu-wa while we were there, just the house. But once they showed up...it came.

"It was so fast, Arthur. We tried to run from it. The woman fell, but the monster didn't even regard her. It's as though it didn't even see she was there. It went straight for the boy. Russ had him in his arms…" Mitch trailed off.

"This is an awful story," Arthur spoke slowly.

"I know you said it strikes at random, but it had us all right there. It could have taken us all out that second. We weren't prepared. Why did it only go for the boy?"

Arthur thought for a bit, recalling all of his knowledge of the beast, and asked, "The woman, does she live in Isolation?"

Mitchell was confused by the question. "No. She's from the city. She was visiting Russell's wife before. Well, she passed also."

"It seems as though your friend is doing worse than most, and that is saying something."

Mitchell acknowledged with a sigh.

"The Tul-chu-wa didn't attack the woman because she is not from Isolation. She has no direct ties with the land and wasn't there when the curse was reborn. Was she Mitch?" Arthur asked knowingly.

"So you know I am the cause of this thing's rebirth."

Arthur snickered. "You are no more at fault for this than an asteroid is at fault for hitting the earth and causing destruction. It happened because it was destined to be so."

Mitchell wasn't sure he fully believed Arthur's words about this, but he knew Arthur was more knowledgeable on this topic than he was, so he left it at that. "Tell me more about why we're still alive."

"The woman has no ties there. The Tul-chu-wa would pay no attention to her unless she attacked it. You and Russell were safe as well because you are Wimpak, though Russell should be cautious. He may not have enough Wimpak blood coursing through him to save him from its wrath next time."

"But the boy, he has the same blood, does he not?" Mitchell pleaded.

"He does, but as you said, Russell isn't exactly full-blooded himself. It might simply be that the boy didn't have enough Wimpak in him. As awful as that sounds."

"Jesus, Arthur," Mitch said. "What have we done?"

"We did what men have done throughout history. White men, black men, native men. We acted out of anger. We acted out of fear, and we acted out of hate. And those that had no part in past atrocities bear witness to new ones. History remembers Mitchell. We don't."

"We, as a people, need to remember our past. Is that what you're saying, Arthur?"

"I'm saying we as a people, as a world community, need to put aside the belief that because we look different or believe different things that we are on our own to fight our own battles. If people would stop fighting amongst themselves and solely for themselves, we could change the history of our future."

Mitchell appreciated these words and held them close to his heart. "If I make it out of this alive, Arthur, I give you my word. I will be the change we all need."

"I hope you are, Mitchell. I hope you are."

"One last thing, Arthur. You've been very helpful to this point, but maybe you can tell me this. Why can't I find the house? I know where we were. I'm sure of it. It's just…gone."

Again there was silence for a short while on the other end of the line. Then Arthur spoke once more. "The creature is of this world and not of this world. It's likely it appears randomly, like the killings. But, it is too coincidental that when you and Russ were out there that it was present, but you have not seen it without him. Perhaps, the creature is connected to Russell and his family somehow. You said he traveled unknowingly. Maybe he unknowingly tied himself to the creature. If you are hell set on going out there, I would insist he go with you."

"Well, that's the thing, Russell…after losing his wife and his son so close together, he…well, he got admitted to the hospital. I don't suspect he'll be back home anytime soon."

"That poor man," Arthur spoke softly. "I will pray to our ancestors that he is cared for. In any event, find something that ties him and his family to the creature. I can't tell you what that is but go to his home and search. You will know when you see it."

Mitchell was frustrated with the cryptic advice, but at least he had a direction to follow. "Thank you, Arthur. You've been a great help."

"You're welcome, Mitchell. Please, take care of yourself. Be safe. And above all else, remember our traditions. They will guide you."

With that, the men hung up. Mitchell sat for a long while looking at the phone and thinking about what the old man had told him. He had to find the connection to draw the monster out of hiding.

He picked up his bag and his rifle and placed them in his truck. He drove down to Tom's place and was surprised to see the man waiting in his doorway, bag, and gun packed and ready.

As Tom walked to the car, Mitch rolled down the window. "You got a key to Russell's place?"

"Ahyup, why?"

"There's something we need to bring with us."

CHAPTER 37

Russell lay in his bed staring up at the ceiling. The blackness of the room felt like he was staring into oblivion, but he knew that was just an illusion that his mind was creating.

How many days had he been here, he wondered. It felt like a lifetime, but if he concentrated hard enough and focused his mind, he knew it couldn't have been more than four or five days. Certainly no longer than a week.

The nurses had removed his restraints earlier that night; he had calmed enough for that small courtesy. He had spent most of the past few hours staring out the window, watching as the night took over the sky. He listened as the insects played and copulated while the peepers spoke loudly in some pond not too far into the woods behind the hospital. It was almost as though they were trying to speak to him, he thought.

No, just my mind playing tricks again.

Russell got up from his bed, tired of staring into the void, and walked over to the door. It was sometime in the early hours of the morning, and all was silent in the halls. Russell knew there was likely only one nurse and one person at the front desk. He pulled at his door.

Locked. What did he expect?

He sat at the end of his bed and put his face in his hands. Sadness washed over him as he thought of his son. Those final moments, with Sam in his arms, had replayed constantly.

Sam looked so confused. Fear had crossed his face when he heard the scream. Russ was confident that Sam felt very little at the end. It tore him up inside, but he was happy Sam didn't suffer. Little Sam. His little boy. He watched the light go out in his eyes like someone blowing out a candle.

He had nothing left. Marie was gone. Sam was gone. All he had was his need to put an end to this thing in the woods. If he could help save his friends, help save whoever was left in that town, he could be satisfied. Then he could be with his family again.

He lay back on the bed with his eyes closed. He couldn't do anything from here, but there was little use trying to get out. He was locked in and hadn't figured out a way to remedy that situation. God only knew how long it would be before he was released.

"There might not even be an Isolation left at that point," he said.

Silently, he lay on the bed, desperately thinking of a way out. Slowly he began seeing a light. A swirling rainbow of mixing colors that he had become familiar with. He was traveling again.

Space and time disappeared, and images of places different from his flashed by rapidly. His heart sank as he knew that he would once again be confronted with the nightmarish creature in the woods. Or Isaac Appleton. Or who knows what else. He couldn't handle it again.

The swirling stopped, and he found himself not in the woods but in a familiar restaurant he hadn't seen in years. He was overlooking Boston from high above. Friendly laughter and chatter took place all around him. A candle burned brightly at the table he sat at. He turned his head from side to side, trying to get his bearings.

Looking for her.

"You look like you just saw a ghost," she said from behind his turned head.

His heart dropped as he slowly turned. Marie was just taking her seat across from him again. She wore the same red dress that she had worn the night he fell in love with her. She placed her napkin in her lap and looked up at him. She giggled when she saw the look of shock on his face.

"Okay, hey, you've already complemented the dress. Any more flattery and you'll have to peel me off the ceiling."

"M-marie. No, it's not that. It's…" he searched for words that would not come.

"Ha, you're silly. Okay, Russ, now tell me, why are we here?"

"Why are we here?" Russ quickly thought of something to say. "We are here because I wanted to treat the most beautiful woman in the world to a fancy dinner. I think you deserve that, don't you?" Russ beamed across the table at her, repeating words he spoke a lifetime ago.

Marie flushed and looked away. "You're a great man, Russell Tolliver."

He reached across the table and grabbed her hand and held it tightly. Her fingers fit so perfectly in his. He never wanted to forget that feeling. He leaned across the table and pulled her hand to his lips. "I love you, Marie."

"And I love you." She raised her eyes to look at him directly. "But that is not why we're here, my love. You're searching for answers."

Russell was confused. "Answers? Answers to what?"

Marie smiled. "Answers to the questions that plague you. How can you get out of that room? How can you get back to Isolation? Why did Sam have to be in the woods that day?"

Russ dropped Marie's hand gently. "S-Sam…"

"Yeah, Dad, Sam. That's me."

Russell's startled reaction as he turned to his right made Sam laugh. "How?"

"This place," Marie said as she took his hand again, "is not reality. Well, not the reality in which you currently live. You've traveled through it before. It is real, yet it is not to your body. Though the connection to your mind affects your physical form. Those that believe when you die in your dreams, you die in reality…they aren't wrong. It is where you seek answers that can't be given to your physical form." Marie now leaned forward and kissed Russell's hand. "And it is where you see loved ones again."

Russell felt hot tears flowing down his cheek. In one hand he held Marie's. In the other, he pulled Sam to him and held him close. If this wasn't reality and he was happy living in a delusional fog forever.

As if she heard his thoughts, she said, "You know you can't stay, Russ. You have to go back and help your friends. Even now, they are trying to figure out how to stop the death. They need you."

"But," Russ looked up at the two of them, "I can't lose you two again."

"You won't. We'll be with you. And one day we will all be together again. But that isn't now. Now, you must go back and stop this creature."

Sam looked at Russ with fear in his eyes. "The night I saw the house in the woods, that scary creature touched my arm. It was awful, Dad. Don't let everyone else be scared too."

Marie looked at Sam with sadness in her own eyes. She wished she could have saved him from that fear. "Your place isn't here. Not yet. Go now."

Sam brightened up just a bit. "Yeah, Dad. You're my hero, now go be everyone else's too."

Russell kissed the top of Sam's head and pulled him closer. He looked at both of them individually. "You two are my soul's devotion. I broke when I lost you both."

"Then let your soul be healed now knowing we're ever present. And we're okay. We will wait for you. We'll be together soon." The scene began to fade away slowly and Russell begged them to come back.

"Wait, but Marie, how am I supposed to get out?"

As the last flickers of Marie and Sam disappeared in front of him, she faintly said, "We're not the only ones with you."

Russell's eyes snapped open when he heard the lock of the door to his room turn. The door slowly opened about an inch, but it was enough to let light and sound in.

Standing by the door was an apparition that he couldn't quite make out. It looked like him, but different somehow. The ghostly figure wore clothes from another time and had longer hair than what Russell currently had, but there was no doubt what this was.

Mitchell had said when a Wimpak travels, he is often visited by his ancestors. Mitchell had seen this ghost before, now Russell was seeing it for himself. The vision was startling but gave Russell comfort. The apparition stared at him before looking back to the door, then stepped back into the corner of the room and slowly faded away.

"I'm going to run to the bathroom," he heard the woman at the front desk tell the nurse.

"Sounds good, Sue. I'm just going to finish up the rounds. I'll get the phone if it rings."

The fog from Russell's mind cleared and he understood what he had to do. He didn't understand how it was possible, but he made a clear decision then and there to get out of the hospital and back home.

He crept to the door quietly and opened it a few inches more. He saw the nurse a few rooms down, standing outside the door looking at her tablet that held the patient's information. After a few moments she took the keys from her scrubs, opened the door and quietly slipped into the room.

Russell didn't hesitate. As quickly and as quietly as he could, he slipped out of his own room and made for the room the nurse had just entered. As he approached the room that the nurse had entered he peered around the corner and saw that the man in the bed had apparently been awoken when she entered the room; they spoke quietly as the woman flipped through his chart.

Russell slipped past. As he approached the front desk, he heard the toilet flush down the hall. He pressed the button for the door that was by the computer monitor and rushed through. He was certain that at any moment alarms would sound and he would be caught. But, as he opened the front door to the hospital, silence greeted him. He broke into a sprint and headed for the road.

Russell didn't stop running until he was well clear of the hospital lights and heading into downtown Berlin. He shook, cold to the bone, as he realized he was only in pajamas and slippers. His feet were already going numb, and his teeth chattered as the cold air blew through his clearly not-windproof pants. A rumbling sound approached from behind, and a large eighteen-wheeler came over a rise in the road; Russell held out his thumb. The trucker stopped a few feet past him, brakes squeaking and grinding as it slowed. Russell said a quick thank you to the night air.

He ran to the cab door and opened it. The trucker, a heavy-set man that looked to be in his late fifties with a mustache that resembled broom bristles, greeted him. "Hey buddy, where are you heading?"

"North. Isolation."

The trucker nodded. "Hop on in. I can get you there."

Russ jumped in the cab and realized the trucker had noticed what he was wearing and sat giving him a cautious look. "What the hell man? You're crazy being out here in just that."

Russ quickly thought about how to explain his attire. "Wife just kicked me out, man. I'm heading to stay with a buddy for a bit. She wouldn't even let me grab a bag."

The trucker shook his head and harrumphed. "Women."

Russell was thankful the man left it at that. By the time they arrived in Isolation the sun was rising. Russell told the man he could drop him off where they were. The trucker hesitated but when Russ further insisted the man relented.

"Thank you for the ride, mister."

"That's no problem. Listen, you get to your friend's house and get warm."

"I'll do that," Russ said as he climbed out of the cab. "Oh, just one more thing."

The trucker looked at him and saw a serious look upon Russell's face.

"Don't stop. Just take your truck and drive right on through. No matter what you do, do not stop."

Russell closed the cab door and let the truck pull away before heading toward Allen Street to his home.

A short time later Russell walked through his front door and into the lonely comfort of his house. He stood just past the threshold and took in the silence. He let the pain sit with him. It hurt, but he needed to steel his heart in order to get through what stood before him.

Mandy had left, he expected that much, but the emptiness still hit him straight in the gut with a heavyweight fighter's strength. He walked slowly around his living room, getting used to the silence that would seemingly forever be with him in his home. Memories of watching cartoons with Sam and snuggling up under the blankets, at night with Marie, once Sam had gone to bed, flashed before his eyes.

How could he live here?

Russ walked down the hall toward Sam's room. The ghostly laughter of a little boy at play echoing in his ears as he stepped closer. He opened the door, bracing for the pain of seeing his little boy's room, untouched since the last time he played there.

Several toys still took up residence on the ground by his bed. The bed, made in a way that only a young child can make, seemed perfectly disorganized to him. His *Flash* posters still keeping watch over the room.

Russell found himself smiling, remembering the joy that Sam brought to the house. As he closed the door to his son's room, he walked a bit further down the hall to where he and Marie shared so many moments. Their room still had the smell of Marie's perfume wafting around. To smell

Marie's scent brought back the night in the restaurant anew. He would make them both proud. He would save his friends and this town somehow.

As he took in the room he noticed a note left on his bed. His heart soared thinking it was perhaps a message from Marie, or maybe Sam. It was an impossible hope, but Russell was a man who dared to dream.

He picked up the note and saw that it was from Mitch. Confused, he read:

Hey Russ, I doubt you'll get this, but something is telling me to leave this note just in case. Tom let me in so I could find something that could draw out that creature so we could finally kill it. That probably makes no sense to you, but I spoke to my old friend again, and he thought it might have a connection to you and your family. I had no idea what to look for, but I found paperwork in your office that showed your lineage. I figure it's a long shot, but right now, that's all we have. Bryce, Tom, and I are out where we found that house before. Meet us there if you get this. Good luck to us all.

-Mitch

Russell read this letter twice. The monster may have a connection to him and his family? He didn't understand but it seemed to ring true somewhere deep within himself.

Suddenly memories flooded forward again. What did Sam say in the restaurant? The monster had touched him when he saw the house. It must have somehow connected with Sam's body, Sam's soul. If it connected with Sam, it was connected to Russ. It was the best connection he could make. They had the same bloodline.

Russell knew he had to help his friends. He didn't know when the letter was written, but he knew where they were and that was a start. He quickly changed clothes and grabbed his backpack. As he headed for the door he stopped and dropped his pack before running down the hall and into Sam's room.

He tucked the Lego house carefully into his bag and walked to the door.

CHAPTER 38

The men had been up for hours and frustration was setting in for each of them.

"I don't fucking understand this," Mitch said angrily to no one in particular. "I know for certain this is where it was."

"You've said that for the better part of two days now," Bryce complained. "We're obviously not doing something right."

The men sighed and sat around the fire that they had built in the center of the circle of tents. Mitch knew it was a long shot, bringing the record of Russell's ancestry, but he had no idea what else to look for. The first time he had seen Russell's ancestral visitor was when they were discussing his lineage, he thought it only logical...

"Why don't we just go walkin' a ways. We know these damned woods can get ya all turned around," Tom offered.

"Ah, Tom. We've walked all over this place. Nothing in any direction. Nothing but trees, trees, and more damn trees," Bryce answered in frustration. "Listen, you guys might enjoy your time out in the woods, but me, I'm more of a comfy chair and a book by the fire type of guy. You know?"

"Bryce, I know it's frustrating…and damned cold. But we're in this together. We all agreed. Hell, you were the one that called me to kick our asses into gear."

Bryce sighed reluctantly. "I know. But what the fuck are we missing? We have the dagger. We're in the location you swear is correct. Yet there has been no sign of the house or even that monster since we've been out here. Why do you think that is?"

"Runnin' outta people to get, I suspect," Tom offered.

The thought of that was terrifying. Isolation was a small town, but it still had hundreds of people at the beginning of this massacre.

Between the people that were killed and the people that left, there must be no more than a few dozen left, Mitch thought.

"Let's just wait here until nightfall. If it doesn't appear by then we'll need to figure out another plan. In the meantime, if either of you have any thoughts that could help us solve this and get our frozen asses out of the cold quicker, I'm all ears." Mitch looked to each of them in kind. Both the men put their heads down and shook them. "Well, until someone comes up with something or the sun sets, let's make the best of it."

Mitch dug through his bag and pulled out an unopened bottle of whiskey. The men smiled as their spirits rose just a little.

"Now that's bound to warm us up a bit," Tom said as he reached for the bottle.

"First sip is mine," Mitch said as he pulled the bottle away from Tom's outstretched hand.

Their spirits were raised as they took turns sipping from the bottle. They dared to laugh and tell stories as they thought of a solution to their macabre problem.

And a few dozen yards behind them, in the shrouded darkness of several large granite boulders, a figure watched and waited for a chance to strike.

Russell slowly drove his car away from his home and turned toward the center of town.

As he looked in the rearview and the sign for Allen Street faded into nothingness, he felt a wave of sadness pass over him. This town that he was so certain he would call home for the rest of his days held a future uncertain for him. Leaving Allen Street now, he wondered what it would be like when he returned.

As he approached the center of town he noticed someone laying in the middle of the road in front of the cafe. At first he thought it was no more than some trash that had fallen out of someone's car on their way through town, but when he saw the contrasting blue jeans to the black jacket, he knew he had been mistaken.

Russ slowed to a stop next to the person laying prone in the road and rolled down his window. He looked down at the body and thought of calling out, in hopes of perhaps getting a response. Somewhere inside though, Russell knew he would not receive one.

He opened the door and stepped out just in time to see Myrtle walking to the door of the cafe, her keys jangling in her hands.

"Don't worry about it, Russ. He's been there since yesterday afternoon. There's no police left. No one to come clean up the bodies."

Russ stared at her with his mouth agape.

"Don't believe me?" Myrtle continued, "Go over toward McNeil's. Ty Merket is strewn out in front of the garage door." She continued to struggle with her keys.

Russ looked from the body back to Myrtle. "Myrt, what are you doing?"

She looked over at him with frustration in her eyes. "Isn't it obvious? I'm opening the place up. I'm already late. Twenty years of doing this I've never opened the cafe late before. I guess there is a first time for everything."

"But, Myrt…why?" Russ asked

Myrtle looked over to him, a soft look crossing her face, and she smiled lightly. "Why not, Russ. I can't just sit around and wait to die and I ain't leaving." The keys finally turned and the door swung open. "Care to come in for a cup?"

Russ smiled back at her. "No, Myrt. Thank you. I need to go find Mitch and the other guys."

She nodded. "Oh yes. Up on the hill. They stopped in yesterday on their way there. Said they were going to put a stop to this killing. They were spouting off some wild stuff. I just wished them luck and sent them on their way."

"Thanks. I'll take you up on that cup later on."

Myrtle smiled as she walked through the door. "I hope so."

Russell got back in his car and drove away from the body lying in the middle of the road. A stark reminder of how much things had changed so quickly. He put his foot down heavier on the gas pedal and made his way out to Wimpak Hill.

"I gotta take a piss," Bryce said as he tossed a few small tree branches onto the fire.

"You shuah you're gonna be able to find the little guy, what with it being so cold and all I mean," Tom joked.

Bryce, who had been frustrated for several hours now, flipped Tom the bird and lumbered off toward the granite boulders a short distance off.

Mitch and Tom laughed together, trying to keep their diminishing hopes high.

"Ah, shit, Tom. You really think anything is going to happen out here. Or are we just pissing in the wind?" Mitch took another sip of whiskey and handed the bottle to his friend.

Tom reached for the bottle and shrugged, slumping forward. "I honestly don't know."

"Yeah," Mitch said as he frustratingly threw a rock he'd been playing with off into the distance. "I think we're just wasting time out here."

The sun was starting to set and the woods began to have an ominous feel about them.

"I hate ta say it, but maybe we should just leave this town. Let nature reclaim it. Kids will tell stories 'bout the abandoned ghost town in tha woods. I don't know if there's any damn thing we can do about what's happening here."

Mitch shook his head. "I know what you're feeling, Tom. But this is home for me. This creature is something my people created out of fear. Something I brought back by mistake. I can't just leave this place."

Tom nodded and went to speak but, in the distance came the sound of something blunt striking something hard, followed by the sound of a body collapsing. The two men looked back in the direction that Bryce had headed.

"Hey Bryce, you okay over there?" Mitch called out.

Silence was the only response. Then a figure appeared out of the shadows and walked toward the two men. It was the boy they had seen in the diner a few days before. This time he carried a bat. Blood spattered along the top portion of it.

"I told you two I'd be seeing you again," Jimmy sneered as he stepped closer.

"What'd ya do to Bryce, kid?" Tom asked, anger spilling over.

Jimmy turned and looked back over his shoulder. "Your friend fell and bumped his head. He's taking a little nap over there."

"You little motherfucker," Tom began to walk forward but Mitch reached out his arm to block his path. When Tom looked over Mitch simply met his gaze with a shake of his head.

Jimmy slowly, methodically made his way closer.

"What do you want, Jimmy?" Mitch asked.

"Oh, the injun knows who I am?" Jimmy spoke with an honest sense of surprise. He stopped his progress to take in the situation.

"I asked around after the other day. People like to talk, you know. Especially in times like these."

"Oh, I'm sure they do. And what do these people like to say?"

"Most people say you come from a good family. That they wouldn't have thought you'd be capable of something like what we saw in the cafe. I even had one woman call me a liar. Of course there aren't a whole lot of people left to question so, small sample size."

Jimmy shrugged. "People are easy to fool if you know how to play the game," Jimmy said as he started toward them again.

Mitch nodded. "So what are we going to do now?"

"Now," Jimmy said as he patted the bat in his hand, "I get to have a little fun."

Tom looked down at the rifle.

"Don't even think about it old man. I'd get to you before you lift that to your shoulder. Besides, my guess is it's empty anyways. A good, honest hunter like yourself would know to not carry a loaded gun in your truck. And I've been watching you since just about the time you all got here and none of you idiots loaded either of those rifles."

Tom knew he was right, but he had to bluff. "Care to find out?"

Jimmy stared at him for a moment while his eyes grew cold. "Yup." And Jimmy ran straight for Tom.

Mitch reacted swiftly, too swiftly, and slipped on the melting snow around the fire. He fell in a heap and Jimmy was on Tom.

Jimmy plowed right through Tom, knocking him to the ground and landing on top of him. Jimmy let the bat fall to the side and proceeded to rain down blows upon him. Tom's military training kicked in quickly as he blocked many of the punches, but Jimmy landed several direct shots to Tom's face, busting his nose and lip.

Mitch finally made his way to his feet and rushed to help. He tackled Jimmy and the two rolled a few feet away from Tom, who took the time to gather himself and stood tall.

It was now Mitch's turn to rain shots from above. The first caught Jimmy directly in the right eye, immediately shutting it. The next, a hook shot to the side of Jimmy's nose, crunching it at an awful angle.

The third never connected as Jimmy's knee came up and caught Mitch between the legs, immediately crumpling him to his side.

Jimmy stood up, laughing. He looked down at Mitch who was clutching himself and wincing. Jimmy spat blood upon the man and then turned to Tom.

Tom stood his full six plus feet and glared at Jimmy. He had known people like this his whole life. People that picked on those smaller than themselves. He had seen them as a kid, he had seen them in the war. And he was not ever going to stand for it.

Jimmy sneered at the man, himself a bloodied mess. The two locked eyes, neither willing to back down. Then Jimmy's eyes caught sight of something else.

Tom held Jimmy's bat in his right hand. His grip tight around the handle. He saw Jimmy's eyes go to his weapon and now, Tom smiled.

"My turn," he said and the two ran at each other.

Tom swung the bat directly at Jimmy's head but Jimmy was younger and faster and ducked beneath it. Before Tom could react, Jimmy was behind him and drove a fist into Tom's kidney.

Tom winced and almost fell to the ground but he caught himself before doing so and whipped around quickly. He swung the bat again but only caught Jimmy with a glancing blow to his left shoulder. Again, Jimmy moved too quickly and caught Tom with a direct shot to his ribs.

This time Tom doubled over, the bat falling from his grip. "You had enough, old man?" Jimmy mocked.

"From a little shit like you? Never." Tom reached down again for the bat, gasping. But Jimmy ran forward and snatched it away from him before he could secure it.

"Ah, ah, ah," Jimmy mocked. "It's not nice to take other people's things." Jimmy dragged the bat along the ground as he walked a few steps away.

"Screw you, kid. Do ya worst. Ain't gonna bother me any," Tom said through his blood stained teeth.

Jimmy sighed heavily, dramatically. "Well, I was always told to do what my elders say." He ran forward and swung the bat low, cracking it against the side of Tom's knee. The old man fell hard into the snow, clutching his leg and screaming.

Jimmy stood over the man and looked down with a smile on his face. "You know, for an old guy, you're pretty tough." He raised the bat to eye level and looked at it. "Oh well." He raised the bat higher and swung down at a straight angle.

But before the bat connected against Tom's skull, Jimmy went flying forward, his neck snapping back as Mitch dove directly into his lower back. Jimmy tripped over Tom's body and collapsed into the snow.

Mitch landed next to Tom. Though in immense pain, Tom nodded at Mitch thankfully.

"Sorry, Tom. That kid got me good."

Mitch stood up just as Jimmy was wiping red snow away from his face. He raised the bat again, ready to charge forward at any second.

"Okay, Chief. Let's play."

Just as Jimmy was about to attack again, a yell from the distance startled the men.

"Hey, what the fuck is going on here?"

"Russ!" Mitch yelled. "Be careful, this kid is cra…"

Suddenly the low bellowing noise that had become so familiar within the borders of Isolation reverberated throughout the forest.

The bat in Jimmy's hand vibrated as though he had hit a ball off the end of it. Shocked, he let it fall to the side. Ice broke off tree branches and fell around the men. Snow shook free and fell softly to the white and red forest floor.

Tom's pain temporarily stopped as he pushed himself upright against a log that he had been sitting on around the fire not that long ago.

Russ stopped in his tracks a dozen yards away from the men and looked in the distance. "Oh shit, it worked."

Mitch followed Russell's eyes and his mouth dropped open. Only a few yards away stood the house, Isaac Appleton's house. The house that Russell had seen in his travels. The house that Sam had seen and built with his toys.

The entire landscape of the forest seemed to change as the four men stared at what had suddenly appeared. A second blast of deep vibrations swept past them followed by the shrill scream of death itself.

There would be no running away this time. They would live or die today.

Russell walked to where Tom lay. "You okay?"

"Been bettah, but I'll manage."

Russ nodded and turned to Mitch. "Guess you got the letter, huh?" Mitch said.

"Guess so," Russ said as he stared back at the house, waiting for a sign of movement. "I think it goes in there to rest. To heal itself. We need to get that thing out here and destroy the house."

"How do ya know that?" Tom asked as he winced through another shockwave of pain running up his leg.

Russell had seen his guide when he stepped foot in the woods. The guide had given him a vision. A vision of the house collapsing to the ground in a pile of rubble. He knew what he had to do. He just didn't know how to manage it. "You're just going to need to trust me on this one."

The men were too busy looking at the house to realize that Jimmy had made his way behind them. He swung his bat as hard as he could into Russell's back. Russ lurched forward and fell to the ground on all fours.

Mitch turned his head quickly to look at Jimmy. Hatred spewed from the boy's eyes like magma from the maw of an active volcano. Blood dripped from his destroyed nose, pooling in his clenched mouth before spilling down his chin.

"Time to die like the rest of your pathetic people." Jimmy cocked the bat back as far as he could.

The scream cut through the air like a dagger. The dark creature burst from the house at amazing speed and cut through Jimmy like he was nothing. Jimmy hadn't even had time to swing the bat forward before the creature split him in two.

The top of Jimmy's body fell to one side while the bottom to the other. The bat made a flat, dull sound as it struck the snow, now melting with every drop of blood that covered it. Russell turned to where Jimmy had stood. Mitch looked down between them at Jimmy's shocked face. He blinked once and was gone.

Mitch took a step back in horror. All three men turned their heads and looked at the hulking monster that stood only feet from them. Jimmy's blood still freshly dripping from its hands, the monster stood there seemingly hesitant. Its massive body heaving as it breathed and took in the situation.

Though the men couldn't comprehend how it was seeing, they had the unnerving sense that it was analyzing them. Its head moved from Mitch to Russ. As it looked at Russell its breathing began to quicken. Its aggression becoming more pronounced, but then it again dissipated.

The massive head continued past Russ and saw Tom laying in the snow, shock beginning to set in. In the heartbeat that passed between its recognition of Tom and its movement forward Russell screamed and dropped the backpack.

"No!"

The creature slammed its fist into Tom's right shoulder. Its hand buried wrist deep within. When the backpack hit the ground and the porch of the house collapsed simultaneously, the creature let out another scream.

This scream was different from the one that was typically heard before death visited Isolation. It was one of pain, perhaps even fear.

The creature withdrew its hand from Tom's shoulder and stumbled to its side slightly. Tom slumped to the side and stopped moving.

Russell looked from the pack to the house and finally understood what his guide had been showing him.

The creature remained looking toward the house, stumbling backward several steps. Russell moved slowly, reaching down to his bag. He unzipped it, careful to not make too much noise for fear of causing the nightmare to turn its gaze toward him.

He pulled out the Lego house, the porch missing, from Sam's perfect creation. When the toy house was free from the bag entirely, the monster turned and looked at Russell.

Russ was convinced the creature would lunge for him before he could react, but instead, it turned toward the house. Its movements were slower now. While still much faster than any man Russell had ever seen, the creature looked wounded.

Russell looked at the log that was before him and slammed the Lego house down upon it. The toy home shattered into hundreds of little pieces. At the same time, Isaac Appleton's home exploded outward leaving nothing but splinters where it once stood.

The creature stopped only steps from where the porch was only moments before. It froze and then slowly turned to face Russell. Its breath was deep and rapid, almost as if it were hyperventilating. Its muscles grew tense, and its head lowered in Russell's direction.

It no longer had the strength to run, but it stormed toward Russell, its mouth wide, showing its razor-sharp teeth. Russell couldn't move. Fear had taken over. The creature slammed a monstrous arm into Russell's chest, sending him flying through the air and landing a dozen feet away.

Mitchell seemed to snap out of his daze as he caught a figure moving off to his left. Bryce was crawling toward him, the dagger in his hand. Mitchell rushed toward him, slipping on the uneven ground as he went.

The creature stood over Russ, looking down at him. Russell's eyes tried to focus, but they could not. Through the dizziness of his half-conscious mind, Marie appeared before him.

Russell smiled at this phantom image that exuded calmness and peace. Marie stood there in her red dress, looking as beautiful as she was the day he met her. Russell's eyes cast down to her side, and Sam stood by her. Sam, who had lived so few years but had taught him so much.

Marie had taught Russell what intimacy was. What loving someone's soul meant. Marie was eternal because her soul was eternally bound to his. Marie had always made Russ want to be a better man. He hoped he had made her proud.

Sam had taught Russ what it meant to have wonder. To see the world through innocent eyes. To see the world in its most romanticized way, even if that wasn't reality. Sam would be by their side in eternity, also. The two smiled at Russ, and it filled him with happiness. Calmness. Peace.

When the creature's hand reached into Russell's chest and raised him high above the ground, Russell's pain was already fading. He screamed instinctively, but he was strong because of the floating memory of the two souls that had guided him in this life.

Mitch screamed as he turned with the dagger and saw the creature impale Russell's body through a broken tree branch that hung high off the ground. Russell's body slumped forward as it dangled. His final breath came quickly. He was home once more.

Mitchell ran straight at the creature but was too slow. The creature, sensing danger, slammed its arm backward toward Mitchell knocking him to the ground by its feet.

He knelt before the creature, the dagger knocked a few feet away, and spoke words that came from deep within. Words that he was unaware of previously. Words that echoed through time.

The creature stumbled back a few steps and fell to its knees. He kept speaking these words until he heard a thunderous rustling coming from deep within the forest. He held his eyes closed as he chanted the words of his people.

He heard a loud roar and a voice that he recognized speak from within his mind.

I knew our time was not completed, Mitchell.

Mitch snapped his eyes open and saw Enok running toward the creature. But it wasn't just Enok. Bears, moose, and deer all ran toward the knelt monster.

They collided with it and sent the monster sprawling backward. Enok tore it, and the deer and moose stomped upon it. The monster let out another ear-splitting shriek, and suddenly, the animals were thrown backward.

The monster stood, giant gashes torn into its body. It walked slowly over to the closest deer, whose leg was broken in a terrible way, and crushed its throat. It did the same with the next deer. When it came to the moose, who was trying to rise once more, it grabbed the poor creature's antlers and twisted until the head was torn asunder.

The animals became fearful and began to run away. Even the bears looked at the situation and fled. All but Enok. The massive bear stood on its hind legs. Blood and blackened flesh hung from his claws. The bear's nose spilled blood onto its fur, but he stood his ground.

Enok, you must run from here with the others, Mitchell spoke without words.

Enok roared. In Mitchell's mind, he heard Enok's words. *No, I will not flee. I told you that the universe would bring us back together for a reason. Remember your people's ways. Remember, Mitchell.*

As the monster approached Enok, Mitchell remembered the dagger. He picked it up and once again spoke words that he had never spoken before. New words. Different words.

And when the monster struck Enok and knocked him down again, the trees began to stir. The creature was focused solely on the giant bear before him and did not recognize the sound of the trees awakening.

Enok, wounded as he was, rose to four legs once more and raised his head high. The nightmarish creature swung back to deal a killing blow to the majestic bear.

The monstrous arm was stopped by a massive tree branch that wrapped itself around. The monster looked at his arm and clawed at the branch with its free hand. The trees reached forward and grabbed the creature's legs, and hoisted it in the air before capturing the free arm.

The monster hung in the air, unable to move by the strength of the trees. It thrashed and screamed in frustration. Mitchell approached it with caution, the dagger in his hand. He stood before the monster that was writhing in the grasp of the mighty trees and looked closely at it. Fearful as he was, he felt the power of his people and the power of nature flowing through his body.

Mitchell plunged the dagger deep into the creature's chest, and it wailed in agony. He pulled the dagger out and again stabbed its chest, this time deeper. The creature writhed against the trees, black viscous blood staining the snow below, until it no longer moved.

The tree branches released their grip, and the creature fell to the ground. Its body began to decay rapidly, fading into the soil beneath it.

Mitchell collapsed beneath one of the trees that had helped him in his battle. He reached his hand to the trunk and patted it. "Thank you," he said.

His eyes began to close from the exhaustion of the battle. And as he began to lose consciousness, he heard something he didn't expect.

The wind blew, and tiny grains of snow pelted the trees.

Somewhere in the distance, the birds were chirping again.

And Enok lay next to him to keep him warm.

CHAPTER 39

As the months passed, winter released its cold grip on Isolation. Though talk amongst the people that remained in the small town said that it was more than just the changing of the seasons that brought warmth back into their community. The creature hadn't been seen since before Christmas, and with the warming weather, Isolation was beginning to feel like the quaint town that the locals had come to love.

The events that took place over that winter were devastating. All told, once a new sheriff was hired and the bodies were all collected, 350 people lost their lives in Isolation and in the woods on Wimpak Hill. Two hundred had left town. Only twenty-seven people had stayed in their homes.

The history of Isolation was further written that winter. And while all but forty-seven people had returned to their homes in the following months, the national and local news never spoke of the happenings in the strange town in northern New Hampshire.

Those who lost their lives left vacant homes scattered throughout. The homes wouldn't stay vacant long, however, as the peace and serenity of Isolation drew people back to it. With no knowledge of the past few months circulating, people flocked to the town, and Isolation began to grow and thrive once more.

Myrtle Cuthbert remains at the cafe, serving coffee to the residents, old and new, that flock to her every morning. Myrtle maintains her upbeat and cheerful demeanor in the face of the public, but those who knew her before the events that took place last winter see a change. A sense of fear and trauma that is likely to last with her until her final days.

Mrs. Annie Granger left the elementary school that once housed so many joyful children. She was one of the lucky few that left the town early. Shortly after the death of little Alex Dinsmore in her classroom, she packed up her things and moved to the south, where she remains to this day, enjoying the warmth and sunshine of coastal Florida.

The Delaney family heard of the untimely death of their son and brother, Jimmy, after an out-of-town officer was called in to check on the residents of Isolation. The officer was called to a disturbance out in the woods on Wimpak Hill, where he found the remains of Jimmy Delaney and Russell Tolliver. The scene was reported as "the worst thing you could possibly imagine."

After they buried their son in the local cemetery, the Delaneys moved eastward to a coastal town in southern Maine. There has been no word from any member of the family since their departure.

The body of Russell Tolliver was buried next to his wife, Marie, and his son, Sam. Only a few of his most diligent fans showed up for his funeral as it, too, like all the deaths in Isolation, was hardly broadcast to the public. Russell was a friend and a good man. I hope his soul is at peace with his family.

As for me, I am not willing to let the events of last winter be forgotten. I am not willing to let history forget these poor souls that lost their lives and the horrific effects of hatred that take place every day in this country. No, in this world. I am writing these entries now, to be published at a later date, months after the creature that haunted Isolation has been dispatched, as testimony to the events that happened.

In a measure of full disclosure and honesty, the headshot that Jimmy Delaney inflicted upon me that day on Wimpak Hill has caused me to often struggle with my thoughts. Oftentimes I need to sit quietly and think hard about the events that took place. But please know, everything I write here is, to the best of my recollection, the honest truth.

I will write more as I reflect further on what took place. But to those who are reading this, at whatever time or location you may be in, please know there are things that happen that can not be explained. Things you may never hear about, but they happen every day. Take heed and beware of what hatred and fear mixed together can bring.

-Bryce Callahan

Mitchell's phone rang and broke his concentration as he closed the book in his lap.

"Arthur, I'm glad you called. You must be getting close."

"Just landed in Boston, actually. In a few hours, I'll be your new neighbor."

Mitchell smiled ear to ear. "That's great to hear. I'm glad you're coming home, Arthur."

"Me too. Listen, would you mind coming over and helping an old man move in? Maybe tomorrow morning? I'll buy the beers."

Mitchell laughed. "Sure, Art. Tomorrow. Just give me a call." Mitchell's doorbell rang, and he rose from his seat. "Hey, Art, I've gotta go. Someone's at the door."

"Sounds good, Mitch. See you soon."

"Safe travels, Art."

As Mitchell walked to the door, he thought of how much had changed over the past few months. Thought of all the loss he had experienced. All the death he had seen. But he was still here, and he had once promised Arthur that he would be the change that he wished to see in the world.

He aimed to keep that promise.

As Mitchell opened the door, he was greeted by a familiar face. "Heyah, Mitch. Care ta join me foah a cup down at Myrt's?" Tom rubbed at his shoulder, the shoulder that had been torn off by the monster in the woods. Months of rehab and months more to come were in front of him, but he was committed to getting back out into the woods to hunt this upcoming autumn.

Mitchell smiled and nodded. "You never have to ask me twice."

As the two men walked toward Tom's truck, Mitchell realized the truth in something Arthur had said. *"History doesn't forget. We do."*

Mitchell would never forget what had happened. And he wouldn't let others forget either.

As the two men turned off of Allen Street, a bright red cardinal landed in the blooming tree on Mitchell's front lawn.

ABOUT THE AUTHOR

Jared Grace currently lives in the White Mountains of New Hampshire, where he teaches high school English and dreams of days yet to come where he can spend his time wandering through the mountains, brainstorming his next great novel for you, his newly established and burgeoning readership.

Jared Grace is the father of two amazing children—Jordan and Wyatt.

This is Jared Grace's first novel, but it will certainly not be his last.

Milton Keynes UK
Ingram Content Group UK Ltd.
UKHW020101040823
426310UK00006B/175